THE McGURK

THE McGURK

A NOVEL

BY

THOMAS MICHAEL BARNES

Printed in the United States of America

ISBN 1440493774
EAN-13 9781440493775

This work is fiction. All characters, dates, times, places and events are fictitious and should not be taken in any other way.

ACKNOWLEDGEMENTS

I wish to acknowledge my spiritual mentor, the former Father Michael J. Garvin of the Archdiocese of Philadelphia, as the reason for this story. May he live a long life and have many grandchildren. I have been writing this story in my head since I met him my freshman year at Bishop McDevitt High School. I want to also acknowledge Monsignor Joseph E. Lynaugh of the parish in which I grew up as the measure of all other parish priests I have ever met. The former Grey Nun and great friend, Maureen Fasey was the inspiration for Sister Martha, and I thank her for her faithfulness to her conscience. I depended a great deal on her friendship when I was facing dark times in high school. She was a wonderful example of Christian womanhood.

I want to thank my best friend from childhood and McDevittt days, Father Victor J. Subb of the Glenmary Fathers and Brothers. He read my manuscript and was friend enough to be kind. He was mostly silent. I am grateful for that, Victor! His cousin, and my classmate through grammar school, high school and later college at Mount Saint Mary's in Emmitsburg, MD, Father Thomas Mullelly of the Diocese of Trenton, New Jersey served as a role model for proper priestly behavior in this story. I have known Tom since the first grade and all he ever wanted to be was a priest. I can say the same for Victor. They have both been an inspiration to me since childhood. They may not be very pleased with everything I have written here, but I can count on both of them to be kind to me. Considering what I have written, that is no small claim to be made about priests one knows!

I also want to thank Reverend Ruth Kirk who was formerly pastor of Saint Peter's Episcopal Church in Glenside, PA for being a good friend to my youngest daughter and oldest grandchild for many years. She showed me true Christian graciousness in very difficult circumstances for family members. It will always be appreciated. She is presently laboring in the Vineyards in Delaware. One can only hope that such a woman will be elevated to bishop someday.

I also want to acknowledge all victims of sexual abuse at the hands of agents of the Catholic Church, whether they were bishops, priests, nuns, brothers, lay teachers or any other person in authority within the church. You have inspired all of us with your courage when you chose to confront this evil.

I don't apologize for the nontraditional approach to Catholicism in this novella. This is a story about human beings, not a treatise on theology to be defended. Let me simply say that although I can no longer be considered a traditional Catholic in any sense, the religion of my youth formed me into what I am today, for better or for worse. That cannot be disputed, not even by me.

Finally, to all the priests, nuns, lay brothers and active lay people in the Catholic Church, I want to say thank you for staying faithful to your vision of Christianity. You are just people and not gods, that is certain. But your efforts are appreciated, even by those of us who no longer feed within your flock. Thanks for all you have done for us.

The McGurk

A HARD WELCOME

"**S**weet Mary, Muther a' God, help me!" screamed the woman in her painful labor. Fionnuala (pronounced "faNEWla"), McGurk, had just delivered her first child, a boy, and the delivery had not gone well. She was hemorrhaging badly and the baby was not crying. The doctor, a Protestant but a good man and well loved by the poor of Enniscorthy, was working feverishly to stem the flow of blood from the mother and start the flow of breath into the child. Neither task seemed to be within his power. He would not look at the mother in her pain for he feared that both she and the newborn would presently die. He quietly said his Reformist prayers under his breath, hoping against all hope that he could save them both. It was in God's hands now.

"Doctor Evans, will they live now?" whispered the Old One who had come from the bog outside of the town to attend the birth. The Old One, although not necessarily needed to assist at the birth of the child in this day of science and medicine, was certainly well within her right as the local midwife to be present at any birth in the local area. It being the Year of Our Lord 1841 within the Pale around Anglo-Irish environs, she seemed out of place and an unnecessary nuisance to the Cambridge educated physician. But she seemed to give comfort and calm the fears of

1

the young mother who was now in such distress, so he suffered her question calmly.

"I think she might live if we can keep her calm. 'Tis the child that I fear will die," whispered the doctor hoarsely. The boy was now almost a minute old and he had not seemed to breathe yet. With that the midwife grabbed the boy and placed him hurriedly on the breast of the mother, who took him in her arms.

"Pray to the Virgin, Fionnuala. Pray now that the boy be given life. Quickly woman, there is precious little time for your pain. We can see to that later. Pray to the Virgin for the boy's life now!"

The young woman screamed woefully with all her heart, "Holy Muther take me' boy inta' your heart, inta' your protection. Give the baby life, I beg ya', will ya' not? If it pleases your Son holy muther, let him live! I'm beggin' ya'now!" The baby gasped. He let out a small screech and started to breathe. The doctor bowed his head in thanks and wiped the sweat from his brow. The midwife took the baby and cleaned him for presentation to the neighbors. The mother softly cried a prayer of thanks to Mary, the Mother of God for saving her son. James Cavan McGurk had just come into the world.

This was just the beginning and a shadow of what was to come for the boy and later, the man. Another Catholic was born in Enniscorthy. It was a time for joy among the poor and humble in heart. It was springtime, 1841. The easy part of young Seamus' life was over. Now the hard times began.

From 1800 until the Famine Time in 1845, Ireland's population grew from about four and a half million to more than eight million, an increase of staggering proportions. By the Famine time the number of poor was enormous but the number of landlords was quite low, about 4,900 or so and almost all of them Protestant English or Anglo-Irish.

As early as 1800 most of the poor in Ireland were completely dependent on the 'Andean' white potato for sustenance. When the fungus *phytophthora infestans* clung to the crop in 1845, the crop failed that year and again in 1846 and into the following year. By 1847 hunger was everywhere and a huge part of the population died from starvation. Many more emigrated between 1846 and the beginning of 1852.

The English government did too little too late to help the Irish population, oftentimes it seemed, even exacerbating an already dire situation for the poor Catholics. So the Irish emigrated, close to a million and a half people. Roughly three in ten died on the journey out of Ireland to places such as America, Canada and other points in the English-speaking world. The overall impact of these hard times in Ireland included the slow death of the Gaelic language and Celtic ways as a viable reality; the annihilation of the landless class; a preponderance of empty mud cabins, often on treeless land; the virtual eradication of small Irish farms and forced emigration out of Ireland, mostly of the poor Catholic peasant. This was the Ireland into which Jamie McGurk was born.

THE WIDOW'S SON

"Young Jamie" as he was known to his mother, and as Seamus to all others in Enniscorthy, (pronounced "ennishSCORtee"), was a sickly lad. His mother Fionnuala McGurk was 16 when she had married her one love, Liam McGurk two years before the birth of Jamie. She was a Haggerty "from home", this being the peculiarly Irish way of referring to a woman's maiden name. She would never love another man for the rest of her life, no matter what others might whisper of her conduct.

Liam had died three months before Jamie's birth in a workman's accident in Enniscorthy. Liam was dutifully following close behind a cartload of stone headed to the work site. He needed this job to feed his growing family and that made him eager to do a good job, so he followed the heavily laden wagon so closely that when the cart split and rocks spewed out onto the road, he could not get out of danger's way fast enough. His death was mercifully quick. At least his pregnant wife could be grateful for that.

All in Enniscorthy said that young Jamie was the image of his father. Jamie grew up strong in mind, powerful in his convictions and intent, his will never bending to sickness or loneliness or even hunger. The local priests often commented on the clarity of mind and singleness of purpose the young lad displayed both in times of trouble and times of calm. It was clear to all that knew him that he would grow into a man to be reckoned with one day.

Father Lafferty, the old kind one with a large heart and patience for children, took in the very poor children for afternoon instruction, three times a week. He taught them to read and write in English. The very smart ones he would instruct in reading and writing in Gaelic and teach them the basics of mathematics with a smattering of science and politics from what he might be able to glean from the local Protestant gentry that he went out of his way to befriend. Their influence could always turn aside a devastating blow to the poorest of the poor and that influence was often needed in Enniscorthy. He often went begging for any periodicals, books or magazines from Dublin or England that they might be willing to donate to his pupils. Since he was a kind and compassionate man to Protestant and Catholic alike, he often came away from their homes with more books and materials than he could carry. His pupils reaped the rewards in the strength of their learning.

But in matters of faith, Father Lafferty could be a hard man. It was the only time he was unbending. After all, this was Ireland and the Catholic faith had seen a hard time of it here; there must be no bending of the rules, unless of course, the Church could benefit from the bending. And that is where Jamie McGurk learned his first lesson in practical spirituality.

One early summer evening after reading the periodicals that the English gentry had donated to Father Lafferty, nine-year old Jamie and Father Lafferty took their evening walk after Father prayed his Divine Office in his Compline prayer book, a necessity and part of every priest's daily duties.

"Compline is the order of prayer for a priest, Jamie," said Lafferty. "Lauds, Vespers and Matins are to be said every day in early morning, at noon and in the evening." Once Father had them said for the day, and after Jamie's lesson, they would often walk to the end of the lane where St. Mary's Church was located and then Jamie would take his leave and hurry home to his mother. But along the way they had an encounter with Old Crooked Pat.

Pat McLoughlin one of the remaining McLoughlin boys from outside the town limits, was now an old man doubled over with arthritis, the last remaining of a family of twelve boys. Never the marrying kind, he lived with his dog in the old family cabin just outside town near the site of Father Murphy's last stand on Vinegar Hill—the proud moment when Irishmen in a people's army stood against the tyrant many years before. No true Irishman ever passed that site without muttering a prayer for the souls of those brave Irish martyrs.

Upon seeing Father Lafferty and Jamie, Old Crooked Pat shouted for them in an urgent way and was hobbling as fast as he could to get to them.

"Good evenin' Father! And good even' young man. Why, if it isn't the McGurk himself!" said Old Crooked Pat, as if the lad were the Crown Prince and this was his realm. Pat had a way of making people feel special. Old Crooked Pat was loved by the town for his simplicity and his willingness to listen to anyone's complaints.

"Father, I have a sadness to share and a question to ask," said the old man.

"And what is it Pat?" Father Lafferty asked kindly.

"Well, Father, ya' see, me' dawg died this morning, old grey Pooka passed on to the Great Beyond and I was wonderin', Faather".... here Old Crooked Pat hesitated before he spoke slowly and cautiously..."Faather, would ya' be willin' to say a Mass for the happy repose of the soul of me' dawg Pooka?"

With that bit of insanity out of his mouth, Pat waited for the priest's response which was very quick in coming.

"Why ya' Old Rapscallion! Indeed! Muise! You're askin' me to say a Mass for the dog that died this marnin'?"

Jamie, whom Old Crooked Pat had called "the McGurk," flinched at the thought of the brow beating he knew that Pat was going to receive from the curate.

"You old fool! You would add blasphemy to your sadness?" The priest simply was beside himself with indignation at the thought of celebrating a Mass for the happy repose of the soul of Old Pat's flea-bitten mongrel.

"Well, then Father, do ya' think that the Reverend Mister Edwards, down at the Church of Ireland chapel would say a prayer or two over me dead dawg?" Pat asked sheepishly.

"Oh, the Protestant clergy might actually do anything. Leave it to them to say a prayer for the happy repose of the soul of a dead dog! Go and ask them, and see what the answer is!" Father Lafferty was now beside himself with consternation at the very thought of such a misplaced use of Catholic sacrament.

"Well, one more thing, Father," Old Pat asked with quiet voice and great humility after sending Father Lafferty's sense of theology awry.

"And what is it now, Pat? Would you have me be comin' down to your cabin to say a Rosary with your chickens or maybe discuss theology with the magpies round your place? Shall I give a benediction to your pigs, for the love a' God!" Father Lafferty said, quite exasperated at this point.

"Well actually Father, I needed your opinion on the point of payment. Do you think that if I asked Parson Edwards to pray over me' dawg Pooka's poor corpse that a payment of twenty pounds sterling would be enough compensation for the good man's time and intentions?"

Father Lafferty gasped and Jamie froze. It was known that Old Crooked Pat was not one to spend a pence if he did not have to do so, but twenty pounds sterling was a fortune. The bishop himself would sit up all night and stare at that sum, if he had it!

"Do you actually have that money, Pat?" Father Lafferty said quietly, slowly and with great purpose.

"Oh I do Father! And more if the Parson asks for it. Nothing is too good for me' old faithful friend, Pooka. I want him to get what I would want for any friend—a good send off into the Beyond!"

Father Lafferty could use twenty pound sterling to great purpose among the poor of Enniscorthy. Father Lafferty drew himself up to his full height of five feet six inches and chided Pat McLoughlin kindly, "Now Pat! Why did you not tell me that the dog was a Catholic? Of course I will say a Mass for the happy repose of his soul! And twenty pounds sterling would be just the right amount of money for such a holy event to take place!"

The two men agreed that Pat would give the money to the parish priest in charge, Father Hanratty the next day explaining only that he wished to donate to the parish and that Father Lafferty would celebrate the Mass on Saturday for Pooka. He told Pat to tell no one. Jamie was to tell no one, and was known after that day as The McGurk.

Young Jamie was learning about the Hard Times. It was 1850 and the famine was now coming to an end. Many had died, many had left and many had simply wasted into nothing, waiting for the end. But twenty pounds sterling in the hands of St. Mary's clergy could do a lot of good for a lot of broken people. And it was all due to the passing of an Irish dog!

FIONNUALA MCGURK'S BURDEN

She was a handsome woman, strong of body, full boned and with beautiful white teeth and long and wavy brown hair and with eyes as blue as the sky on a summer Sunday. She was in fact the envy of women in Enniscorthy. A widow now, she found employment as a housekeeper with the very same young doctor who had delivered Jamie on that hard day.

It was not untrue to say that the doctor had saved her life, stitching and binding her in time to stop the flow of blood and make the hemorrhaging cease. He was also a widower, although his marriage had been less than idyllic. A Welshman who had married a high born Englishwoman and then emigrated to Ireland, he took over the practice of an old English doctor. The old fellow had written his old medical school for a younger doctor to take his practice as old age stole the man's strength. Fionnuala felt drawn to him since the day Jamie was born. He being a Protestant and married, she knew to keep her thoughts to herself.

The doctor's marriage had been hard. His English wife was constantly pining for home and never really happy either being married to the doctor in Enniscorthy or even being married at all. She was not really made for marriage and the constant compromises and willingness one needs to put one's partner first. She was too much of an aristocrat to really do the work that a marriage requires. So it was sad that the doctor's wife had caught fever while home visiting her family in England the next year and died suddenly. In truth, when she died, the doctor was secretly relieved. He would never marry again, he promised himself.

Still, he had the needs of a man and Fionnuala would fit those needs well. Neither of them ever spoke of it but both of them knew what would eventually happen in the secret quiet moments of the afternoons in his small manor home when the cook retired for the evening and before Fionnuala left for her small home in town in the evening. And one afternoon it happened. Not much was spoken to start their loving. It just happened without so much as a word being spoken between them. No words, no others would ever know, even they themselves would barely mention it or allude to it in any manner. It was their quiet secret. It would carry on for a full eight years that way.

The doctor would always ensure that he withdrew himself from her before pregnancy could result and then he would insist that Fionnuala wash herself inside with warm water. They never had issue from their union. It was their way. Still it was a secret she could never tell in Confession and she hid it from everyone. Taking communion was hard for her, but she had to do this to avoid suspicion. It was the only way an Irish woman could remain above the talk of the town in this regard. So she swallowed hard and took communion at Sunday Mass, knowing full well that she was living in a state of sin.

Fionnuala's burden was knowing that she was the mother of a special one, a good boy with a Christian heart. She herself was all too human and too needful of a human embrace in order to get through the pain of living. Her burden was that she was fully and completely a human, a woman and a lover and deeply involved in human affairs. There was no place for her to hide her humanness, even from herself. So she made herself scarce to most people, especially women, in order not to have her frailties found out. She needed the doctor's embraces as often as possible. The penalty for that need was to keep her joys secret and her life narrow. It was the only way to protect her son from the wickedness of those who would find her out.

The time would come some day to leave the comfort of the doctor's arms. For a woman as full of life as Fionnuala, this would not be easy. But it must be done and she knew that one day, the day of departure would come.

THE DAYS IN IRELAND
BEFORE AMERICA

And so Jamie McGurk grew in height, strength and wisdom, even some uncommon insight into life and the human condition. His mother mostly kept to herself except when she was working at the doctor's manor; she spent her time with the normal household chores of an Irish widow raising a son alone. She was quiet and did not speak often but it was apparent to all that Jamie was the center of her life and she was the center of his.

Father Lafferty spent as much time as he could with Jamie, and by the age of fourteen Jamie could read English, Gaelic, had a working knowledge of Latin and even some Greek. His mathematical skills were basic and sharp. He had even done some reading in the sciences from the periodicals and books that the English gave to Father Lafferty. For a poor boy from Enniscorthy, Jamie was uncommonly educated and keenly observant of the human condition.

By the age of 16 he had found good and solid employment as apprentice and aide to the local barrister, Edward Farnesworth. Squire Farnesworth had just enough business that he needed a sort of runner between his various affairs during the day while he stayed near the docket. Jamie, now known exclusively as The McGurk to the people in Ennsicorthy, was trustworthy and the squire rather admired his tenacity and strength of spirit and his hunger for learning. Father Lafferty secretly had hopes that Jamie McGurk might consider entering Maynooth to study for priesthood, but he had yet to bring this up in conversation with Jamie.

Jamie was a daily attendant at Mass in the parish, often serving as the only altar boy in the early morning for the priest celebrating it. His thoughts were his own, he never spoke of a vocation to the priesthood, but the priests watched him closely and often talked to each other openly about just such a possibility.

Jamie was hearing voices of the angels and saints in his head. He was wise enough to keep his gob shut. He knew that to speak of such things would invite ridicule or even worse than that, even here in Papist circles in Ireland. Yet, he heard voices, of that he was sure. He saw things at night while in his bed, in his head and behind his eyes when they would close from exhaustion. He knew enough about life to know that he was either crazy.... or something else, something unique, something that he could not share with other people that it was going on. He was either touched or he was one of the Chosen. He did not know which it was, but he prayed every day to his God to let him know.

AMERICA

When Jamie McGurk reached the age of seventeen, he had earned enough money and placed it away so that he and his mother could travel to America. He had heard that many Wexford Irish were living in Philadelphia. And so in the spring of 1858, Jamie and his mother sailed away from Ireland to America, first to New York and then by train to Philadelphia.

Their trip across the Atlantic was typical and even serene. Their reception in New York was uneventful except for one memorable incident. Father Lafferty advised him quietly when they were alone just days before his departure with his mother for America that things would be different and that he should stay close to his God, his Faith and his Church. Jamie promised that he would attend Mass as often as he could in that faraway Protestant country and that he would never forget that he came from among the poor but proud people of Ireland. That seemed to please Father Lafferty greatly. The good priest promised to write often and Jamie said that he would return the favor.

Jamie McGurk was afraid of the new things he would find, and at the same time elated at the prospect of a new life. Jamie was not afraid of hard work, he kept his own counsel, was an ever-observant student of life and never had the bad humor to speak ill of others. He was a sort of working class gentleman in his manners and demeanor. This had always served him well in Ireland and would continue to serve his needs in the New Country.

While waiting their turn to be checked by the Health Service doctors and staff, about five people in front of them, waiting to be checked by a doctor were two Irishmen speaking loudly to each other. Jamie McGurk thought perhaps they might be drunk.

The men were about twenty years old, and apparently related, perhaps cousins. One had an Irish newspaper, under his arm. It soon became apparent that one could read well and the other could not.

In a heavy Galway accent the one began to read old obituaries in a strong voice to his friend, "Dennis, do ya' see that? What an odd thing to be happenin' in death!"

"And what is that, Francis?"

"Well, look at the listings of all the dead for tha' week. They all died in alphabetical order!" Dennis said nothing, but slowly folded the paper and placed it back under his arm with a look of studied impatience on his face. They were almost up to the head of the line and would be speaking to the Health Officer in less than a minute. It did not seem to be the right time to Dennis for him to be telling his friend that he was a lunatic. They soon were accepted and moved on through.

Jamie McGurk and his mother passed the examination without incident, walked into America and took a train to Philadelphia. The ride took two days. They stopped three times on that train ride to buy food, and the food tasted strange to them. "America has its own taste," thought Jamie McGurk. He would have to grow used to it.

Once in Philadelphia, their lives began anew. The Irish of Philadelphia had just received newly arrived kin.

IRISH PHILADELPHIA

Irish Philadelphia in the late 1850's was replete with a dying Fenian movement, spawned by the Irish American politician in the various Fire Brigades and Irish owned saloons throughout the city and the ever present Irish bishops attempting to keep control over the growing Irish and Irish American citizenry.

There were also various Irish gangs in the City of Brotherly Love like the Schuylkill Rangers who were linked to arson, murder and extortion and could trace their beginnings to the anti-Irish disorders of 1844 in the Schuylkill and Grey's Ferry areas of the city when the Irish in these areas banded together for defense.

The Rangers under the leadership of Jim Haggerty forced tribute among the merchants on the barge wharves and coal yards up the river as far as Pottsville. They were also accused of a counterfeiting operation, robbery along the river and constant warfare with the Philadelphia Police.

And the Rangers were not the only Irish Philadelphia gang to flourish in the Irish slums and tenements of Philadelphia in those days. Other gangs such as the Bouncers, the Tormentors, the Killers, the Spitfires, the Smashers, the Flayers and the Kensington

Blackhawks vied with the Rangers for notoriety. They all had a reputation for violence and struggled for control of the Irish crime scene in Philadelphia.

By the 1850s the Democratic Party in Philadelphia had a large base of the Irish on which it could depend to get out the vote. It was based on the party devotion to the workingman, hostility toward the privilege of the Whigs' worldview, and patronage to the poor. In 1854 the Act of Consolidation was passed combining all city and county boundaries in Philadelphia, having the practical effect of bringing more Protestants who were better educated and monied into the city boundaries. This was a deliberate attempt to offset Irish influence in Philadelphia politics and city machinery.

Although the Irish were important to the Democratic Party it was an uneasy marriage. In city government in 1858 only 8 of the 85-member Common Council for the city were Irish and only 2 of the 27 member Select Council were Irish. The Irish were needed for a Democratic win in Philadelphia politics but they were a far cry from being a dominant force in the city's political scene on the level of office holder.

Unfortunately, because of the Yankee Abolitionists' alliance with the British anti-slavery movement and the threat of Negro competition for jobs, the Irish in the City were not strong anti-slavery adherents. When the Civil War broke out in 1861 all of this gave the Irish a hard time in being seen as loyal Unionists.

It was into this maelstrom of poverty and Irish/Irish American chaos that Jamie McGurk and his mother Fionnuala settled into Philadelphia to start their new life. It would not take them long to realize that the world that they had left behind in Enniscorthy, County Wexford was a very different, very rural world in complete and utter juxtaposition to the rough and tumble world of urban confusion and constant movement of the City of Brotherly Love in 1858.

ST. KEVIN'S

It was late in 2002. St. Kevin's time was over and done. The old buildings were being knocked down, after it was decided to close the parish and merge it with a neighboring parish. It was a difficult decision for Marco Cardinal Bertelli, but there was low school enrollment and the parish rolls had dwindled to a couple of hundred people. The Catholic Church in Philadelphia was changing some said dying.

St. Kevin's was now an organizational cadaver and the buildings had to be razed to make way for a new parking lot. The cardinal archbishop had made his decision. So the demolition began in late December. The building was over a century old, built by an immigrant Irish priest who some said was a saint. His bust on his gravestone in the churchyard would have to be moved, and his body would have to be exhumed and interred in the Holy Sepulcher Catholic Cemetery at the edge of the city.

The church was deconsecrated and readied for demolition by the clergy and the wrecking ball made short work of the buildings. During the mess, the wrecking ball dislodged a piece of the ceiling unintentionally which fell onto the stone altar below and split the altar open, clean down its middle. Inside the altar was found a set

18

of books, diaries actually, that were wrapped in leather and bound with a red string and sealed with a wax seal, the parish seal.

One of the construction workers, Stanley Skindileski who was a member of St. Luke's parish, saw the books, noticed the seal and picked them up. He placed them aside until he could take them to the rectory at St. Luke's that night. He told the young priest, Father O'Bardon what had happened and with a bit of awe in his voice gave the books to the newly ordained cleric. The priest took them to his bedroom and set them on his desk while he attended to his prayers that evening and then went to sleep, ignoring the diaries sitting on his desk.

In the night, he dreamed. A light was shining into his eyes from the books on his desk; not actually into his eyes, more like into his forehead. A narrow beam of yellow-golden light was coming from out of the books and into his forebrain. He awoke with a start. He was sweating. He turned and looked at the books on his desk. He looked at the clock on his dresser—4:00 AM. He walked over to the books, unwrapped the leather and broke the seal. Inside the leather wrapping were three volumes. He started to read the one with the earliest dates.

"In the Year of Our Lord, 1874, I being a priest of Jesus Christ in the Catholic religion, do hereby begin to set down this account of my priesthood in Philadelphia, Pennsylvania of the States United, the date being September the first..." He read until it was time to shower and get ready for his day, starting with early service at 6:30 AM. After celebrating Mass at St. Luke's, Father Liam O'Bardon took the train from Glenside down to the Chancery Office in Center City Philadelphia where he worked as an aide to Monsignor Bill Glenn, special assistant to the Cardinal Archbishop in the matter of sexual abuse of children and clerical misconduct.

Monsignor Glenn lived in the neighboring parish, Our Lady Queen of Peace in Ardsley and they would often ride the train into work together, as they did today. Father O'Bardon was very quiet on this morning's ride. Monsignor Glenn's thoughts wandered to the crisis-of-the-day that he would have to handle for the Cardinal Archbishop. There was always a crisis, and the young priest has been a great help. Then the heavy-set monsignor fell asleep for the rest of the ride into the city.

THE CARDINAL ARCHBISHOP

The priests walked to the Chancery where they worked. They had a new boss, the newly appointed Cardinal Archbishop of Philadelphia. Marco Joseph Cardinal Bertelli, the Archbishop of the Roman Catholic Archdiocese of Philadelphia, was Brooklyn born and bred. From a respected Italian family, he was a perfect fit to lead Philadelphia's Catholics. Armed with a law degree from St. John's University, this son of immigrant parents had risen above his humble beginnings. In Italy, his father Luigi was laying bricks for an aqueduct in Calitir, in the Province of Avellino, when he met Maria Cucci who worked in her parent's bakery shop. They married in 1909, journeyed to America in 1910. They first lived in Harford, CT and then in Brooklyn, NY and then in Queens, New York. They had eleven children ending with Marco.

Marco was a fine student in Catholic schools and he entered seminary in 1943 and was ordained in 1949 in the Cathedral of St. James in Brooklyn. He was sent to the Vatican to study canon law and graduated in 1956, later earning a masters degree in political science in 1962. In 1975 he earned a law degree from St. John's University in Queens and the right to practice civil law in the courts of Pennsylvania and New York State. Marco Bertelli was not a man for the people.

As Father O'Bardon and Monsignor Glenn began to learn the ways of the Archbishop, the fallout from the sexual abuse crisis was growing into a hurricane from the off shore storm it had once been. Things were starting to get very ugly very quickly. Just weeks after Christmas, in the New Year, 2002, he Boston Globe released its article on Father John Geoghan's pedophilia in Boston. Philadelphia would not be far behind if the facts were known, the Cardinal thought, with never ending revelations about pedophile priests, nuns and lay brothers and the bishops who protected them at all costs.

Bertelli was sure that he could handle the situation. His credentials were impeccable. He'd been appointed archbishop of Philadelphia in December 1987 and installed in February 1988, then elevated into the College of Cardinals by Pope John Paul II in June 1991. It was the opinion of the media in Philadelphia that this archbishop was much like all the other American bishops relative to his actions concerning children that were abused by priests and nuns. He was more concerned with the reputation of the Church than with the safety of the children. It was a sad story that would repeat itself all over the world within the ranks of the episcopacy and the leaders of the religious orders. The names changed, the locations were different, the bishops' background information might differ but they were all involved in a cover up of massive proportions. The media would be ruthless and they tried hard to keep the bastards honest.

Throughout the ever expanding global sexual abuse crisis within the Church, which eventually metamorphosed into a crisis of authority against the magisterium itself, these men (and women) showed the People of God over and over again that they were absolutely clueless as to what the real meaning of Church is. Ultimately, this man would line up with his brother bishops and the men and women who were Religious Superiors in his complete misunderstanding of the authority and position that their God had entrusted to them. They were ultimately mercenaries in the Army of God. It was clear from their actions that they never took a true soldier's oath to serve faithfully their King. They never served their King, not really. They merely put on the uniform and served the Army.

But all of this insight was to sadly overcome the People of God in the Catholic Church at a later time. In early 2002 this organizational cancer and narrowly focused leadership paradigm was not yet evident. It would be fair to say that Marco Cardinal Bertelli did not even suspect himself that he was not up to being the bishop he was called to be. It would also be true of his predecessors, especially the mercurial and somewhat odd John Cardinal Kraske, the Polish-American Archbishop of Philadelphia who had immediately preceded the Italian-American now in place.

Monsignor Glenn entered the offices of the Archbishop in the Chancery building and asked his secretary if he was in today.

"He is," was all she would say.

"May I see him?" asked the Monsignor gingerly since he did not want to upset this woman, who held more power with the archbishop than most Catholic clerics in the city.

"Let me ring him" she replied in a familiar monotone. Juana Marta Rodriguez understood power and knew how to use it, sparingly and softly. It scares more people that way.

Monsignor Glenn entered the Cardinal Archbishop's offices.

"Good morning, your Eminence. How are you feeling?" he said with a forced smile on his face.

"Great. Now what do you want? You are interrupting my morning coffee and my one daily vice—devouring the Inquirer. What in the name of God can you possibly want of me at 7:30 in the morning?"

"Your Eminence, we've got problems!" Glenn said with a touch of alarm in his voice.

"We always have problems. We're priests!" the archbishop countered with not just a little irritation.

"Yes, Eminence, but this time I am not sure we are going to handle them very well", and with that he proceeded to explain. "It seems that the latest developments in the sexual abuse lawsuits that are now beginning to come to the surface against the archdiocese are huge. Another problem for us as well is the District Attorney's decision to start an investigation into clerical child abuse within the school system and clerical infrastructure run by the Catholic Archdiocese of Philadelphia."

The archbishop, a lawyer himself, wore an increasingly darkened face as the aide continued delivering his briefing.

Glenn continued, "Things are not good, not good at all. In the best-case scenario, people could be convinced to be quiet and resolve this out of court, out of their loyalty to the church. In the worst case scenario, buildings and property will have to be sold to pay the lawsuits. Either way, our organizational behavior is not something anyone would want to defend in court. We are in serious trouble, no matter how one looks at this!"

By the end of their discussion which lasted two hours, the Cardinal Archbishop said, "Get O'Bardon involved in this. He is newly ordained and a virgin to this sort of thing. It is time he had his Baptism of Fire. Keep me posted and get out of here. I want to finish reading my newspaper!"

The priest could not help thinking as he left the Cardinal's office suite, 'Today is the First Day of the rest of my life'. He had seen that slogan printed on countless altar banners in countless churches over the past three decades. "What an odd thing to think at a time like this" he said to himself under his breath.

THE DIARIES

"It was a strange day," thought Father Liam O'Bardon. Monsignor Glenn had instructed him sternly on his duties as a priest to be ever faithful to the Church and protect her against the forces of anti-Catholicism. Then he touched on what his new duties would be, basically dealing with the District Attorney's Office for the Archbishop and handling the media to contain the sexual abuse scandal as best he could. It all seemed so unnecessary to the young priest.

"Why couldn't these old bastards just keep their peckers in the pants?" he blurted out to Monsignor Glenn. The older priest shot him a look. O'Bardon took the cue from the older priest to keep his personal misgivings about clerical misconduct to himself.

And so, he hurried home to St. Luke's that night, ate his dinner alone and in silence, thanked the housekeeper for the meal and retired to his room for the evening. He saw the diaries where he had left them, sat down in the Queen Anne chair in his bedroom and began to read. He read until midnight, devouring the books. They were written in an uncommonly clear hand, the letters easy to decipher and the wisdom within them hard to ignore. The diaries started with recollections of Ireland.

"Having been born poor, Catholic and Irish in Enniscorthy, County Wexford, Ireland in 1841 and living under the rule of the stranger, I yearned at an early age to become a priest. For it was in Enniscorthy, in the time of my grandfather that Father John Murphy and his brave compatriots served both Church and Country in attempting to drive out the stranger. In 1798 he failed in his attempt to subdue the savagery of the oppressive Yeomanry along with other great Irish patriot priests such as Father Michael Murphy, Father Mogue Kearns and Father Philip Roche all of them being Wexford priests and rebel generals. But in his failure he inspired us, the Irish of another generation, to hope for freedom and live as free men even while under the weight of the foreigner. Ireland shall be free. One day, she will be home to free men and not simply serfs to the will of others.

"I never spoke of this to anyone, not even the parish priest, for I feared that my sweet mother would attempt to deter me, her only son, from his pursuit of Holy Orders. I also feared that the parish priests would inflict heavy penalty upon me if I should show that I was not up to the task of studying for priesthood, which was in fact a difficult task to complete, as I would later learn. So, I kept my own counsel throughout my childhood, occupying myself with the simple task of staying alive in such a poor and tortured country. I worked hard and long and studied under the local curate, a Father Finnbar Lafferty, who proved to be an able teacher, a kind priest and sound theologian, as well as a wise old man. It was because of Father Lafferty that I became a priest at all, for it had not been for his support, his prayers and his influence, I would not have entered seminary at Maynooth, or indeed anywhere at all! It is a rebel priest that inspired my pursuit to the priesthood. It is a rebel priest I aspire to become. I will willingly endure any sacrifice to bring Peace and Christ's justice to the poor and oppressed, be it in Ireland or any other place.

"And so the good cleric, Finnbar Lafferty taught me to read, to have some knowledge of numbers and science, to have a basic understanding of English, Irish, Greek and Latin and to understand that people are generally not evil, but almost always broken. When the time came to leave Ireland in 1758, I did so in the company of my sainted Mother, Fionnuala Haggerty McGurk. She was a beauty to behold, the envy of beautiful women everywhere and the finest mother on the Earth. She was a fine and committed Christian and a role model for a good man to emulate.

"At the age of seventeen I arrived in the company of my mother in these States United. Settling in Philadelphia among the other Wexford and Waterford Irish that preceded us, we soon began to see our fortune and deliverance in this Nation and its people. Although there was much to yearn for in the quiet and pastures of home, there was a sense of urgency, of excitement of prosperity for all in this new land. Even though the Irish were oppressed here in their poverty and in their lack of education, they had a way out of their situation here when desire to succeed was coupled with hard work and hope. This is something none of us knew from home—hope. America offered hope. Home offered only memories and many of them were skewed with the sentimentality of homesickness which often obscured the pain and chilling poverty with which we were once surrounded. Home was best left behind in most cases.

"Father Lafferty never forgot us and would often write to us in care of the local priest at the parish here in which we attended Mass, St. Michael's. It is to be understood that Father Lafferty was lobbying for me to return to Ireland and take up my studies for the priesthood. I would have done it immediately, but there was no money and I could not leave my mother alone in America. And there were other problems that had to be taken into account.

"The decade that we arrived in America, the 1850's, were a hard one for Philadelphia Catholics, especially the Irish. The anti-Irish denunciations and anti-Catholic sentiment of a certain group of American tyrants formed us in Philadelphia as it did in almost no other place in America. The story is a hard one to read but one that must be told in order to understand our place among Philadelphians and my place among my own.

"The tyrants that formed us in Philadelphia were called the 'Know-Nothings'. I write of them now and their deeds so that their hatred will never be forgotten and for all who read this tome to understand that whatever failings we Irish have or had, our character was formed in one unending boiling soup of hatred both in the Old Country and in the new one.

"It was the 'Know-Nothings' that gave us power by trying so hard to keep it from us. They inspired us here in the new country, as the English inspired us in the Old one, to fight on and on and on to beyond the beyond if need be, to secure our personal safety and the right to livelihood of our families and kin. They attracted a large share of attention in America during the decade mother and I arrived in Philadelphia, the 1850s. It was the remaking of what was sometimes termed by journalists as the Nativist Movement which, had actually had a long history among the Anglo-Saxon Protestants that took the colonies away from Britain and made them self sufficient in mercantile concerns and independent in political ones.

"Their principles, other than outright hatred of the Irish seemed to be the proscription of those who professed the Roman Catholic faith and the absolute and hateful forbiddance of the foreign-born among us from all offices of trust or political influence in the government, whether federal, state, or municipal. In truth, I must say we Irish seemed to earn special hatred from this new group of oppressors.

"This Nativist spirit could traced back to the founding of this new nation for in many of the colonies were found laws of penalty which forbade the practice of Roman Catholicism, and these laws remained in force down to the time of the revolution.

"I was to learn through extensive reading at the behest of Irish parishioners who had an interest in such things that this was not simply a problem in Pennsylvania, the national district in which Philadelphia resides. For completely up to 1833 the union between Church and State in the Commonwealth of Massachusetts was extant, only being dissolved that year. And only in that year were Catholics officially excused from the burden of taxation for the support of the Protestant Church within the confines of that district. Even the neighboring district of New Jersey had an official anti-Catholic Constitution until the year 1844. It was not until 1877 that Catholics were allowed to hold office in the district of New Hampshire, that law being written into the district Constitution until that year.

"Even in many other districts throughout the States the spirit of anti-Catholicism would often rear its ugly head in official documents and pronouncements. Freedom of religion as oft times spoken of as written in the National Constitution was not completely acceptable to Americans in theory, and even less in its actual practice among the citizenry. This was the confused state of affairs extant in the Republic in the early years that my mother and I arrived here to live out the rest of our lives. It often seemed to us that we had left one anti-Catholic den of thieves for another.

"Things were so hateful that the oft spoken of John Jay of New York, who was later to be elevated to the exalted status of the Chief Justice of the United States, hung upon the Constitution of the New York district an iron-clad regulation which denied the privilege of citizenship to every foreign-born Catholic unless he would first 'abjure and renounce all allegiance to the pope in matters ecclesiastical'. The early Americans known as the Federalists were the Nativists of their day, and Know-nothingism, was simply the latest venue of these tyrants and social miscreants. Their hatred could be traced directly to the views and prejudices foisted by the Federalists upon foreign-borns and especially in their trademark intolerance of their fellow countrymen professing the Faith of the Church of Rome. Being a Catholic always seemed a hard way to go among English speaking nations.

"These prejudices against Catholics were old prejudices in this new country and the 'Know-Nothings' of Philadelphia had many worthy ancestors espousing similar hatreds in this land. Previous to the arrival of these latest bigots on the scene, Catholics and other foreigners were denounced, mainly from the wealthier Protestant pulpits, as enemies of the American ideals meant to be circulating throughout this Republic. It was not all that far from the views of the English overlords to us, the Irish, back at home.

"Periodicals and even some books intended to inflame passion against the Irish and other Catholics were circulated among the citizenry. Roman Rite Bishops and their priests were very often viciously maligned, their 'odd' religion misrepresented, ridiculed and derided in public, and violence was often committed against Catholics and property belonging to them with the police usually choosing not to see what was plainly in front of their noses. An Ursuline Convent at Charleston, in the district of Massachusetts was burned to the ground in 1834, by a Nativist mob of hateful miscreants, and their cruel and hateful treatment of the terrified nuns and their pupils, were open wounds in the sickness of religious bigotry in America. Father John Murphy would have understood the scene perfectly. I was not all that far from Wexford after all. There were tyrants here too. And perhaps they also needed a John Murphy to appear among them to lead.

"The depth of the hateful wonder of the Nativists appeared horribly in the murderous riots of Philadelphia in 1844. This was a full fourteen years before our arrival in America but the Philadelphia Irish still spoke of it when we arrived here and do so even today, even as I write these notes down in this journal. It was then that several Catholic churches were attacked by a Nativist and murderous cohort, and two of those parishes, St. Michael's and St. Augustine's, were deliberately set afire and destroyed. Public worship by Catholics was suspended by order of Philadelphia's Bishop Kenrick, and the horror was so incredibly extensive that on Sunday, 12 May, 1844, all Catholic churches in this, the City of Brotherly Love, were closed. Many houses containing within them any number of the Catholic Gael were sometimes set ablaze, many of the residents were shot down like dogs at their front stoops and church vestibules, and a number of otherwise law abiding citizens lost their lives in the chaos of this religious bigotry.

"The party whose members were known to the general public as "Know-nothings" was officially organized in 1852 in the Grand City of New York, in the national district of that same name. It was totally anti-Catholic in its intent and by laws and in its desire to maim and injure and disenfranchise any Catholic that it could find unprotected.

"The Nativists had successfully put their man in office in various elections in Philadelphia, Baltimore, San Francisco, New Orleans, and New York City. In 1854 the 'Know-nothings' held around forty seats in the national legislature, the Congress, and elected their candidate a Mr. Gardiner, to the Governorship of Massachusetts, with the aid of an active Nativist legislature. In 1855 New Hampshire, Connecticut, and Rhode Island each elected a Know-nothing governor, and the party carried the day in nine different national districts. By the time mother and I arrived in Philadelphia, 1858, their influence was largely gone but the scars they left would last for generations.

"For reasons that are hard for me to understand, the 'Know-Nothings' started to evaporate in their influence in the face of Democrats and Republicans arguing over issues of slavery and a coming civil war. The country had bigger problems than the hatred of Catholics. By 1856 they were largely ineffectual but they had done tremendous damage to the prospects among the Irish and Irish-in-America and their hopes and dreams. They had set back Irish futures at least a generation. And now, on top of their hatred, a civil war was brewing. We Irish were caught between hatred and death. But then of course, this was not a new experience for us. We were marching with grit and determination toward war in both North and South. Philadelphia's commitment to the war would be key to our legend and promise as new Americans.

"From 1858 until April of 1861 when the war started, mother and I found employment and no small amount of happiness among the Irish of Philadelphia. I worked as a clerk for a lawyer in the city center and the good Doctor Evans had a classmate from Oxford living in Philadelphia who needed a housekeeper. He wrote to him, a wealthy businessman named Harrison, and he employed mother as his chief housekeeper in a large house in Philadelphia's more wealthy section. Life was returning to normal and I was approaching my twentieth year and yearning for home and priesthood.

Several young lasses had caught my fancy but I could not shake the call to priesthood from my mind and I did not want to do so. John Murphy and the other hero priests of Wexford were calling to me in my dreams and in my quiet times. I could not betray their hopes and dreams for me due to my own infrequent desires for family and a lover. No, somehow or other in a way I could never explain to a woman who was interested in me, I was meant for something else. I knew that. And I did not attempt to dissuade myself from the notion. I fully accepted my fate and placed my life in the Hands of God. This was an odd way for a man of my age to act, I knew. But it was my way. I also knew that.

"I wrote often to Father Lafferty back home. We openly discussed my enrollment at Maynooth, the only Catholic seminary in Ireland and his own school. I was making real plans to return to the Olde Sod. I would go home and take priesthood upon my self and shoulder the burdens, the emptiness and the fullness and happiness of priesthood. They were all entwined and could not be separated. To accept one was to accept the other. Then everything changed. I would not being going home to Ireland, at least, not yet. I would instead serve in the army.

The Diaries Continue

The War Between the States and My Involvement Within it

"A Civil War had started in April of 1861 with the secessionists firing upon Fort Sumter and I was about to be conscripted along with other Irishmen living around Second Street in the Fishtown section of the city. So I joined the 98th Pennsylvania Volunteer Infantry and was placed into Company A. We were infantry and walked everywhere and slept in the mud. Army food was terrible so I remained thin throughout the war.

"We had been formed from the remnants of the 21st Pennsylvania Regiment which was disbanded after its three months service at the end of July 1861 by Colonel John F. Ballier with men who were left from the 21st and those of us who were new recruits from Philadelphia. Most of the men of the regiment were recent German immigrants except those of us in Company A, who were mostly Irish and American born Irish Catholics. We would serve in the Army to free the slave and save the Union. That was our war cry. It seemed to me to be the duty of every Irishman who had known bitter tyranny under British rule back at home to serve in this endeavor here.

"We spent that winter encamped in Maryland and in March of 1862 we marched to Hampton, Virginia and joined the Third Brigade, First Division of the Fourth Corps in the march up the peninsula. We came under the fire of rebel guns for our very first time on the Fifth of May 1862. I lost two friends from my company that day. One died in my arms. The other was simply blown to bits. He disappeared into thin air except for his legs which were left over from the force of the cannon ball striking his frame. There was not much left of him.

"On the First of July of that year our Regiment fought hard at Malvern Hill and we lost perhaps sixty killed, wounded or missing or otherwise unaccounted for. We were ordered to march back to cover the Federal retreat from the battle at Bull Run and we hurriedly did that.

"We just missed the fighting at Antietam and we established winter quarters near a place known as Falmouth in Virginia. While there we half-heartedly participated in a slovenly way with Burnside's shenanigans at Fredericksburg that December and had a famous muddy march to nowhere in January 1863.

"Old Joe Hooker took command of the Army of the Potomac soon after that and the Regiment was transferred again to Third Brigade, Third Division, Sixth Corps of the Federal Army. We fought for Marye's Heights and also Salem Heights on the Third of May and our colonel was wounded and so Lieutenant Colonel Wynkoop took command of the regiment. I too was wounded that day, although I was merely grazed by a Confederate ball in my left leg and received barely a scratch. Two men on either side of me died clean when rebel balls smashed through their heads. They were dead before their bodies hit the ground. Thank God for that. They suffered no pain. There was death everywhere.

"We were sent back home to Pennsylvania to a sleepy and lovely spot known as Gettysburg. We thought we could rest but the most decisive battle of that horrible war raging east of the Mississippi River took place there. Our Brigade, the Third, was posted on the extreme right of Little Round Top and when Sickle's Corp was driven back we held our position and did not run. We were exposed to the horror of enemy artillery and we received casualties for it, but we held and held strong. We wintered at Brandy Station. We were a proud unit and over 230 soldiers reenlisted on December 23rd. Only one hundred of us went home when their enlistments were done.

"It often struck me as odd when we would sight Irish brigades with their green flags flying over on the rebel side of the ramparts that Irishmen were also fighting to keep the negro enslaved in the South. How could Irishmen have such confusing feelings when they were sore oppressed themselves back home? I have never been able to answer that question satisfactorily to myself.

"Once at Gettysburg I happened to stroll among rebel dead picking up armaments after we repelled a Confederate attack upon our position when I heard a groan from among the fallen bodies of the southern lads. I stooped down and held up the head of a dying rebel and spotted a wooden rosary falling out of his pants pocket. I gave him water from my canteen and he said 'thank you' in a whisper, but I could clearly ascertain the brogue. He was an Irishman and dying on a battlefield far from home. We talked for a minute before he died. He begged me to pray for him and the happy repose of his soul and also to write his mother in Clare to tell her of his death. He told me that I was to say that his last thoughts were of her. He handed me her last letter to him with her address in the note. He died saying an Ave with me. I wrote his mother that evening. I never received a return post from her. I did not expect it.

"In January we marched to Charlestown, West Virginia and soon afterward we left for Philadelphia for our first and only furlough of the war. That May the regiment again took to the field of battle under Colonel John Ballier and we fought at the Battle of the Wilderness, again at Spotsylvania, and in North Anna and in Cold Harbor. In just five weeks our casualties were three officers and twenty-four infantrymen killed and six officers and one hundred and two infantrymen wounded. Pain and misery was everywhere among us.

"We were billeted at Appomattox when Lee surrendered his Army of Northern Virginia to Grant and our unit was given seven hundred newly drafted recruits and we were sent to Danville near Carolina and then we marched back to the Capital in Washington to be mustered out of the Army at the end of June 1865 when Johnston surrendered to Sherman.

"We had seen many a battle and many of us had died. As for me, I was promoted to Corporal in September of '61 and then at the end of the war in April of '65, I was promoted again to Sergeant and I was mustered out of the Army with most of the regiment in June of '65. I had received a small wound for which I would receive an equally small pension. Many friends and companions died within my sight and some within my arms. One good friend, one Tom Barnes, returned with me to Philadelphia and remained my lifelong friend. He had been wounded twice and still stayed fighting within our regiment to the end. As for the others, they will always remain in my heart. Many of their names I did not know but their faces I shall never forget.

"I don't think of those days much now. The bravery of those young men seems wasted in the times that followed that tragic war. But for us Irish and other immigrant groups, our participation in that War was our ticket to acceptability, at least on the lowest level of regard, by the Protestant overlords that run this Republic. At least we foreigners had won the right to be free of open molestation in most districts.

"I had not attended Mass or had regular prayer time in over three years and I had only seen my mother once. Still beautiful as in her youth, she was however thin and seemed faintly sickly to me. She did not speak of any pain and I did not ask about it, still I worried about her. I yearned for regular Mass attendance and a calm life after the chaos of war and the horrors of it. I wrote to Father Lafferty and again resumed my plans to attend Maynooth in Ireland and study for priesthood.

"In January of 1866 I received a letter from Father Lafferty at mother's home in Fishtown on Second Street telling us that money had been secured from a wealthy English Catholic family for me to travel to Ireland and study for priesthood at Maynooth. I had since taken a job as an apprentice to an ironworker in a mill in Kensington. It paid the bills.

"The patron bought me a ticket that summer for a ship to take me from Philadelphia to New York to Nova Scotia to Galway along with other passengers returning to Ireland and England. I was not sure how I was going to leave mother alone. How would she pay the bills in America alone? She offered that I should not worry and that the parishioners at Saint Michael's had offered her work and money if she should need it. Assured that she would be all right in my absence I left for home.

"I arrived in Ireland that August and traveled immediately to Saint Patrick's College, Maynooth to study for priesthood in the Fall of 1866. I was twenty-four years old and coming hard onto twenty-five. I passed all examinations required of me for placement and I started studies for Holy Orders immediately. Finally my journey of the soul was to begin.

"Ireland was still suffering from the aftermath of the Penal Laws which were passed by an English Parliament in order to suppress Catholicism in Ireland. They were in force legally from 1691 until about 1760. Although not actually enforced in any real way in the late 18th Century, they remained on the books until Catholic Emancipation in 1829. The upshot of all of this hooliganism in the English court system forced upon the Irish people was a sort of inward looking fear that all Irish nurtured relative to their Faith. They both loved it and feared for it at the same time. Their experience as Catholics had been hard, even and especially in their own land and because an Irishman could not study for priesthood in Ireland (it was punishable by death) Irish lads were seminarians at Irish schools in Spain and France. The "French taught" seminarians tended to be quite radical in their outlook and often saw their role in post-revolutionary terms. Such were the priests in my part of Ireland, the Pale.

"So even though it was much later than this time that I was to take up studies for priesthood in my own homeland, I was bit different than most. I was imbued with a sense of righteous radicalism that only an Irish cleric could understand as Godly. People didn't need a God who talked out of a sanctimonious book. They needed a God who lived in a priest. They needed a human to be the hands and feet of God, to act in His Name, to be his stand-in for persecution if need be. It was not enough to be like the Christ for a priest. A priest had to actually be the Christ. That was my view of priesthood gleaned from the Irish priests that I had known as a child in Wexford.

"I studied hard and found Greek and Hebrew to be more difficult than I expected but I persevered and eventually conquered the basics of these subjects. I resumed my informal learning of the Gaelic language by seeking out constant conversation with Gaelic speaking seminarians, mostly from the West of Ireland. I was older than most other men in my class but

I cannot say that I was the best student. I was not. I was somewhere in the middle of the class in intellect and understanding of the subject matter. I had to be careful to study hard and not dally too much in idle conversation. I took the two-year course in Philosophy studies and then moved on to the four-year course in Theology.

"I had to be equally careful that my radical political ideas not be seeing the light of day at Saint Patrick's College, Maynooth for the seminary itself had been started with grant money from English Parliament in 1795 and it was being continually watched by Englishmen and Irish bishops for any hint of radicalism. One William Kelly had been expelled from the seminary with great public attention being paid to the situation when it was found that he openly supported the "Young Ireland" Movement. No matter, he applied to the Jesuits and was accepted and was later ordained a Jesuit priest about 1863. He became a great preacher in Australia and later came home to Ireland to prepare young Jesuits in their seminary. Although it was hard to find them at Maynooth, I did have kindred spirits there.

"I at one and the same time did most certainly believe in Christian charity and Christian manliness. Turning the other cheek seemed to me to be blasphemy when your own kin were being starved off the land by absentee landlords who were more interested in pastureland and sheep then the starving Catholics who tended them. This had been true in the years I was formed in an Irish childhood filled with stories of starvation, deprivation and anti-Catholic hatred. Now that I was back home in Ireland, many of the old resentments and feelings would often float to the surface of my soul and I had to fight hard to keep my gob shut in order to maintain mental and spiritual balance to finish my studies. I was studying for the Catholic priesthood in an Irish seminary built with English money sent by Parliament and the oddity of it all was not lost on any of us. Control was always an issue with the patrons in the English government and their enforcers among the Catholic bishops of Ireland. A fine line of hypocrisy was being walked by all concerned. We took English Parliament's money for the school's survival

and in turn, we promised to be good lads. We were to be good and holy
priests without a hint of French radicalism extant in the generation of Irish
priests ahead of us. It was all manure."

The Diaries Continue:
The Vatican Council of 1869–1870

"I had been at St. Patrick's College, Maynooth, only three years when the Holy Father Pius IX convened a Council. The Pope and his council were all the talk for two years at Maynooth. He convened this Council of bishops by issuing a Papal Bull Aeterni Patris, on June 29, 1868. The council met for the first time on December 8th, 1869 and stayed in session in Rome until July 18th, 1870 and it was all quite controversial. The basic thrust of the Council was to issue a proclamation on papal infallibility. During these seven months roughly 750 bishops sat in the council, with 19 from Ireland. This was about three quarters of the Catholic bishops throughout the world and many good bishops saw the doctrine of infallibility in matters of Faith and Morals as inopportune to put forward at that time. Frankly they thought that we had outgrown the need for this intellectual tyranny and hubris. It was this sort of thinking that made so many Catholic bishops and churchmen hated throughout the Continent. But this did not stop the Pope and his cronies, many of them Irishmen.

"Those bishops who openly opposed the proclamation of infallibility seemed to number about 200 of the Council's sitting bishops. In the last of the meetings held on 13 July 1870, (called General Congregations) those bishops opposing the proclamation would cast 88 opposing votes, while another 76 stayed away rather than vote. About a fifth or more of the sitting Council bishops opposed the proclamation outright. The proclamation passed muster with the episcopacy in attendance, including Paul Cardinal Cullen, Ireland's first Cardinal, he having been elevated to the College of Cardinals in 1866. There were several proscriptions concerning many obtuse matters. It was an error to say that God is not the creator of all things. It was an error to say that God cannot be found in nature. It was an error to say that Divine Revelation cannot be made apparent in outward signs. It was an error to say that miracles cannot and do not exist. It was an error to say that there are no divine mysteries and that God can be fully explained by natural means.

"I must tell you, I was secretly shocked at the shallowness of the Council. I had grown into manhood clinging to my Catholic Faith for hope and strength in the face of constant and never ending dire economic strangulation and social persecution at the hands of the heretic overlords from England. The best my church could do when meeting in General Council was to ratify old attitudes that were extant prior to the Revolution in France and were the same attitudes that had made clerics hated in the eyes of European peasants for centuries. The bishops did not seem to grasp that theology is blasphemy when it was exercised on such high planes, completely devoid of any connection to the sufferings of the Believers and completely meaningless in the lives of the Faithful. They were engaged in semantics while many of the Faithful throughout the world were engaged in dieing, starving and persecution. What a load of chicken drop.

"The bishops were simply talking theology while the Irish and the poor Catholics of the world were suffering for the Faith. Instead of using their influence to right the wrongs heaped upon the backs of their lay co-religionists in the pews, the bishops at the Council were indulging themselves in theoretical theological nonsense. I really don't think the typical Irish Catholic in Philadelphia (or anywhere else) really cares about this hosh-posh. It is not in any way helpful to his faith or his life. Bishops are idiots.

"I was quietly disgusted with this display of ecclesiastical and episcopal hubris, but I decided to say nothing to anyone. It was now a tenet of the Catholic Faith. I shuddered when I thought of how I would now have to adhere to this pre-Revolutionary prattle of the overarching reach of the Church. What made the matter even worse is that one of the professors at Maynooth to whom I had great affection, Father Patrick Murray, was at the Council and was one of the leading theologians supporting and lobbying for the Doctrine of Papal Infallibility. I felt personally betrayed by this pre-Revolutionary stance of an arrogant few by the assistance of an old theologian who was personally quite good and whom I personally knew and liked, but again I said nothing. The Church yearned for the days that existed before the French made governments as important as the curia. John Murphy was somewhere in heaven looking down on this theological nonsense and shaking his head in disgust. What idiocy theology is when men are starving and the voiceless need a voice! Theology is a poor substitute for justice. Certainly the bishops knew this. Did they even care? I doubted it.

"I felt that that I understood the mindset of Father John Murphy now more than I ever thought I would. When the Yeomanry finally captured him on Vinegar Hill, they tortured him, burned him alive, decapitated him and placed his head on a pike. I felt the same would be done to me, at least metaphorically, if I openly talked of my disgust at the Council's findings. This was Catholicism at its finest? Says who? It was a shallow attempt to reassert our right to speak for all of Western Civilization in matters of Faith and Morals by claiming absolute authority over the same, just like we had done in the Middle Ages. What a ridiculous tenet to hold forth in the age of science and research and academia. We wanted to be the sole voice shouting in the Wilderness concerning man's relationship to God. The real problem was that Man had moved past even believing in God. Our job now was to win Man back into the fold of the Believers, not to tell him how he should believe. Man did not believe. That was the problem. And that was our challenge—to give him a reason to believe once more. Like Nero, we were fiddling while Rome burned. Certainly someone had to tell the Cardinals that they were about as useful as yesterday's newspaper...all that could be done with them was wrap fish.

"I was now more determined than ever to be that Catholic priest I needed and wanted to be, at one with the Healer and Teacher from Nazareth and completely divorced from the nonsense that too much organization among human beings seems to enhance ad infinitum. Sometimes humans simply take their place in the Universe too seriously. We really are not that important when all is said and done. It is the creation that is important, not this or that piece of the whole broad cloth. The bishops saw their role in the Universe on a much larger scale than they had any right to see it. And this nonsense out of Rome was proof of it. I knew better than to say this. I simply let it burn into my soul. God knows that I hated the insight I had been given. The Church was only The Church when it served the People of God and actually behaved like the Church. When it served the arrogance and hubris of the bishops it was a tragic comedy. I loved the fact that I would be a Catholic priest. I hated the fact that I would have to feign belief in this nonsense in order to be one. It was my personal compromise, my personal crucifixion; I had to pretend to believe in this insanity in order to be ordained a priest of Christ.

"The normal course of study at Maynooth was seven years. There were three years of philosophy and related studies and then four years for theology. There was also an extra year for fools like me who had no real formal education to catch up on learning as best they could before the real studies started. I was not formally educated in a proper school, so the course of study was eight years for me, the faculty wanting to ensure that I was of sufficient intellectual weight to carry the Faith to all who might argue against it. This is all to say that I studied hard and I studied constantly. The food was bad, the apartments sparsely appointed and cold and the days were long which seemed to imbue us all with a seriousness that to me seemed out of place for clerics imbued with the Holy Spirit. There seemed to be little lightness to the place which in turn seemed to be its trademark. The poet W.M. Letts as early as 1802 wrote the following verse of seminarians at Maynooth. 'The men of Maynooth are like the rooks, with their solemn black coats an' their serious looks." Sixty four years after the poet posted this verse, the same could be said of the student body to which I belonged.

"Finally, after eight years of study and nothing but letters to and from my mother and Father Lafferty's annual visit to me at Maynooth and one short visit from Old Crooked Pat, I was ordained a priest in the newly built Catholic St. Patrick's Cathedral in Armagh by Archbishop Daniel McGettigan and set straightaway for Philadelphia again to take up my priesthood in America. I was now almost thirty three years of age, more than slightly old for a newly ordained priest but ready to take up the challenges ahead. I was glad to be done with seminary. It was the summer of 1874 and I had started studies for the priesthood in August of 1866. I did not find the experience very enjoyable or very enlightening, but I was grateful for the education and itching like a wool sweater to put it all to use."

O'Bardon finished reading and fell asleep in the chair. Morning came and it was time to shower, celebrate morning Mass and catch the train for Center City. O'Bardon was growing closer and closer to this strange and independent minded priest born 140 years or so prior to his own birth. He knew that he should deliver the diaries to the Chancery immediately, but he wanted to read them first. The diaries were somehow becoming central to his own view of his own priesthood. This was a dangerous thing and he knew that. But the honesty of this strong-willed Irishman was too much to overcome. He knew that too. Father McGurk was no one to ignore or with whom one should trifle, not even in death.

THE PHILADELPHIA GRAND JURY INVESTIGATION

April 2002 and Philadelphia District Attorney Linda Abramson was stunned into silence. A Jewish woman, highly intelligent and known for her squeaky clean record in attorneys' circles throughout the city, she was shocked at what she knew to be happening to Catholic children in the city at the hands of Catholic clergy and nuns.

At least eleven grand juries nationwide had already commenced investigations of dioceses, and absolutely none resulted in criminal charges against presently presiding bishops relative to their universal failure to properly deal with sexually abusive priests under their control. Still, a few bishops facing prosecutorial inquiries or legal action of some kind reluctantly entered plea agreements that created funds to partially compensate victims or allowed oversight and monitoring of a diocese by law enforcement or the court system. And several of these same investigative panels, including grand juries in New York and in Boston where the Catholic Church's sexual abuse crisis erupted in 2002 due to the investigative efforts of reporters from the Boston Globe, issued lengthy and often lurid reports.

It was found that many church leaders had transferred guilty clergy from parish to parish without notifying parents or law enforcement authorities of the entire situation. Put simply, bishops and their minions in the various American chanceries had routinely and systematically put Catholic children in harm's way for decades, some as far back as the 1920s, in order to protect the 'reputation' of the Church. It was the ultimate ecclesiastical sin of omission. When the report was finally released September 2005 the city would be stunned. It was found that 63 priests molested children over several decades within the jurisdiction of the Archdiocese of Philadelphia, some of them were serial molesters with an uncommon degree of cunning, and all of them were protected in one way or another by the bishops and the Catholic Church's organization extant at the time in the city. The report's opening paragraph said," Some may be tempted to describe these events as tragic. Tragedies such as tidal waves, however, are outside human control. What we found were not acts of God, but of men who acted in His name and defiled it."

A full three years and more before the release of the final report from the District Attorney's office and Father Liam O'Bardon was now part of the cover up and he knew it. He was too honest a man to lie to himself or anyone else about the true nature of the situation in Philadelphia.

As for the District Attorney, she kept her own counsel on the matter until the report was released. In 2002 the cover-up and obfuscation was fast and furious. Now knowing that there would be a thorough investigation and final report, priests' personnel files were 'doctored' routinely in order for the Archdiocese to be able to claim to insurers and investigators alike that "remedial therapy" had taken place, when in fact, no such thing happened at all. The Archdiocese of Philadelphia, a Catholic diocese under the guidance of an attorney-bishop, was lying through its teeth.

Linda Abramson was born in 1941 and she had been the District Attorney of the City of Philadelphia since 1991. She took her undergraduate degree from Temple University and also received her law degree from Temple University Law School. Abramson served as the head of the Philadelphia Redevelopment Authority during the administration of Mayor Frank Rizzetti.

Abramson had been a judge on the Philadelphia Court of Common Pleas, and a former assistant D.A., Abramson was elevated to District Attorney in 1991 to fill the vacancy created by the ousted D.A. Abramson was elected to a four-year term in 1993 and was re-elected in 1997, 2001 and 2005 defeating every challenger. She was one of the longest serving D.A.'s in Philadelphia history

Liam O'Bardon would come to learn in the 40 months that he dealt with the D.A.'s office that Linda Abramson was an honest woman who simply wanted to get to the truth of the matter and stop the abuse of children. Although technically his adversary in the game of "protect the Church at all costs", O'Bardon had a grudging respect for the D.A. She was honest. He was not.

Riding into Center City on the train with Monsignor Glenn that morning, Father O'Bardon was again given instructions on how he was to proceed as the Monsignor's assistant in dealing with the D.A.'s office. He was to protect the Church and her reputation at all times, that was his primary assignment from the Cardinal Archbishop. Monsignor Glenn told him twice that he hoped Father O'Bardon understood the trust and faith that the Cardinal Archbishop was placing in him. Father O'Bardon said he understood. In fact, he understood all too well, and he was now resigned to this particular personal crucifixion. He would have to plumb the depths of his soul to find out how he could ethically carry out this assignment. It might not be possible.

For the first couple of years, all that was really required of O'Bardon was that he answer letters via Archdiocesan lawyers to the lawyers down at the District Attorney's office concerning a particular priest, nun or lay brother in a specific situation involving an alleged sexual abuse victim. That was not all that difficult since O'Bardon simply wrote the responses and then routed them through the lawyers for approval. It seemed almost automatic.

The District Attorney's staff of lawyers would ask a question and the Archdiocesan staff would do everything in its power to not answer the question. It was the typical legal game of cat and mouse. All of this seems normal to lawyers but is maddening to people who live on the edge of urgency and desperation, like abuse victims. It is the kind of legal environment that makes no one happy, gives little real information to anyone but is highly successful in protecting against estate and tort issues. In the end, Catholicism at its worst was reflected in the success of the church's lawyers in keeping property from being sold to pay off legal settlements and O'Bardon played a big role in this "success." He knew it and he was not proud of it.

But by the beginning of the third year of the investigation, matters were boiling over. Things were not good from the Archdiocese's point of view. The District Attorney's investigation was getting close to the real meat of the matter, that is, that people in charge of the Archdiocese and working in the Chancery were not properly supervising very sick priests. The reasons for this did not matter to the D.A.'s office, the damage to hundreds of lives was apparent and that was all that mattered. Children were being treated as unintended casualties in a war over the church's "reputation", as if that mattered in a case where a child is raped. The deeper the D.A.'s office dug, the more ugliness was found. There seemed to be no end to this.

All during these three years O'Bardon began to question his priesthood commitment in the face of the obfuscation in which he was daily involved. He came to realize all too well that he was a liar, a con man and a priest, all at once. And because of his ability to manipulate the truth his star was rising, the Cardinal Archbishop liked his work, his attitude and his willingness to soldier on, to do anything that needed to be done to "protect the Church." The irony of it all was not lost on the priest. He was beginning to hate himself and to question what it meant to be a priest. He had grown deeply ashamed of himself.

In the course of this three-year assignment to Purgatory, O'Bardon had grown close to a young nun who worked at the Chancery. She was young for a nun at 26 years old when they first met. She was cute and she had strong Polish facial features framed in light brown hair sticking out from her modern nun's wimple. Her name was Sister Martha Konscikowski and she was a good human being with a good heart. Tall, thin and serious in her demeanor she was almost as tall as O'Bardon who was six feet one himself. They would work together for hours, preening through priest's personnel files, reading what was contained therein and trying to put the best face on the situation involving this or that particular sick individual. Their job was to make the file as clean as possible without actually breaking the law. O'Bardon could not deny the fact that she attracted him. But he tried to keep that to himself and not show his affection for her. She was a woman so she noticed that the priest, three years her senior, was attracted to her. Being a nun she pretended not to notice. The chemistry was there between them and both attempted to block it out, to turn it sideways, to ignore its implications. They both tried with all their might and for a while, the ruse they played with themselves held.

But one afternoon, Sister Martha missed her bus back to the convent near the Cathedral of Sts. Peter and Paul. She would have to walk back to the convent from the Chancery offices in the dark of the winter night. Father O'Bardon had driven to work that day in his new car, a compact car his parents had bought him the previous summer. He offered Sister Martha a ride back to the convent and she agreed. They were both secretly pleased at the small amount of time it would give them together in his car alone, although neither of them dared to admit this to themselves.

"Hard day?" Sister Martha asked him as she entered the car and looked at her friend behind the wheel. She buckled herself in to the car and watched his face grow solemn.

"Sister, all my days are hard days. And yours are too. I sometimes ask myself, what are we doing and why are we doing it? No matter how you slice this, no matter how many times I try to convince myself that we are protecting the church, it all comes down to money. We are doing everything we can to 'doctor' files to limit the legal liability of the Archdiocese once the Grand Jury Report is published. And both of us know that. What are we doing?" O'Bardon said with uncharacteristic candor. He had actually never talked to Sister Martha like this before. She was startled.

"But don't we have the right, the duty even, to protect the Church?" she said with apparently forced conviction.

"Protect the church from whom? Attorneys? And besides what is *the church* anyway? Aren't these small boys and girls in our grammar schools that have been raped and molested by priests, brothers and nuns 'the Church'? Is the church what the Cardinal Archbishop says it is?" O'Bardon blurted out, in a soft voice, but still forceful, almost as if he was talking to himself. The nun's face reddened.

She knew that he was right and that he was only mouthing what she had already said to herself many times over. They spent the rest of the ride in silence. Enough had been said between them and it was not what either one of them feared (or hoped) the conversation would contain. The night was long for both of them. Neither of them slept that well that evening.

Three years went by and both Sister Martha and Father O'Bardon worked diligently cleaning files, answering queries from the Grand Jury and media making sure that as little information as possible was given out. They knew that they were the first line of defense against the enemies of the Church in those quarters. Their job was to protect the Church. And they did that. They grew closer and closer during those years, making a regular habit of eating lunch together and once, the summer before, they had run into each other while both were vacationing at the Jersey shore and they made a dinner date. Neither was wearing clerical garb and they enjoyed each other's company at dinner immensely. They were human and needed what all humans need, a sense of belonging to someone, in their lives. They were growing close to each other now and nothing could stop that. They both feared and cherished the closeness.

It was Spring of 2005 now and the Grand Jury was calling witnesses. The pace of the tragedy and its unfolding was now about to pick up. They had done all that they could do to protect the church. It was now up to the Cardinal Archbishop and the attorneys. Their combined actions would now determine the church's reputation for decades to come.

For a week and a half that the Cardinal Archbishop was called to testify in front of the Grand Jury on his official behavior and that of his predecessor, John Cardinal Kraske, about the sexual abuse of children under his pastoral care throughout the Archdiocese. He was found to be obtuse in his answers, not remembering all sorts of things a reasonable man would be expected to remember and generally evasive in his answers. The Philadelphia Inquirer posted the main points of the District Attorney's findings when the Grand Jury Report was released. It was damning.

Father O'Bardon and Sister Martha both read the newspaper account of the District Attorney's finding with great shame. They were deeply involved in this mess and they knew it. They acted out of a sense of loyalty to their church, to her leaders and to their sense of childlike simplicity that what was said or done by a bishop was the Will of God. If the Cardinal Archbishop wanted them to obstruct justice with the manipulation of priest personnel files, then so be it. They learned late a very hard lesson in life. I am my brother's keeper and I must obey the mandates of my heart, not the Cardinal Archbishop if it goes against my conscience. That responsibility cannot be delegated "upstairs." We all must claim it for ourselves.

"A Continuous, Concerted Campaign of Cover-Up"
Excerpts from the Grand Jury's Report
Philadelphia Inquirer
September 22, 2005

"Many of us are Catholic. We have the greatest respect for the faith, and for the good works of the Church. But the moral principles on which it is based, as well as the rules of civil law under which we operate, demanded the truth be told.

Some may be tempted to describe these events as tragic. Tragedies such as tidal waves, however, are outside human control. What we have found were not acts of God, but of men who acted in His name and defiled it.

Grand jurors heard evidence proving that Cardinals Bertelli and Kraske, and their aides, were aware that priests in the diocese were perpetrating child molestations and sexual assaults. The Archdiocese's own files reveal a steady stream of deceptions.

After reviewing thousands of documents from Archdiocese files and hearing . . . from over a hundred witnesses, we, the Grand Jurors, were taken aback by the extent of sexual exploitation within the Philadelphia Archdiocese.

For any who might want to believe that the abuse problem in the Philadelphia area was limited in scope, this Report will disabuse them of that impression. The Jurors heard from some victims who were sexually abused once or twice, and from many more who were abused week after week for years.

Indeed, the evidence arising from the Philadelphia Archdiocese reveals criminality against minors on a widespread scale—sparing no geographic sector, no income level, no ethnic group. We heard testimony about priests molesting and raping children in rectory bedrooms, in church sacristies, in parked cars, in swimming pools, at St. Charles Borromeo Seminary, at the priests' vacation houses in the Poconos and the Jersey shore, in the children's schools and even in their own homes.

Cardinal Bertelli, Cardinal Kraske and their top aides all abdicated their duty to protect children. They concealed priests' sexual abuses instead of exposing them.

There is no doubt that the cardinals and their top aides knew that Philadelphia priests were abusing children. There is no doubt that these officials engaged in a continuous, concerted campaign of cover-up over the priests' sexual offenses.

Sexually abusive priests were either left quietly in place or 'recycled' to unsuspecting new parishes - vastly expanding the number of children who were abused.

Documents clearly established that Cardinal Bertelli knew that the priests had admitted abusing minors. They also established that he alone was responsible for subsequently placing or leaving the priests in parishes where they would present a severe danger to children.

Cardinal Bertelli had a strict policy, according to his aides, that forbade informing parishioners. The Cardinal, in fact, encouraged that parishioners be misinformed.

Cardinal Bertelli was trained as an attorney. The Grand Jurors find that in his handling of priests' sexual abuse, Cardinal Bertelli was motivated by an intent to keep the record clear of evidence that would implicate him or the Archdiocese. To this end, he continued many of the practices of his predecessor, Cardinal Kraske, aimed at avoiding scandal, while also introducing policies that reflected a growing awareness that dioceses and bishops might be held legally responsible for their negligent and knowing actions that abetted known predators.

To protect themselves from negative publicity or expensive lawsuits—while keeping abusive priests active —the cardinals and their aides hid the priests' crimes from parishioners, police and the general public. In his testimony before the Grand Jury, Cardinal Bertelli was still attempting to evade responsibility for placing known sexual offenders in parishes where they had easy access to hundreds of children. He often suggested he might not have known all the facts and that he delegated the handling of these matters to his Secretary of Clergy. He repeatedly claimed to have no memory of incidents and priests we on the jury will never forget.

What makes these actions all the worse, the grand jurors believe, is that the abuses that Cardinal Bertelli and his aides allowed children to suffer—the molestations, the rapes, the lifelong shame and despair - did not result from failures or lapses, except of the moral variety. They were made possible by purposeful decisions, carefully implemented policies and calculated indifference. In its callous, calculating manner, the archdiocese's 'handling' of the abuse scandal was at least as immoral as the abuse itself.

Archdiocese officials at the highest levels received reports of abuse. They chose not to conduct any meaningful investigation. They left dangerous priests in place or transferred them to different parishes as a means of concealment. They never alerted parents of the dangers poses by these offenders. They intimidated and retaliated against victims and witnesses. They manipulated "treatment" efforts in order to create a false impression of action. They did many of these things in a conscious effort to simply to avoid civil liability.

It didn't have to be this way. Prompt action and a climate of compassion for the child victims could have significantly limited the damage done. But the archdiocese chose a different path."

O'Bardon was the pathfinder. He was deeply ashamed of his part in this debacle. After reading the article and knowing their part in it, they braced for backlash from their fellow nuns and priests.

It did not come. The clerical culture would not allow for it. They might not be heroes with their colleagues, but they certainly were not villains as far as other priests and nuns were concerned. Such was the dark and horrid heresy that "love of Church over all" had made of the clerical mindset and had now overcome Catholics in the pew. It was better to lie and cheat to protect the church from lawsuits than to protect children from lecherous priests and nuns. The angels must have been screaming in pain. Priests and nuns throughout the Archdiocese certainly were not. Such was the 21st century view of Catholicism among Catholics. Shame knows no religion. It exists in them all. It seemed to take up a long residence within the Catholic Church in Philadelphia and elsewhere at this point in history.

"What would Jesus have said of all of this?" O'Bardon could not keep himself from thinking. Jesus wanted a millstone tied around the neck of anyone who would harm a child and then have them thrown into the sea. He plainly stated that. The priests and nuns and pew Catholics of Philadelphia must have missed Mass the Sunday that this particular piece from the Gospel was read. They did not seem to be familiar with the passage. O'Bardon felt deeply ashamed of himself and his church. His church did not seem to know what the concept of "church" really was to Catholics it seemed to mean the clergy; it certainly did not seem to include the children.

MARTHA AND LIAM

"What now?" was all he could think. Liam O'Bardon's role as Chancellor of the Lie was coming to an end with the publishing of the Grand Jury Report. Philadelphia Catholics were uncommonly quiet and unmoved by it all. That fact disturbed him even more than the evil it bespoke, Sister Martha had been immediately reassigned to teach a fourth grade class at the Cathedral parish as soon as the Grand Jury report was published. The sooner she is out of the storm's eye, the better, thought her superiors. Priests openly and resolutely had preached that the media was anti-Catholic throughout all of this and some even continued to do so when the Grand Jury Report was published, Linda Abramson coming under particular fire for her alleged anti-Catholic stance. But O'Bardon knew better. If being a Catholic meant someone who resolutely seeks justice then Linda Abramson was the most Catholic person in Philadelphia despite her Jewish Faith, and O'Bardon knew it.

O'Bardon took a vacation to Ireland to see his mother's family directly after the Grand Jury Report was published. He was out of town for over a month while the heat rose directly into the face of Monsignor Glenn and the Cardinal Archbishop. That was fine with the Chancery since O'Bardon had not been discovered as a key player in the whole mess by the District Attorney's office and he was not subpoenaed as the Cardinal Archbishop and Monsignor Glenn were to be. They did not fare well with the city's lawyers and came off looking like liars and con men. Whether they actually were or not made little difference. They looked like they were and the media had a field day.

O'Bardon's mother was a Haggerty from Wexford, actually from Adamstown, about fifteen miles or so outside of Enniscorthy. Most of the Philadelphia Irish were from Wexford or Waterford in the Pale. His mother had been a devout woman and loving and was a major influence in his decision to become a priest. Liam O'Bardon would usually travel to Wexford to visit family, the American branch of the family and the Wexford branch of the family being reunited in the 1950s when his uncle Edmund visited Ireland again after a family exodus in the 1890s. He visited 'the family' and found them open to him. The reunion was sweet and the two families considered themselves cousins after that visit. There was a strong family resemblance to Liam O'Bardon and many of his Irish cousins that was undeniable.

He would often stay in Treacy's Hotel in Enniscorthy and then get someone from town to drive him into Adamstown for the day to spend with family. Usually, he would spend two days with family in the week or so he was in Ireland. He would travel to Galway or even Ulster sometimes, and always to Dublin. He would spend a lot of time on trains and buses in Ireland, seeing the sights and enjoying riding with the Irish in a style in which they were accustomed to travel. He loved the Irish. After all, he looked like one of them, even though the O'Bardon's had been in America since the Famine times. Apparently genes do not recognize geography as much as they do bloodlines.

But O'Bardon stayed a month this time, and most of it in Galway by himself. He would walk the strand and think and pray and wonder what it was he needed to do next to redeem himself from the part he had just played in this whole sordid drama. He did not know what to do with his priesthood or even his life. He had lied and manipulated for the Cardinal Archbishop by laundering personnel files and the Chancery had been caught in the lie by the District Attorney's Office. He was an unknown offender but he was still an offender. He felt dirty. It was really as simple as that. What does a dirty priest do to redeem himself? O'Bardon did not know. He prayed and prayed and he still felt empty and dirty and unholy. At least he was honest enough with himself to feel ashamed. The same could not be said for all the clerics in the Archdiocese.

MCGURK DIARIES CONTINUE: BACK TO AMERICA

Father McGurk left Cork, Ireland sailing in the summer of 1874 and returned to Philadelphia and his mother after an absence of eight years. He had left Philadelphia as a young veteran of the Union Army in 1866. He had returned in 1874 as an Irish priest with a heavier brogue and a more Irish temperament than when he had left. He went straightaway to his mother's home on Second Street in Fishtown upon arriving in Philadelphia on the train from New York and the meeting was long awaited by both of them. Upon seeing each other for the first time in years, they fell into each other's arms and cried unashamedly. Her boy was home. His mother was with him again. That was all that mattered now.

The Roman Catholic diocese of Philadelphia was created in 1808 with Michael Egan, OFM, pastor of St. Mary's Church, elected as the first bishop. An ongoing and never ending controversy over the concept of trusteeism had embroiled St. Mary's parish since about the year 1796 and controversy would continue to blemish the episcopacies of Friar Bishop Michael Egan

(1810-1814), Bishop Henry Conwell (1820-1830), and Bishop Francis Patrick Kenrick (1830-1851).

Before it was raised to an archepiscopal see, the (now) 'Blessed' John Nepomucene Neumann served as its fourth bishop (1852-1860) and James Frederick Wood as its fifth bishop (1860-1883). Wood served as first archbishop of the metropolitan see (which at that time covered the entire state of Pennsylvania) until his death. Bishop Patrick Ryan (1884-1911), who was then coadjutor bishop of St. Louis, succeeded Bishop Wood as archbishop upon Wood's death. It was in 1874 that Father McGurk returned to Philadelphia and he initially served his church under Bishop Wood. He and Bishop Ryan would get to know each other quite well over the remaining years of their time serving Christ together in Philadelphia. But his first bishop under which he served as a priest would be the convert who had made a name for himself in American banking before studying for the priesthood in Rome.

The pattern for the Catholic church in Philadelphia was a rigorous and militant Catholicism forged in famine-shredded Ireland. It was tightly held together against all reason and relaxation by the general "us against the world" posture of the 19th-century papacy. The Irish-born bishops who almost completely dominated the American hierarchy shrewdly, almost cunningly, adapted the American Church of Rome to American conditions and imposed its particular form of Jansenist discipline on other immigrant groups, some of whom arrived enjoying more relaxed versions of the faith.

Jansenism was an odd child of mainstream Catholic thought which emphasized the doctrine of original sin, always was more than aware of human depravity and the necessity of Grace. Oddly enough its proponents believed in Predestination, much like the Protestant Calvinists. This school of thought was born in the writings of the Flemish cleric Cornelius Otto Jansen and it formed a distinct movement within the Church of Rome from the 16th through the 18th Centuries. It was eventually condemned as heresy by the Church mostly through the efforts of the Jesuits. The Jansenists had tremendous influence on the education of the French clergy and therefore by extension, on the Irish seminarians that studied in France for priesthood. Jansenism was to infect Irish Catholicism for hundreds of years, making an already difficult religious observance almost impossible to provide spiritual comfort.

So Irish Catholicism grew to be a Jansenist thing, a terrible, lonely, shame based view of the Catholic Faith that was often worn as a badge of honor among the many sufferers who lived it. In many respects it differed strongly from the Catholicism brought to America by other Catholic immigrant groups from Catholic Europe, but the Irish in Philadelphia imposed their Jansenist views on the others without exception. Much of the clergy in Philadelphia's Catholic Church were Irish and by force of numbers alone, they could impose this form of stark Irish Catholicism on the other groups.

The key vehicle in which it eventually came to exercise influence throughout Philadelphia was a parochial school system that had no parallel anywhere in the world. But the schools were not the only venue of Catholic power in the City of Brotherly Love. For all the seasons of the year or dates on the calendar; for all the phases in a Catholic's life and all and any crises the body, mind or soul, the Catholic Church of Philadelphia offered devotions, social services, Catholic organizations and authoritative and unchallenged counsel to the Catholic in the pew who was paying the bills with his working class donations and tithes.

It is not too much to say that the Catholic Church in Philadelphia would one day become very much an adjunct of the Catholic Church in Ireland, regardless of what immigrant group was actually worshiping in the church buildings or what language was spoken by the priest to the people in the sermon at Mass. The Irish were to rule supreme in clerical circles here and their ways would be the rule, not the exception. The Catholic Church in Philadelphia was to have an Irish mindset. It was really that simple.

To be Irish Catholic in Philadelphia was to be hooked into the Catholic power base, at least in a cultural sense if not in reality. One understood the ways of this particular kind of power and the particular mindset of the bishop and his minions if one were a Gael.

That fact would both help and hinder The McGurk throughout his priesthood in this city. To be a cultural insider could be a blessing or a burden, depending on how deeply one felt about an issue. To know what your friend was thinking because he shared your heritage, your paradigms, could be a blessing; to know the same about your adversary could scare one to distraction. The McGurk would know both situations.

For all the talk of Irishmen, Bishop Wood was an American born convert from Unitarianism whose father was an Englishman. He was received into the Church in Cincinnati, Ohio in 1836 and left a senior position at a bank immediately to study for priesthood in Rome. He rose very quickly within the ranks of power in the priesthood and served as a chief financial advisor and coadjutor bishop to Bishop Neumann of Philadelphia with right of succession. Stepping into a financial disaster when he arrived, complete with an unfinished cathedral and unfinished buildings all over the diocese, he essentially made the diocese financially sound and completed the Cathedral as well as started the seminary buildings. He was a sound and intelligent money man, with a shrewd sense of how money works and how the diocese could make its money make even more money and he was also a sharp theologian. In fact he had been an American advocate of Papal Infallibility. This fact was not lost on McGurk.

The diocese of Philadelphia was elevated to the status of an Archdiocese in the Fall of 1875 and that fact made Archbishop Wood a much more important man in American Catholicism. It also made Philadelphia a much more important place in American Catholicism. This type of left-handed status leached down into the priesthood itself, giving any cleric who was already full of himself an even greater reason to be self righteous in his thinking about his own place in the Universe. The McGurk was not impressed with the new archdiocesan status because he was too busy learning to love the people at Saint Michael's parish on North Second Street. He was one of their curates now and they were learning to love this quiet Irishman quite fondly.

The McGurk was assigned to work among the Irish of Saint Michael's parish by the bishop when he arrived in America and reported to the Chancery for permission to use his faculties in Philadelphia. The bishop welcomed him. The Irish needed him and his realistic and pragmatic approach to Catholicism and priesthood. His sermons were short and to the point, with very little fluff but not much thunder. For a serious man, he had a warm streak in him for the People of God. It was very rare that he would ever raise his voice or talk sternly to anyone.

Although he was no pushover and no bumpkin, he was very kind and compassionate and usually said nothing if a parishioner was out of line or needed correction. He had a certain look, the kind of look a grandfather gives to a grandchild when they are in the wrong. He used that look a lot in times of correction and people came to understand that staying within the bounds of a Christian life was their responsibility to accept, not his to impose. Actually, he was rather saintly in a very manly and quiet sort of way and the people of Saint Michael's were appreciative of that fact. He could have been a tyrant if he chose and many other priests did choose that route to clerical oversight of their parishioners. Instead he chose to look at priesthood as a sort of brother-in-arms to the people in the pew who were actually carrying Catholicism into the world through their behavior in the world. He was the curate but they were the Catholic Church in the world. He would never forget that.

Now that he was an ordained priest, he had to be even more circumspect about his radical social opinions and political and theological leanings than when he was as a seminarian at Maynooth. There had already been two plenary councils in America by this time, both of them held at Baltimore the primal see, to ensure that American Catholicism reflected the values and beliefs of the Universal Church. The first council was held in May 1852 and essentially reconfirmed the universal nature of the American church, pragmatically meaning that it should look exactly like the European church and behave in a similar manner. That is it should behave in an authoritarian and uncompromising manner on all levels. Upon studying the council's decrees, they sounded autocratic and divorced from the real needs of the people to McGurk. The second plenary council was held in October

1866 during the McGurk's first year at seminary. He followed it findings closely in the press that was sent to him in Ireland by his mother. Basically it reinforced the absolute control over property and decision making processes of the bishop and the pastor over the parish trustees. The McGurk thought this was nonsense and more pre-Revolutionary reactionary power grabbing from an already over-arrogant hierarchy, but again he kept his opinion to himself. He had more pressing and practical priestly duties and obligations to carry out.

At Saint Michael's parish less than a month, the McGurk was now deeply involved, even enveloped, in his priestly duties. Now completely involved in hearing confessions, celebrating the daily Mass, making parish visitations, counseling parishioners, being faithful to his prayer life in the Divine Office and all the many other things a priest's day encompasses, he was to learn how exhausting priesthood can be, even to a man so young. It all reminded him of how he felt when he was on a forced march as a soldier in the Army of the Potomac. He was a different kind of soldier now, but just as tired as an infantryman on the march most of the time. Priesthood could be exhausting.

But it could also be lighthearted and exhilarating. Once while reading his breviary for evening prayers he was interrupted by a young man who seemed to constantly be in a sort of spiritual crisis of one sort or another. This young man suffered from too keen a conscience and it was hard to dissuade him about his sinfulness once he had decided that his soul was in danger over some imagined spiritual assault by the Devil Himself.

"Excuse me, Faather", young Peter Dolan said, "can I speak to ya' for a minute?" The McGurk nodded and young Peter started in, "Ya' see Faather, I am having trouble keepin' me' mind on me' work and I am usually thinking of other things that I might be doin', if ya' know what I mean Faather! So's, I was wonderin', do ya' think that a man can live a good Christian life on three dollars a week?" which was Peter's salary.

The McGurk looked quite seriously at the young man and finally said, "Peder, on three dollars a week, that is *the only* way a young man can live!"

Another time, while engaged in conversation with the pastor of Saint Michael's concerning a family in the parish that seemed to be constantly down on its luck, the McGurk received a special assignment. The parents being both from County Wexford, the McGurk was assigned to look in on them from time to time and see if there was anything the parish might be able to do for them. Once, while visiting the neighborhood, he found only the old grandmother home and he was invited into the house with great formality by the old woman. They conversed for over an hour and found that they both shared many fond memories of the Olde Sod. At one point the McGurk asked old Mrs. Finnerty to count off the names of her many grandchildren. There was Michael Terrence, Edmund Terrence, Padraig Terrence, Anne Theresa and Sean Terrence Magee. When the McGurk asked her why the boys were all given Terrence as a middle name, the old woman seemed confused. Since they were all named by her son in law, she really had no idea. But not wanting to disappoint the young priest in his earnest desire to know, she simply stated sadly, "Faather, we are a poor family. We can only afford so many names!"

Once while hearing confessions, a middle aged man was droning on and on about his sins, none of them being of any particular weight. He seemed to have an endless string of venial sins and no mortal sins at all to report. The McGurk realizing that there was a long line of penitents behind him waiting to be Confessed, finally said to the man, "Is that all? No mortal sins? No stealing, lying, unjust anger, adultery?" The man seemed startled for a minute at the sound of the last sin and finally said haltingly and even a little sheepishly, "Ah, well...no Faather. No adultery or anything like that....but thanks for rattlin' me brain; I just remembered where I left me' hat!"

And so he passed his time as a young priest throughout the remainder of the 1870s and into the 80's working happily and ceaselessly to bring some hope and comfort to the Irish men and women of Second Street and its environs around Saint Michael's parish. He was loved by most, respected by all and feared by a few who might take advantage of the weakest in his flock. He was a man's man, quiet and unassuming, humble and strong at the same time. He was quietly comfortable around any human being who was trying to be genuine with him. He lived a quiet, humble life of service and he was happy with the basic simplicity of that arrangement.

One Sunday he was asked to celebrate Mass for the pastor. The pastor was ill and it was a hot July day and the younger man was seen as the natural stand in under those circumstances. It was not at all unusual for Saint Michael's to have the odd Sunday visitor now and again for Mass with people traveling through Philadelphia for one reason or another or even a visitor from a neighboring parish. And that was the day that The McGurk met his one true lifetime love, "Contessa" Bibiana Capricia Calandra. Although not actually a countess, but from a wealthy Genoese family, Bibiana was breathtakingly beautiful. Her dark Italian beauty was truly magnificent. Once a man saw her, he would never forget her. Never.

Loosely translated, her name meant "She who is fully alive, ruled by whim and has a good singing voice." No woman in the history of the human species was ever named more accurately. The Contessa was in Philadelphia to linger awhile at the first American parish for Italians, Saint Mary Magdalene De Pazzi which was in South Philadelphia.

In 1855 the Bohemian immigrant and bishop of Philadelphia, Bishop Neumann, had purchased a Methodist Church building and gave it to the city's Italians for their church. It grew over the years to serve their needs as a cultural center quite well. The first Philadelphia Italians were artisans, stonecutters, masons and some very educated people, mostly Genoese. Many of them had been able to mix with the city's elite before the Revolution. By 1875 the parish was integral to the life of Catholic Philadelphians in every way. Tuscan plasterers, who were known for their beautiful renditions in wealthy homes in Philadelphia, began to arrive directly after the Civil War and they brought their families with them. The Contessa was of this group.

Arriving in 1879 with her father and mother, Bibiana was a thirty-year-old widow who had lost her husband in Italy to a fatal sickness. With no children, having inherited her husband's estate and in the company of her wealthy parents, Bibiana opened up a dress shop for the well to do in the Center City area off Market Street. Saint Michael's parish was directly on the trolley line from Second Street to Center City and she would often pay a visit to the church to pray. She often prayed for she was lonely and desperate for happiness. Being beautiful only made her plight worse since she had traditional cultural obligations of an Italian widow, forcing her to honor her husband's memory by staying unmarried for a significant time after his death.

The McGurk would often see her praying in front of the statue of the Madonna in front of the church. She would light a candle and pray, sometimes for hours, in the face of that statue. Her face glowed in those moments of devotion. The McGurk was in love for the first time in his life. He knew it, was not ashamed of it, but somehow knew he must not mention it to anyone. Such was the secret life of a 19th Century priest in America.

But by this time in the city's history, Southern Italians mostly from Naples and Sicily were starting to emigrate and found themselves in Philadelphia. These were a different type of Italian, usually uneducated or semi skilled and from a completely different region of Italy than the Northern Italians from Tuscany and Genoa that had preceded them. The northerners had trouble mixing with the southerners and found their rough, peasant ways very difficult to accept or abide. Sometimes, they would worship at Catholic Churches other than Saint Mary Magdalene's in order to feel more comfortable.

So Bibiana would often frequent Saint Michael's, gracing the Irish with her presence and incredible beauty. Father McGurk was simply caught in the web of her elegant beauty and eventually, he would have to deal with his feelings. Even he knew that, as uninitiated in the ways of love that he was. For five years he loved her quietly, silently, rarely speaking to her and secretly thrilled at her silent attentions to him at any Mass that he might celebrate in her presence. He wanted desperately to be a priest and that meant there was no place for a woman in his life.

As for Bibiana, she was so beautiful that she had no lack of suitors, lovers or even paramours. She was after all, a beautiful and educated European widow of some means. She lived life to the fullest, albeit quietly and with great discretion. But no matter what fine Italian or American gentleman might have been in her life at any given moment, there was always that Irish priest, Jamie McGurk, in her heart. She was woman enough to admit that fact to herself and Catholic enough to keep that knowledge isolated from any other human being, including the priest she loved. She spoke to no one about her love for the Irish priest. McGurk was in the same position. Their love was unspoken and they both hoped, unnoticed.

But whatever may have been his secrets for now, the McGurk had pressing matters to deal with, because he had been asked by the bishop to act as a scribe at the third plenary council in Baltimore. It was held from early November to December 1884. Much had to be done and Father McGurk was instrumental in helping prepare the Archbishop of Philadelphia for the council. In the end, the third plenary council would be more of the same as were the first and second. It solidified the hold on church property within the hands of the pastor and bishop and clarified sacramental issues to the satisfaction of the priestly caste that used them as their ticket to power. The priests needed the sacraments to remain powerful and central in the lives of the Catholics under the care to maintain their hold on temporal power, such as money and church property. And they taught the average Catholic that the sacraments were necessary to enter heaven.

This was a very tidy and neat little circle and The McGurk had always suspected that it was deliberate obfuscation for the ultimate benefit of the priestly caste. There could be no sacraments without the priesthood. The sacraments made the priestly caste indispensable and necessary at all levels in order for Catholic spirituality to exist at all. It also gave the priest a sort of wizard's power over the masses of peasants he could lord over. If there were no priest, there could be no Eucharist, no Confession, no Extreme Unction, no marriage, nothing sacred at all. It was a neat little niche that they first created and the exclusively occupied and it gave the priestly caste tremendous and unchallenged power.

Being Irish, it always reminded him of the social power of the Druidic priests over the Celts to whom they administered their magic. Without Druids there could be no appeasement to the gods of forest and water and sky. He often wondered if this was the same with the 'magic' he offered to the people in the sacraments. Since ancient times, the job of any priesthood was to control the gods with sacrifices and offerings. Was this then any different? He was beginning to see his role as "priest" very differently than the one for which he had prepared. He was having a hard time separating sacramentology from magic, separating priesthood in his church from priesthood in the Druidic mysteries. "What is the essential difference?" he would often ask himself.

It was hard to preach the theology of a set of sacraments necessary for salvation to people who had not enough to eat. But it was demanded of him. Theology was his first line of defense against the questioning Catholic who came to him for answers. If he could not give him answers that would ease his pain, at least he had theology to offer. The whole prospect made him sick to his stomach. Where was the Christ in all of this semantic nonsense? Where was the vibrant healer? Where was the loving and focused teacher? Where was the salve to the pain and wounds of a hard and often cruel life for the suffering Catholic? It certainly was not to be found in theology. That was for sure. But theology reigned supreme.

This was all very well for church discipline and good order, but completely out of the realm of experience for the average Catholic in Philadelphia. The church was living in a theological fantasy and The McGurk knew it. As the years went by he found himself more and more a prisoner of a paradigm that made less and less sense to the average Catholic trying to live a good, decent and meaningful life in a world that could often be vicious. The hard lives of the Philadelphia Catholics demanded more compassion and less theology. But to McGurk the Church seemed all theology and very little common sense. He was afraid of becoming a walking and talking museum piece, and he knew that his church was already at that point and had been for many, many centuries. "Where was the Jesus in all of this?"; this was often in his mind. He was proud of being a priest. And he was also ashamed.

"How much theology did the Apostles have at their disposal?" he would often ask himself under his breath. Theology is nonsense when it is substituted for a living Faith and the McGurk knew that more than anyone. Words are meaningless when they do not convey action but only the unrealized ideals of a dreamer. Even Father McGurk knew that with his basic seminary understanding of Christianity. Theology was now officially entrenched in American Catholicism, substituting "reason" for charity and Christian action in the world. The supremacy of theology and all things theological and ecclesiastical would prove to be very dangerous for the Catholic Church to come.

The American bishops, most of them Irish or Irish-American by this time, were addicted to a theology that consistently placed them above the people and out of reach of any control or influence by the people in the pews who paid the parish bills. Every plenary council that they had held in America only served to reinforce their exalted status of themselves with its final proclamations. It was hard enough to be a priest when one had to consistently preach the Gospels of Jesus to an unbelieving world, often thought McGurk. Being a priest could be an impossible job when adding episcopal arrogance to the mix and fancy wording and semantics was the order of the day when it came to helping Catholics find realistic solutions to life's problems.

These clerical barons called themselves "Excellency" and the title of "Eminence" was used for any rare Cardinal that might be among them, sent to them from Rome for any number of oversight situations. And the sad thing was, they actually *meant* this! This was not mere semantics, these were real accolades spoken from one arrogant and delusional overlord to another. These men were not merely out of touch with the spiritual needs of the faithful, they were rich, entitled, arrogant and out of touch. Most of them lived in a lordly manor that reminded The McGurk of the strangers' in control of Ireland. These men were more barons then bishops. "Where is the Jesus in this?" the McGurk would painfully wonder. He never found an answer to that question. The bishops never provided an answer.

It was hard to be Irish and harder to be Irish Catholic and perhaps even harder still to be an Irish Catholic priest serving in Philadelphia who admired and emulated the great Father John Murphy. Murphy lacked the backing of the Irish bishops when he went to his death as an Irish rebel general. But he never lacked the support of the people and he was much more loved by them than any bishop would ever be. He was an Irish hero and an Irish priest. The bishops were substitute Englishman who were willing to keep the Catholic population in check for limited and "reasonable" accommodation to Catholics in Ireland from the English Parliament. At this point in his priesthood McGurk began to wonder if things were all that different for Catholics and their bishops in America. One called the tune, the other danced to it. Would it always be like this he wondered?

THE STATE OF FATHER
O'BARDON'S PRIESTHOOD

ather O'Bardon was now back at work at the Chancery, sans Sister Martha. He missed her presence but he kept that secret to himself. He worked long days for Monsignor Glenn who in turn worked long days for the Cardinal Archbishop. The archbishop was nearing mandatory retirement age and would be leaving soon. His replacement had already been named. The Archbishop was coming from St. Louis, Missouri and he would be another Italian American.

Anthony Cardinal Bertelli had dishonored himself along with his predecessor, John Cardinal Kraske. They had simply lied. It is no more complicated than this. They had spent huge resources of time and money hushing the up the chorus of sins committed by priests, nuns and lay brothers in their diocese. They were more or less like all the other American bishops. Their concept of 'the church' was fatally flawed.

Julian Cardinal Renatto was born in April 1930 in Los Angeles, California. He was ordained in 1961, studied for his canon law degree in Rome and was named Archbishop and ordained personally by John Paul II in 1985 when he was named to head an important Pontifical Institute. In January 1994 he was appointed archbishop of St. Louis and in July 2003 he was named Archbishop of Philadelphia. He was to receive the red hat of a Cardinal in September of that year. In short, this man was cut from the same cloth as all the others. There was no expectation of change when the new archbishop arrived. O'Bardon was now wise enough in the ways of the world and aware enough of the clerical culture to understand the message being sent to Philadelphia by the Vatican. It was business as usual. Philadelphia Catholicism was still firmly under the control of the Old Guard.

So O'Bardon prepared to help the departing bishop retire and the arriving bishop take the reigns of temporal and spiritual power in the archdiocese. Suddenly, he hated being a priest. It was becoming all formality and all organization and very little to do with Jesus of Nazareth. "Where is the Christ in all of this?" he would mutter to himself. He was beginning to find priesthood to be more and more formality and style and less and less substance. Father McGurk was having an influence over Father O'Bardon that could not be denied.

He drove home to Glenside up the winding Lincoln Drive through Fairmount Park and onto Wyndmoor. The drive then took him to Cheltenham Avenue overlooking Holy Sepulcher Cemetery, a left onto Easton Road, past Arcadia University and Cheltenham High School and up to the rectory at Saint Luke's. He said nothing to the housekeeper except that he was not hungry and would not be down for dinner. He told her that he would make a sandwich later that evening if he was hungry. She did not answer him. Mrs. Schlessinger was hard of hearing and often did not answer the priests. He grew used to that. He hoped that she had heard him.

O'Bardon entered his bedroom and took off his clericals and put on a pair of jeans and a flannel shirt. He sat at his desk and reached for the second journal of the McGurk's diaries. He needed to be with a fellow suffering priest tonight. He started to read.

The diary entries continued. O'Bardon read them carefully and slowly. He took in every word.

"It was in the Year of Our Lord 1874 and in the month of July I set sail back for America and Philadelphia arriving in August. I met my mother for the first time in eight years and she looked sickly and old. She had been lonely without me, but said 'nary a word to anyone about her loneliness. We fell into each other's arms and cried, we had missed each other that much. I was soon assigned to Saint Michael's parish on Second Street and was at home again with the Irish of Philadelphia.

"In the course of my many priestly duties I was to sight a beautiful Italian woman of means who often came to Saint Michael's to pray. So as not to belabor the point or be unduly dramatic, suffice it to say that I fell in love with her and am in love with her even today as I write this down, so very many years later. Her name was Bibiana Capricia Calandra and she was the most beautiful woman I have ever had the pleasure to know in my lifetime. She was the reason that I am fully alive as a man, the reason that I was to more fully understand my calling as a priest and the reason that I stayed a priest to this day. She was my angel and she is with me even now, even from the grave. I will never forget her and I will always love her, even as I am now a priest of Jesus Christ.

"So that there is no misunderstanding on the part of whomever might read these journals, I want it to be understood that Bibiana, like all beautiful women everywhere at all times, had many lovers, admirers and suitors. I was of course, not one of these, since I am a priest. Although I never had the pleasure of her embrace I want it to be known that she was the one true love of my life. Once I met her, she was never once out of my thoughts, out of my care or out of my life.

"The first five years after I met her, we did not even speak once. I would see her enter the church and she would see me watching her from a distance and know that I could not help myself, her beauty was that powerful. I never spoke of her to anyone and never told her that I loved her until the day that she died. I confessed my love for her during her final confession to me so many years later. Her response to me was, "Oh Father. Oh Jamie. I know. I

73

know. And I have always known, since the very first time that you looked at me." Then she told me simple words that I shall never forget and somehow always knew. "And I have loved you Jamie since the moment your eyes looked into mine. There was never another. There never could be. I loved you as hard and as well as I could from the distance that I was required to keep. I love you, Jamie." She spoke to me like this, took my hand, and died peacefully. I blessed her, closed her eyes, and left her to her family and friends. I celebrated her funeral Mass and prayed over her grave. She will always live in me until the moment I die. If I had not been a priest, I would have been proud to have her as my wife. I am not ashamed of this. It gave me strength through many lonely years of priesthood.

"She helped me to deeply understand that God loves us all, in our imperfections, our hobbling gait and our crooked souls. We are simply human. God is the Eternal between us, we are the temporary that He has chosen to deal with in a fatherly manner. Our lives belong to Him and He belongs to Himself. It is sometimes a hard thing to understand and accept, but Bibiana and the people I have served throughout my priesthood have taught me this one lesson. It we calm ourselves and listen to His voice within us, we need never feel alone or isolated. We are part of Him and He is part of us.

"Some may have spoken of her quietly as a woman of ill-repute, others may have styled her a courtesan or even something worse. But I knew her deeply and utterly. She was the kindest, most compassionate and truly lovely woman that I have ever known. No one will ever know the depth of her kindness. She had tremendous wealth that was left to her from her husband and later from the business concerns of her wealthy parents and she used it unsparingly and anonymously in the service of others. So many people who may have been slandering her were helped directly by her charity through her alms to her own, Saint Mary Magdalene's parish and also Saint Michael's. She literally kept both parishes afloat for many years. She was unsparing in her criticism of small minded and unkind people, and she was just as willing to forgive if they showed any sign at all of Christian charity. Whatever weaknesses she may have had born of loneliness and desire, her willingness to secretly buttress anyone against hardship and want never faltered throughout her life. She was a saintly and ultimately a Godly woman. I will always believe that. I loved her deeply. And I do so now as I write this. If there ever was a Magdalene among us, it was her. If there was ever a woman that I would have cherished as a wife, had I been in any other life circumstance, it was her. If my heart ever beat in another's breast, it was hers. She made my priesthood bearable and she gave meaning to my loneliness. I thank God for the gift of this woman in my life.

"I also came to love the poor and often dispossessed people of Saint Michael's parish and the surrounding neighborhoods around Second Street. They were my people in every way, even the Protestants and the occasional Jew. And that is saying something for an Irishman! They were poor in the pocket, but never in their spirit. For they were the most solid, wonderful and completely real people I have ever had the pleasure of knowing. They were truly the 'salt of the earth' and I loved them for it. If it was my great privilege to serve them on this Earth, I thank God for the lessons that they taught me about humility, about bearing up under hardship for the good of the Church, for the good of their families, friends and fellow man. They could not be broken, and in their strength, they gave me hope. They were more of a priest to me than I ever was to them.

"One story comes to mind almost immediately as I write this to illustrate my point. My old Army mate, Tom Barnes, had been wounded twice and the wounds never really healed from the War for Secession. They would weep constantly and he was always in pain, usually hobbling with a cane. He was drunk more often than not, just to kill the pain of the wounds. He wore his blue Union kepi almost all the time after the war and I would often see him hobble by the front of the church, where he would doff that kepi if he saw me nearby, slide up close to me and whisper "Good Marnin' Faather!" and then laugh with an almost childlike chuckle. He had known me as a private in A Company and I had fought many a battle along with him and the fact that I was now a priest bemused him to no end. He found the whole thing comical for years after the war.

"It was with great shock that I met the news that he wanted to become a Catholic! A non church-going Episcopalian, Tom had finally decided at the age of 35 to become a Catholic since practically all of his friends and acquaintances around Second Street where of the Catholic Faith. I suppose he did not want to be left out! I tried heartily to talk my old friend and fellow war veteran out of it, saying that I did not think that the Faith suited him, but he would have none of my blather. I told him that he would have to take the Catholic Faith seriously or that I would not proceed with instruction and he agreed solemnly. So I prepared him and accepted him into the church and he attended weekly Mass for years until his death. I must admit, he was not so much a believing Catholic as he was a dutiful one. Always one to keep his word, he never missed Mass nor set aside his Easter duty of one Confession per year.

"His brother George would become a Catholic too, on the sight of Tom taking the Faith. I suppose that George felt the same as Tom, if living among the Irish, why not believe like them? And so when George married an Irish girl from Second Street and they eventually had a child, his brother Tom was asked to stand in as the Godfather for the child. Tom agreed.

"His wounds were serious, his health was bad and he was almost always drunk so the chances of him ever marrying or having issue were slim to none. He must have known that. So, bearing all this in mind, as I was baptizing the baby boy, his nephew, the time came for me to ask, "And what is the name of this child of God?" and Tom solemnly answered "Thomas" so I being the priest and Tom being the Godfather I took him at his word and baptized the child Thomas.

"Later that day, the child was in his mother's arms (she could not attend the baptism as she was not well) and she was sitting among her many friends and neighbors delightfully telling them of her son, William.

"William?" they asked, "why he was baptized Thomas!" and they would know the child's name since most of them were at the church for the baptism. She immediately looked around the room for the now drunken Godfather, Tom Barnes my mate from Army days, and she screamed. "You drunken sot! You named me' lovely boy after' yerself! Why you're the Divil' himself!"

"With that she threw a shoe at the now unconscious drunk. The brogan hit him in the nose, blackened his eyes and the force of the blow threw him back in the rocker within which he was sitting. The pain of it all woke him up out of his stupor but he was dazed and could not see clearly, and he stumbled up slowly out of the chair holding his head with both hands. Still being unable to clearly see, he then immediately walked over to the second story window which was open to allow air into the hot apartment since it was the depths of summer.

"Thinking the window was the door, he stepped into the window, his knees smashing the wall beneath the window and in his drunken stupor and unable to see, he fell out of the window entirely altogether. Luckily, there was an awning below onto which he fell since the flat was situated above a bakery that had just installed the new green canvas awning to bring in more business. He fell straightaway onto the awning and ripped a hole in it as he fell onto the wooden sidewalk beneath it and in front of the building. He did a lot of damage to the awning but it did break the force of his fall and probably saved him from getting a broken neck. He did however receive a broken nose from the fall which he had the rest of his life. He had the look of a boxer about him for the rest of his days.

"It would be months before his sister in law would allow him back into the flat that she shared with his brother and their son. But after about six months, bygones were bygones and all was right with the world in the Barnes' family. And old Tom Barnes had a namesake. It was worth a broken nose.

"For years, young Tom Barnes would come to Mass on Sunday with his Uncle Tom. They were inseparable until the old man's death. In later years my Army mate would tell me that he had paid such a high price for giving the young man his own name that there was no way he was not going to have a hand in his growin' up! The younger Tom Barnes has become a bookkeeper with the Reading Railroad. I have been told that he likes to drink. 'Tis small wonder.

"And I did love these people so! They made my priesthood meaningful and filled my life in a way that I cannot fully describe. I was often told how wonderful I was to them and how they depended on me for all the important times in their lives; the marriages, the baptisms, confessions and Extreme Unction at their deaths. But the truth is very different. The truth is that they were wonderful to me because they truly needed me to be their priest. And what a wonderful feeling that is for any man! They needed a priest to administer to them in their pain, their joy and their sojourn in life. I was that priest. I can think of no greater honor and no greater joy.

"But I do not wish to give an impression that all was grand and fine. Certainly it was not. I had my haters, my disbelievers, my ne'er do wells and blaggards among the people that I served. There were the ever present drunks, those who beat their children and wives when life was too difficult to handle, those who gambled away their money and whose children depended upon charity in order to eat, those who never took marriage vows seriously, those who dallied with young children for pleasure.

"I am even sorry to say that I knew priests who set themselves upon children. I would take them aside and speak sternly to them. I would threaten, I would cajole, I would shame them. It never made any difference. They were a protected class and they knew it. No bishop would undo them, no parishioner would believe that they had committed such evil and no priest or nun had power to deter them. Even the police refused to believe such a thing could happen. It made my own priesthood sad to become increasingly aware of this evil among my brother priests and even among the nuns and teaching brothers. Many young lives were simply destroyed in this ever present and darkly creeping evil. I was largely powerless to do anything about it. Simply put, no one believed me and Canon Law forbade a priest to go to any authority other than the bishop in such a case. I was sewn in. I was blocked. It was that simple. I hated the Church during these sad times. I was a prisoner of my own beliefs.

"But there was one time, a brightly lighted day, that this was not so. A priest in a neighboring parish, an Irishman, was caught abusing a child in an unspeakable way. He was caught by the child's father in the sacristy. The priest was in the company of seven altar boys in the middle of the day. He had them all removed from class, and he told the nun that he was going to have them practice their skills as altar boys since they were all new to that status. She gladly consented.

"The priest removed them from class and took them directly to the sacristy. Most of them were about ten or eleven years old. He had them remove their clothes, then he removed his cassock and stood there among them in his under garments. He gave them altar wine to drink and was about to start abusing each one when the Good Lord must have decided to intervene, just this one time. A fluke occurred, one of the parents of one of the boys, a Mr. Flaherty, was a working man in the area of the church building. He stopped to make a visit to the Blessed Sacrament at lunch break and heard giggling from the sacristy and a man's voice. He, being a member of the parish, found the entire situation odd and walked beside the altar into the sacristy to investigate. There he was to find the whole sordid scene.

"The priest in question froze in fright. The Irishman told the boys to dress and the sagart (priest) did the same. Mr. Flaherty dismissed the boys and sent them back to the classroom. He immediately walked the silent priest to the parish priest and explained the situation. The parish priest asked the curate if such a thing happened. The curate hung his head in shame and said nothing. Within a week the priest was sent to a monastery for penance. I have been told that he is still there, all these years later, doing penance for his sins. This is as it should be. But I must sadly say, this is a rare occurrence. Most of these evil priests have many a chance to engage in their horrible sinfulness throughout their entire priesthood.

We all know it and we are all shamed by it. We never speak of it among ourselves. The children are sacrificed for the 'good of the Church'. All and everyone involved are silent. I am deeply ashamed of myself and my fellow priests and Catholics on this account. This is the work of the devil and Canon Law forbids us to address the problem on pain of excommunication. Someday, we will all pay for this. God will not be blind forever. The Holy Spirit will one day descend upon us in vengeance. We cannot escape our day of reckoning. I hope that I am dead when that day arrives for I am as guilty as the rest for keeping silence. May God have mercy on my soul. And may the children forgive my cowardice, for coward I truly am. My only defense is that under Canon Law I can only approach the bishop with such a situation under pain of excommunication. I sacrificed these boys in order to maintain good order in the church. I pray that they someday forgive me. It is my only hope in this regard.

"It is also true that the parish priest has complete control of all monies collected from these good hardworking people and there is little oversight, if any at all. Many a priest has become rich when he should have been content to witness to the poverty of Christ, the poverty he agreed to live within at his ordination. But many of us do not, perhaps even most of us. What is so wrong with us as priests that what we want to do with so much fervor we simply cannot do? Is it that we are so weak, so unprepared to carry out the promises of ordination? Or is it that we decide "what I have to give is enough" and do not hold ourselves accountable to our own goodness, our own ability to rise above the mundane and make ourselves more Christ-like? We are like soldiers who are proud to wear the uniform but afraid to engage in combat. So often we are phony and artificial. We are often unsure of our mandate as Christian priests and unwilling to engage our darker sides in the combat necessary to truly know the divine within us. Being a good priest is so hard. Being a bad priest is lethal. It is that simple.

"To be frank, although women have been a strong temptation to me, I was never so sorely tempted as to break my vow of celibacy. When I was a young priest it was because I was so tired from the work of a priest as to make the act almost impossible. When I became an old priest it was because I was so tired from being an old man! But in either case, I was one of the lucky few. So many of my priestly colleagues have strayed in this area it is almost cliché to mention it among us. We are simply not what the people think we are in practically any area of our lives. I am actually more astonished at this then ashamed.

"Bibiana was always so gentle with me. Although I never asked her to lay with me and she never hinted that she would, she was always so much of a wife to me in so many ways. Caring, supporting and loving for me in so many ways, she truly was the closest thing to a wife I ever had. I think that we were had been married it would not have been as perfect as it was. She was a true saint and I trusted her and needed her support in anything I might have accomplished as a priest. She taught me so much. I love her so even to this day. I miss her so much.

"But now comes my moment of intellectual truth. Now I must state to the reader why it is that I have written a note to the reader and appended it to the cover of these books which I have bound together with the parish seal and asked the finder to give these journals to the bishop when they are found. For the truth of the matter is this, I have not lost my Faith now at the end of my priesthood as I write these final notes. I have simply lost my God.

"As I write these journals it is the Year of Our Lord 1911 and I am seventy years old. The doctors tell me I have not long to live, perhaps two months or a little more. I have a cancer and I suffer from the miseries. I am in pain all of the time now. And so I sit down to write these journals and I will hide them in the high altar of Saint Kevin's. Perhaps one day years from now they will be found.

"I will state my case simply. After almost thirty-seven years as a priest I can no longer believe in the physical reality of a man-god called Jesus, who is known as the Christ or Jesus of Nazareth. After a lifetime of prayer and meditation and study and service in His name, I do not believe Him to be real, at least not on the physical level. In short, I believe that he is folklore, a human embodiment of a Jewish ideal of Messiah that needed a time in place and history to sway the opinion of the Gentiles who eventually took Him up as their own. To state it simply, Jesus did not exist, but the Christ always did. I believe that now.

"I will not belabor the point or go on and on trying to convince you, the reader, of my points of contention with the traditional Gospel story. None of it is true. It is all broadcloth of the same fabric as the other Middle Eastern religions coming out of Egypt and the Levant. Perhaps the German theologian Doctor Albert Schweitzer said it best at the beginning of his book of 1906, "The Quest for the Historical Jesus." Here he showed us unequivocally that early Christianity was not concerned with any idea of an historical Jesus. They awaited their Jesus who was to come at the end of time. And it is evident from even a mere cursory reading of the Acts that Paul, the Great Missionary, had no idea who an historical Jesus might be. The whole concept was foreign to him. I must admit that this bothered me even in seminary days. The Jesus that Paul met on the road to Damascus was pure spirit. It was the only Jesus Paul knew. And there was good reason for that, an historical Jesus had not been invented yet. He was to come later, much later.

"At the end of his book Dr. Schweitzer tells us of his mentors in this quest for truth. They were many theologians and historians with names like Hase and Bahrdt and Venturini, Reinhard, Strauss and Reimarus, Hess and Paulus. They were honest intellectuals of the early parts of the last century who saw the truth and spoke it plainly. Only it was that theologians were hearing but not really listening because it would mean the end of their reign over the minds of men if they should acknowledge the truth of what they had read in their works. They were keepers of the story and had no real power in it. They suspected the secret but never shared it for fear of losing their position, their power, their frame of reference.

"I must be forgiven for taking this coward's way out! The very same thoughts that I express here ruined the life of Strauss. He thought people would accept his explanation of his Christ of mythology. They did not and his life was ruined, and the horror for him started at the young age of 28 years. But he remained proud of his intellectual honesty on the matter, as well he should have. For he was truly a voice crying in the wilderness. And now I must state my case as I see it.

"The New Testament still has vestiges of the original Jesus in the Gospel of John. That Gospel has nothing to do with reality. It is a Jesus of the Spirit who will come at the end of time. This was the Gospel of the Jewish apocalypse and its believers. They were to become the Church at Jerusalem when the Jewish community there expelled them from the synagogue.

"Then there are the Gospels of Matthew, Mark and Luke. They are the Gospels of the Greeks who were accustomed to god-men among them, the sons of god in whom they believed such as Hercules, Apollo and even Mithras. So we have two Gospel strains for two types of mythology. One is based on Jewish versions of the end of times and the other is based on Greek mythology in a Jewish context. There, I have said it. An historical Jesus is nonsense and makes no sense to me as a practicing priest of Jesus Christ. I have lived my life for His glory and he never existed in the flesh. I am not ashamed of this statement and will not recant. It is time for reason to reenter my religion.

"I take this to my death but plainly speak it after my demise. The Jesus of History is a fairy tale for children. The Jesus of the Spirit is what we must rely upon to reform our lives. He is all we have and all that stands between us and moral decay. The Jesus that Paul of Tarsus spoke of never lived. Paul knew that. And now we must admit it to be intellectually honest and win back the hearts of men.

"And so now, dear reader, you understand why I wrote these diaries. They are my last attempt to be intellectually honest on the one central point of my life, the one question my life has sought to answer through service to others, who is Jesus? And the answer is this; He is no one. He is everyone. He is nowhere. He is everywhere. Take your choice and then live your life accordingly. That is the choice every one must make."

O'Bardon fell asleep with the book against his chest. He slept at his desk until dawn. He arose and celebrated Mass. He drove silently to work at the Chancery office and did not even turn on the radio in the car. He prayed. The emotions that he felt had no names. He was simply overwhelmed.

A BIGGER PROBLEM

Julian Cardinal Renatto was now the Archbishop of the Roman Catholic Archdiocese of Philadelphia. He was not to be trifled with, for he was a man accustomed to the use of power. He rose quickly through the priesthood's ranks and was plainly aware that he had always been a Vatican insider. But now, that very same perk had him assigned to a committee that would drain his resources and time. In fact, it could very well be the end of a lot of things for the Church if Renatto did not get this assignment right.

It was true that his first attempts to blunt the District Attorney's Grand Jury Report were clumsy and seen as hostile to the victims. He overcame that blunder fairly well by calling in all Philadelphia priests to the seminary for a day of prayer and penance at the Seminary.

But something else was brewing, another storm was coming toward the Church, something ultimately even more dangerous than the bad exposure that child rape had been. The Vatican wanted several groups investigated and "dealt with." They were considered to be dangerous to the Faith. The Vatican monopoly on the "Jesus Story" was being seriously challenged by intellectuals, biblical exegetes who generally had no church allegiance or affiliation and film makers catering to a newfound interest in these things among the average theatre goer. What made matters worse was that most of the intellectuals involved in this growing cultural phenomenon were renowned scriptural scholars who had spent their lives in historical Jesus research. To use a military analogy, this was not a bunch of corporals griping about the food in the mess tent, this was a bunch of generals refusing to obey orders. Things were starting to get very serious. The Church fathers were slowly descending into a sort of existential panic.

The sex abuse scandal was going to take a back seat to an even more pressing problem for the Faith, if in fact that was even possible. In the Church's view, it seems that in the United States and Britain, several groups of theologians with an existential phenomenological and secular humanist approach had taken scriptural redaction and historical research too far in the study of the Gospels and Acts. In fact, their ranks were becoming increasingly filled with world-class theologians who were now beginning to write books, give television interviews and give public lectures on their views of Jesus as myth, as only a man or at least, as *not* the physical Son of God. For an organization that held a monopoly on a Western worldview for so long, Catholicism and by extension all of Christianity was now being seen more and more as just one point of view among many competing points of view. Knowledgeable people other than clerics had opposing views of the Jesus Story. This was not good relative to the Church's power position concerning story rights. The organization could unravel relatively quickly if it lost its primary right to tell the Jesus Story. The Church's proprietary rights to tell the Jesus Story were now growing increasingly endangered. Something had to be done quickly to regain the primary right to tell the Story. The Church was essentially anchored on the right to tell the story as the primary authority. Once that was gone, the Church would soon follow. The Curia realized this immediately with growing alarm as the 20th Century drew to a close and the new century unfolded.

Some scholars participating in the retelling of the story said that Jesus existed but that he was a Jewish Cynic or shaman many even an Iscarii Zealot, that is, a terrorist. Others said that he was a healer and political problem for the Romans and the Sanhedrin and perhaps even a political messiah of sorts; therefore he had to be killed. Still others said that he was a shaman or a healer or an itinerant rabbi of sorts, a Pharisee, an Essene, a Ebionite follower of John the Baptist who grew to compete with him and many other similar things. Another name for the Ebionites was 'Nazarene'. Most people find that fact more than interesting.

But some few others said that Jesus did not exist at all. They claimed that he was a literary construct of Jesus ben Pandera of a century before the supposed "Jesus of Nazareth" and Jesus bar Kochba, of about century after Jesus of Nazareth was supposed to live. The real and central problem was "primary source documentation", or more specifically, the lack of it. For the reality of Jesus' existence, to put this bluntly, there wasn't any proof. There were no writings, no first person accounts of his existence that were believable or reliable. There were no extra Biblical sources that were completely and undeniably reliable and authentic that spoke to his existence. There was nothing that a scholar could point to as irrefutable evidence that this man ever walked the planct. The intellectuals were chipping away at the story itself and doing it with reason and scholarship. A change in civilization itself was in the balance.

The biblical scholars were gaining a following among the believers across the world. Belief was turning to doubt and the point of view of the scholars was changing Faith to mere Reason for many people. And most important of all to the church fathers, money was starting to dry up in church coffers around the planet. Mass attendance was dropping quickly. Catholics and Christians in general were becoming more of a type that were adherents to a culture than believers in a religion. The Church's ability to influence human behavior was waning.

To make matters even worse, fundamentalist Christianity was taking away large slices of the Catholic population all around the world. Their belief system was simple, straightforward, apocalyptic and very, very close to the magical thinking that terrified people tended to embrace in a crisis throughout human history. And modern life, if it was anything at all, was one continuing crisis. There did not seem to be any respite that ever came forward to calm the fears of nuclear war, the ascendancy of technocracy, the isolation of the individual from the community, worldwide natural devastation, the disintegration of the traditional family, traditional community and even the traditional national identity or even something as global as planetary climate change. Fundamentalists had a belief system which superseded all of this tragedy. God was coming and very soon. Watch for Jesus in the sky.

Fundamentalists believed the Bible to be literally true in all respects. From a traditional Catholic point of view, they had more of a Faith in magic than in a Loving God. But it worked in a big way because it was perfect simplicity. God spoke through the Bible, period. This was now becoming a real war of ideas and the Catholic Church was losing on many fronts. First it lost to the scholars, then the magical thinking literalists and then the lawyers suing for millions for raped children. Something had to be done quickly to turn things around and put the Catholic Church back in control of the war for minds and hearts.

But the problem for the Vatican at the moment was to control or counter the output of information to the people that the scholars were now routinely presenting through the media. And this is where Cardinal Renatto entered the picture. He was given the job of retaking for the Catholic Church all of the ground that had been lost to the scholars. His job was to win the Public Relations War between the Church and the scholars. This was the problem in a nutshell.

The problem was not new, but it had only become a problem in a big way since the founding of the Jesus Seminar and the publishing of its findings in the 1990s. A scholarly enterprise of the Westar Institute in California, the Jesus Seminar was a sort of clearing house for scholarly information concerning the historical Jesus. It was staffed with theologians and biblical exegetes of the highest caliber. And they were intellectuals and scholars with very little allegiance to the agenda of the "Faithers", the traditional believers in the Jesus Story. The Jesus Story as it is traditionally told was folklore to most of these people. And they openly stated as much. The Bible, both Old and New Testaments, were simply seen as literature and treated as such. Their job as they saw it was to bring the theology that had been taught to the divinity students and seminarians out to the people in the pews. It was about time. The world was about to change relative to the Jesus Story. There was probably no way to stop this, but the Church had to try.

The scholars saw much of early Christianity as being formed in the mold of Middle Eastern Gnosticism which predated Christianity by perhaps as much as a thousand years or more. Christianity was just one more vehicle for Gnosticism to make its points to people in the area of the Fertile Crescent.

Ancient Gnosticism among Christians and Jews was brought to light in a big way in the 1940s. Certainly when the thirteen Nag Hammadi manuscripts were found in the desert of Upper Egypt in December of 1945 by a peasant who was looking for kindling, Christianity and its relationship to Judaism was seen in a new light. It was actually quite disturbing to scholars. The disparities that it brought forward relative to the traditional Jesus Story were unmistakable.

Together with these documents, the roughly 870 partial documents eventually called the Dead Sea Scrolls were found between 1947 and 1955 in the wadi Qumran on the Dead Sea. They are the only surviving Biblical documents written prior to 100 A.D. and they tell of a very different proto-Christian Church and Jewish theology than we had ever imagined. Some of the documents are of the traditional Jewish type relative to theology while others speak to the beliefs of the Essenes, a splinter Jewish group and a possible forerunner in most ways to what was to eventually be known as Christianity.

An actual movement of Jews that was very similar to Christianity was now brought to light and it predated the Jesus of Nazareth Story by at least 150 years. To state this simply, "Christianity" was much older than the traditional storyline about Jesus himself ever indicated. Something was wrong with the storyline that we had been told in Bible school and Catholic grammar school. The dates didn't line up. The facts were very different. There were major players in the story that we had never been told about and pre-Christian sects that seemed to match the ethos of Christianity in their belief systems almost exactly. No Jesus of Nazareth was involved in any of this. How could this be?

The facts seemed to infer a completely different timeline of events than we had been taught and frankly, what might loosely be termed today the "Jesus Movement" or as they termed it then, "The Way" was much older than the alleged Jesus himself. Something very significant was out of kilter. There were people talking, acting and believing very much like Christians long before the "Jesus of Nazareth" story supposedly took place. And some of them were disaffected Jews who seemed to be arranged in a sort of three tiered order of proto-monks, married people of the community raising families and itinerant preachers going around the countryside like the prophets of old. This was all perhaps 100 years or so prior to the protagonist of the Jesus Story even being born, supposedly at Nazareth. This was coming from solid archeological finds and the study of the aforementioned manuscripts.

But much of this had been discussed openly in the highest levels of theological discourse since about the middle of the 19th Century. Alternative views of Christian history and origins were starting to be taught, at least in general terms, in all the seminaries of the Western world by about 1955. But it took almost 150 years for the same ideas to reach the people in the pews. And they had nothing to gain by feigning ignorance. They were not priests whose very livelihoods were depending upon the child's version of Christianity that they had been taught in Sunday School or in Catholic grammar school. The people were now demanding answers concomitant with a highly educated population, a population of church goers who for the first time in history were often much more educated than the priests and bishops themselves. Things were starting to get out of hand. People were beginning to suspect that they had been deceived. They had been. Perhaps this was not done with evil intent, perhaps only to keep order and discipline within the church. But one thing was for sure, to some degree or other, the early Church Fathers were more than aware of these discrepancies. To some degree they worked to hide them. That was now an established fact.

A favorite subject for Cable television history shows and for blockbusting book sales, the search for the Jesus of History was now a cottage industry for theologians, historians and advocates of virtually every theological point of view. But the Jesus Seminar in California at the Westar Institute was making huge inroads in the psyche of the common Christian or those people who had at one time considered themselves a churchgoer but no longer attended church. These were world-class intellectuals and many of them had been active priests and ministers and even rabbis prior to the seminar being formed. Some were believers, some were not. Their academic credentials were impeccable and although each scholar seemed to represent a different point of view concerning an historical Jesus, virtually none of them told the same story as the churches.

Since the agenda and storyline of the Catholic Church more than any other Christian denomination was heavily invested in an historical Jesus since the very beginning of its involvement with the Jesus Movement more than 2,000 years ago, it had the most to lose financially and in terms of membership if this intellectual cancer (as the church saw the situation) grew any bigger. The Old Order thrashes in rage when a New Order arrives to call them all liars. It is always like that.

So the Vatican asked the Italian-American Cardinal Archbishop of Philadelphia to come up with an answer to the challenge this academic free-for-all presented to the church. Like all corporate leaders who have too much to do, the cardinal archbishop of Philadelphia delegated the job of research to his right hand man for this sort of thing, the 'clean up man' named Monsignor Bill Glenn. Glenn of course, like all good middlemen, did exactly what the rest of us would do if handed this slippery football. He punted directly into the arms of his assistant, Father O'Bardon. O'Bardon was now the point man for the Archdiocese of Philadelphia in its search and destroy mission against the revisionist Gospel writers in America; lucky him. There was just no rest for the weary.

To make matters even more complicated, O'Bardon was starting to doubt the value of his own priesthood. A priest less than eight years now, he was often lonely and tired and yearning for some sort of normalcy, some sort of inner peace in his life, something he had not seen now for almost five years. The sex abuse scandal had knocked him down. This latest assignment might knock him out.

And to make matters even more raw, he had read the diaries of Father James McGurk, a priest of Philadelphia more than 135 years before the present set of crises. That priest died believing in a very different Christ than the one O'Bardon was preaching about in his homilies. McGurk's rough and tumble priesthood of over 130 years previously had taught him that the Jesus Story of tradition was not enough to salve the wounds of his parishioners. They were in pain and needed a real spirituality to get them through the vale of tears that was their life. They needed more than pious stories made up about a man who may or may not have existed. And if he did exist it was now clear he lived in a manner that was different than the way he had been presented in the Gospels. What Catholics needed, thought McGurk, was access to the power that the Jesus Story talked about...power to heal sick bodies and sick hearts and broken minds. Simply telling them that one time it all happened was not the kind of spirituality that they could use. They needed something real, something tangible, something they could actually use to heal. Power does that. Stories do not. McGurk saw no evidence that the Church held that sort of power.

This was getting serious, very serious. O'Bardon's belief system was starting to unravel. If Jesus existed at all, it was now abundantly clear that the Gospel Story was more of a broadside for propaganda consumption than it was history. It was in effect a collection of urban legends written some sixty to ninety years after the death of Jesus. It was myth, pure and simple. Although O'Bardon knew some of this from his seminary studies, he was never before living beneath the blade of this intellectual Sword of Damocles twenty-four hours a day. He had frankly never considered all of this academic retooling of the Jesus Story to be all that important. Now he realized how important it was. Other people were starting to tell the Jesus Story in a very different way than the church does. A lot of money, power, and credibility rested on who won this battle for the right to tell the Story. That much was clear. What was not clear at all to O'Bardon was what he could do about it.

THE CARDINAL'S ORDERS

"Come in Fathers and sit down. We have a lot to discuss this morning." With those words, the newly appointed cardinal archbishop of Philadelphia invited Monsignor Glenn and Father O'Bardon into his office suite and had them sit directly in front of him on his office couch. He pulled a chair up close to them and sat down. He had just come up from exercising in the Chancery gym, so he was still dressed in his gym clothes and slightly sweating. This meeting was so important that it could not be put off to a later time. The cardinal archbishop of Philadelphia was to hold the most important meeting in the priesthoods of these three men, and he was to do it in his gym clothes. There was a certain oddity to that. It was not lost on either O'Bardon or Glenn. This was going to be a very unusual morning they both thought.

"Well, where to start?" Renatto intoned. "I guess at the beginning" he answered himself. He continued without waiting for any sort of acknowledgment from his staff lieutenants. "The Holy Father is very concerned that new elements that have appeared within the theological spectrum of discourse in the last twenty years are now getting such a hearing as to drown out our message of salvation and truth in the Son of God, Jesus Christ. The Holy

93

Father is afraid that our message of Christian truth and justice will be lost in the unending minutiae of biblical pseudo-exegesis that is coming out of the media, especially cable television, and is aimed at "humanizing" Jesus of Nazareth so that he is more 'acceptable' to the modern mind. This is unacceptable to the curia and is seen as running counter to the authentic Gospel story of salvation from sin and Faith in Jesus Christ."

He took a deep breath, sighed heavily and even sadly, dropped his head a little and continued. "I have been given the job of trying to find a way to get our message out over the din of confusion portrayed by the media. Since most of this is coming from the English-speaking world, it is only fitting that an English-speaking bishop be given the task of straightening out the confusion. And the confusion is great and its waters run deep."

The Cardinal Archbishop then proceeded to outline the entire scope of Historical Jesus research in the past 180 years or so. He was a scholar and brilliant and he was in charge of the facts. He knew his stuff. O'Bardon was so impressed with the Cardinal's command of the facts that he could not hide his surprise. The Cardinal talked for twenty straight minutes and was in complete command of literally dozens of names, dates, book titles, lines of research, schools of thought and dangerous lines of inquiry. It was small wonder that this man was trusted by the Vatican with such an assignment. The man was a walking repository of information concerning the historical Jesus.

He continued without even making eye contact, staring at the ceiling while slumped backward in his chair, hands locked behind his head. "The Jesus Seminar at the Westar Institute in California is the main perpetrator of this extra biblical view of Our Lord and Savior, but by no means are those academics the only contributors to the confusion. What we need is a plan to combat this new heresy, this new and never-ending string of Jesus Stories that are openly competing with our version of events at the end of Second Temple Judaism. Let there be no doubt in your mind, this is about the life and death of our Church, our traditional message, our right to speak for Our Lord as his representatives. If they are right and we are wrong, then who are we to claim primacy rights on the Story?

We must win this battle for the minds and hearts of the Faithful. We are losing them to pop theology streamed out to them on cable television shows in a never ending cacophony of rebellious voices who have no interest in the traditional version of the Gospels."

He stopped speaking and looked at his two men. They sat there unmoved, unblinking and not knowing what to think, what to say. What could they say? Finally, Monsignor Glenn said slowly and deliberately, "So, your Eminence is saying that Father O'Bardon and I are to...? to? To do *what* exactly?"

The Cardinal Archbishop of Philadelphia laughed out loud, an almost maniacal laugh. "I have no idea what you are going to do or how you should do it. But whatever the answer is, find it quickly and write an implementation plan. Have it in my hands so that I may deliver it to the Papal Nuncio in Washington D.C. for presentation to the Holy Father no later than next Christmas. You have less than one year. Good luck, gentlemen." He then got up slowly, smiled at them and left the room for the shower. The two priests sat on the couch and looked at each other, eventually Glenn left the room and O'Bardon was sitting there alone. He sat there for ten minutes, alone and stunned. " Now what?" he thought. He had no idea how to answer his own question.

He spent the rest of the day researching the Jesus Seminar and planned to travel to the Westar Institute in Santa Rosa, California as soon as possible to discuss the various points of view with as many scholars as he could find. He made plans to fly to California in three days. What was this place, this Westar Institute? He did all that he could to find out about them before he departed.

According to its own website, the Westar Institute is a member-supported, non-profit research and educational institute dedicated to the advancement of religious literacy. It claims a two fold mission: that is "to foster collaborative research in religious studies and also to communicate the results of the scholarship of religion to a broad, non-specialist public." It was this last idea that scared the Church.

The website went on to explain that until a few years ago, essential knowledge about biblical and religious traditions was hidden in "the windowless studies of universities and seminaries—

away from the general public. Such research was considered too controversial or too complicated for laypersons to understand. Many scholars, fearing open conflict or even reprisal, talked only to one another. The churches often decided what information their constituents were "ready" to hear." O'Bardon was beginning to feel very uncomfortable reading this and was gaining a new appreciation for the Curia's fears.

The website continued. "Through publications, educational programs, and research projects like the Jesus Seminar, Westar has opened up a new kind of conversation about religion. This is an honest, no-hold-barred exchange involving thousands of scholars, clergy and other individuals who have critical questions about the past, present and future of religion. "

"Some of the principles guiding the work of Westar are:

All serious questions about religion—including biblical and dogmatic traditions—deserve research, discussion and resolution; no inquiry should be out of bounds. The scholarship of religion should be collaborative in order to expand the base of decision-making, cumulative in forming and building on a consensus, and genuinely ecumenical."

"Religion and bible scholars should conduct their deliberations in public and report the results to a broad, literate audience in simple, non-technical language.

Westar is not affiliated with any religious institution nor does it advocate a particular theological point of view."

O'Bardon realized immediately that this would be a fight to the death.

SEEING MARTHA AGAIN

Father O'Bardon needed to see Sister Martha. He had made up his mind when he read the diary entry concerning The McGurk and Bibiana. He needed Martha and he admitted that to himself for the very first time on awakening the morning after the last diary reading. He was a priest true, but he was also a man. Somehow, someway, in some fashion that he would have to be able to live with, he needed Martha. It was just that simple.

Father O'Bardon phoned the Trinitarian Convent that served the Cathedral parish at the Cathedral of Saints Peter and Paul. He asked for Sister Martha. She was attending class at Saint Joseph's University that evening and was not available, the nun that answered the phone told him. Father O'Bardon identified himself to the nun who had answered the phone and asked what class she was taking. The nun told him that Sister Martha was taking a psychology class in the graduate school and that this was all she knew. O'Bardon thanked her, hung up the phone, went to his car and drove to Saint Joe's on City Line Avenue. He needed to see Martha. It was just that simple.

O'Bardon parked the car, found the registrar's office and asked the Sister in charge of the office where he could find Sister Martha. She helped him find Sister Martha by checking the records and directed him to the building. He waited on the steps of the building until class was over at 7:00 PM. Martha walked out the door and was surprised to see him. She was very surprised. They had not seen each other or spoken in many months.

"Martha, have you eaten yet?" he asked. Martha nodded that she had not. "How about I buy you dinner at the Student Union building?" he said. Martha nodded yes and they both walked silently toward the cafeteria. They passed a few minutes in small talk, got their meals, took their trays to a quiet corner in the room and sat down at the table. No one was near them, O'Bardon made sure of that. He was wearing clericals and Martha was in her habit.

"Liam, what is this all about?" Martha asked. She had never before called him by his first name.

"Martha, there is no easy way to say this. I am having real doubts about myself, my manhood, my priesthood, my entire Faith system. I don't know exactly what I believe anymore on any number of levels! I need to talk and I need to talk you alone. I need you to just listen. You don't have to say anything. I just need you to listen...after you listen to me I will drive you home, so don't worry about missing your bus. Can you do that for me?"

"Of course!" she said and started intently into his face. Liam began talking in a low voice. His eyes scanned the table, the walls, the ceiling and her face alternately as he talked. He was clearly troubled and searching hard for the right words to explain his predicament. Martha could see that.

And so he told her. He talked about the diaries, The McGurk and his influence over him lately, his shame over their part in the cover up of the child abuse scandal in the archdiocese, his new assignment to find a way to deal with the media and its differing versions of the Jesus Story and finally, almost hesitantly he said this, "...and along with all of this, I have found that I have feelings for someone that I cannot hide from myself any longer. I am constantly thinking of her and I do not know what to do about it."

Martha's face reddened deeply; she was obviously interested, concerned and paying very close attention.

"Do I know her?" Martha asked just as hesitantly.

"Yes. You do."

"May I ask who it is?" Martha said with all honesty and sincerity.

"I am thinking about you all the time Martha." Martha let out a small gasp, and put her hands over her mouth. She dropped her gaze. She said nothing. She sat there not knowing what to say.

"Don't say anything Martha. I don't expect you to say anything. I just needed to get this off my chest." They finished their meal, walked to O'Bardon's car and he drove her home to the convent. As she got out of the car, without looking at him at all, she grabbed his hand and squeezed it tightly. She held it for about ten seconds while looking out of the passenger side window. She got up and left the car without saying anything. She did not look at O'Bardon. The message had been delivered. O'Bardon and Martha were both in big emotional trouble. And they knew it. This storm had been brewing for a long time and it was about to break wide open. There could be no going back now.

O'Bardon flew out of Philadelphia International Airport for San Francisco, California that next Friday. He would drive down to Santa Rosa to meet some of the Board of Directors of the Westar Institute. He was going to meet with the enemy. This was going to be the opening engagement in a long and secret war and both sides were vaguely aware of the stakes. Academic battles are always like that, brutal and congenial and never, never ending. The battle between those who absolutely know and those who absolutely question was about to begin.

MEETING THE ENEMY

ather O'Bardon was met at the airport by biblical exegete John Dominic Cusack, a leading theologian and writer and major member of the Jesus Seminar. A former Dominican priest, now laicized and married, "Dom" Cusack was an Irishman by birth and by temperament a scholar. He was a good man, kind in disposition and long suffering of fools. That was a good thing, because O'Bardon realized by simple force of reputation that he was in the shadow of a giant in the field of biblical exegesis and he felt humbled that he was being picked up at the airport by a world class scholar, albeit wearing a flannel shirt, jeans and white sneakers. A man of about 65, Cusack was perhaps the most famous face of the Jesus Seminar group and that face was known throughout the world as a major force in Jesus Story research and the retelling of the story.

"Father O'Bardon?" Professor Cusack asked.

"Yes, Professor Cusack?" Cusack nodded affirmatively.

"I recognized you from the photo on the book cover of your last book. I read it from beginning to end in two sittings. Wow!" O'Bardon was impressed with Cusack's grasp of so much minutiae and how he could place it all in one cohesive matrix of explanation concerning the historical Jesus. Cusack took the priest's bag and walked with him toward his car, a new compact car. Cusack looked at the young priest, chuckled to himself and finally said,

"And I recognized you by the black suit and Roman collar!" and both men laughed. Their temperaments were similar. That was a good sign.

"How do I rate being picked up at the airport by John Dominic Cusack?" the priest asked.

"Well, the truth be told, the Board of Directors is meeting today and the Chairman, John McGaughey asked me to bring you there straightaway. They are interested in exactly why you are here. It is *very* rare that Rome sends anyone our way. You are something of an enigma. This never happens. The Vatican usually does everything possible to ignore us or blunt our influence. You are a celebrity over at the Institute at the moment, Father," Cusack said, mildly chuckling.

On the way to Santa Rosa, about an hour and half away, O'Bardon fell asleep. Cusack had been a priest for too many years not to recognize that the young man was troubled. "This will all play out in time" the older man thought.

They arrived in just enough time for O'Bardon to rush to the men's room to wash his face and hands and meet the Board Chairman. He was immediately asked to address the Board. O'Bardon had prepared notes to give to the chairman and did not expect to speak.

"Good morning ladies and gentlemen. I am Liam O'Bardon and I have been sent here by the Cardinal Archbishop of Philadelphia who has been tasked by the Holy Father to find a way to use the findings of the Jesus Seminar to further the Catholic message and mission." Everyone sitting around the boardroom table looked at each other in mild amusement at that last remark. Asking this group to be sensitive to the philosophical needs of the Catholic Church was very much like asking the fox to guard the henhouse and all of the people in the room knew that. They all smiled and some even allowed themselves a small laugh. O'Bardon got the irony of his request and smiled with them. He continued.

"Roughly 26 percent of the American population identifies itself as Catholic. That is a lot of people, approximately 78 million Americans. I have come here today to discuss the impact of your research at the Westar Institute on these people and others."

"There are roughly 19,500 Catholic parishes in the US. These parishes often have a church building, a school, an auditorium and provide education, worship and social services at some levels to the surrounding community. There are 230 Catholic Institutions of higher learning in the US and they have over 600,000 students enrolled. There are 615 Catholic hospitals in this country and there are over 2,400 Catholic grammar schools and high schools in the US and over 315,000 of those students are non-Catholics within the total enrollment. 27 percent are minority students numbering almost 657,000 students for a total enrollment in the US Catholic School System of about 2,628,000 students. Caring for these students alone provides about 19.5 billion dollars a year in tax relief for Americans supporting public schools. 97 percent of Catholic secondary school students go on to post secondary education. 99 percent graduate."

"In 2003 about 6.5 million people received some sort of assistance from Catholic Charities. $38 million dollars was given to Hurricane Katrina relief alone by Catholic Charities in 2005–2006. About $1.3 billion dollars has been collected since 1983 by the various dioceses to be further disbursed throughout the world for Catholic missions, many of them social outreach to people of all faiths and many of them in support of Western political objectives, such as aid to Eastern European churches. In short, the Catholic Church and its various arms and institutions are a very large part of the American Dream and social safety network in this country and elsewhere. It would be hard to replace, perhaps even impossible to replace."

"The work of the Westar Institute, although admirable in academic terms, has an enormous impact on the social outreach and public communications aspect of the Catholic message. In short, it is a series of competing messages that is placing our mission-at-large in harm's way. People are looking to academics and the media more and more to tell them about Jesus of Nazareth and they are neglecting the message and ultimately, the ethos and mission of the traditional Church more and more as every week goes by. In short, there are now many competing voices jockeying for position in the race to tell the Jesus Story first. The Catholic Church does not want to lose this race. There is too much at stake, not just for Catholics, but for the country and the world."

"My mission here today is to find out what the Catholic Church can do to make your findings here at the Westar Institute serve the greater purpose of Christian outreach and the Catholic message. We are trying to find a way to enlist the findings of the academic world in our outreach efforts. I hope that through our conversations and our discussions with each other, we can find mutual ground on which to stand as we tell the Jesus Story together." He stopped reading, looked at them politely and stepped from behind the podium.

He thanked them for their patience and quietly left the room to polite smiles and absolute silence. Dom Cusack sat down with him to talk.

"Well, you made your statement. How do you feel? Do you think it was received well?"

"I am just grateful that they let me speak. That was totally unexpected. Do you think what I said will have any effect on them?" O'Bardon asked.

Dom Cusack said, "I think it will have no impact on them at all. They were scholars before you entered the room. They are scholars now that you have left the room. They will continue to do what scholars do. They will be walking question marks. They would not be scholars if they followed an agenda, no matter how worthy. Their job is to find the truth and then report it. No more than that. The church's job, and therefore your job, is to have an agenda and bring it forth. They are involved in one set of problems and you are involved in another. You really cannot expect them to help you with your problems. Asking them to do that is kind of like driving your car to a bakery and then getting angry when you cannot get an oil change."

Both men laughed. O'Bardon offered to take Cusack to lunch. The older man gladly accepted. A friendship was being born. Father Liam O'Bardon felt strangely at ease with this former priest that was twice his age. He also felt relieved in some way since he had been allowed to fire the opening salvo in this war with academia and he was received politely and with courtesy. Somehow or other, O'Bardon felt that he had now done his duty.

LUNCH WITH DOM CUSACK

"What do you want to eat?" O'Bardon asked. "How about Italian food?" Cusack said.

"I know just the place" said the older man and he drove them both to his favorite local Italian restaurant. They had a wonderful discussion over lunch which helped Liam place the work of the Jesus Seminar into proper perspective.

O'Bardon quickly got over his awe. Cusack had a way of putting people immediately at ease with his easy smile and Irish brogue; it was obvious that he had been a priest because he still had priestly ways.

"So, what can you tell me on the foot soldier level about the Jesus Seminar?" O'Bardon's question was simple and straightforward and right to the heart of the matter. Cusack laughed,

"Well, let me get a few mouthfuls of this pasta and I will answer your question!" Cusack dove into his meal with great gusto.

"This man really does enjoy Italian food, no doubt about that," O'Bardon thought as he watched Cusack devour his meal. Having studied at the Vatican as a seminarian and later as a priest-scholar, Cusack was no stranger to Italian food, Italian culture or the mindset of the Vatican.

"So you want to know the insider's view of our work? All right then, sit back and hang on. This will be a bumpy ride I am afraid! There seems to be nine major groups in the Jesus Seminar. You must remember that by definition, most of us accept the Jesus of history as factual. That is, most of us think he actually existed. A few of our scholars do not. The groups could probably be broken down this way: Jesus as The Heavenly Messiah, Jesus as the Literary Mystic Everyman, Jesus the Greek Hero, Jesus the Political Threat, Jesus the Wise Man, which is the group in which I fit, Jesus the Spirit Man, Jesus the Socialist of sorts, Jesus the Doomsayer and Jesus the Savior of Men."

"There are roughly four or five of us who have international standing and credentials as biblical exegetes that do not believe that Jesus actually existed. They have various points of view as to how, when, why, where this all happened, or more clearly, this did *not* happen. The rest of us, numbering perhaps 23 or 24 writers, scholars, professors and researchers believe in various points of view that proclaim that such a man *did* exist, but not in any way that would resemble what we have been taught as children. Almost no one in the group would publicly state that the Gospels are completely reliable history. This can cause trouble because some of us are still practicing clergymen. This is not an easy thing to do. Core values fall like apples from a tree every time somebody returns from the Middle East with a new find!"

He continued. "My group sees Jesus as a sort of mystic traveling cynic which was common in the Middle East in those days. Our point of view is basically that Jesus was not all that uncommon relative to the life he lived and the things he said." O'Bardon was surprised at that. Cusack caught the look on his face. "Yes, its true. Other people of his time were saying very similar things."

"About five of us believe that Jesus and by extension Christianity was simply a Hellenized version of various Jewish movements that were birthing at the time, such as the Essenes, the Nazarenes, the Ebionites and a few others. It is still not clear what the exact relationship, if any, between these various groups was. Were they one movement that was called different names? Were they various sects within a general movement like Protestantism is today? We are not clear yet on any of these questions."

"I want you to note something. It is really instructive for you to understand how this is more or less indicative of the entire process of biblical exegesis as it relates to the historical Jesus. I can give you a hundred examples. But I will give you one that will stay with you. Let us take the example of the Mandaeans. They still exist today and are the modern day followers of John the Baptiser, who Catholics refer to as St. John the Baptist. They are Gnostics, dualists, have a loosely defined set of scriptures, a priesthood, secret rites, a very small population throughout the world of perhaps 70,000 people, and are a very closed and secretive society. One cannot become a Mandaean. It follows matrilineal blood lines, as does Judaism, and one must be born into the religion in order to practice it."

"Mandaeans do not recognize Moses, Jesus or Muhammad as true prophets but only Adam, Noah and John the Baptizer. They have a hierarchical clergy, practice frequent baptism in the manner of the Essenes and worship on Sunday. They believe in a peaceful life above all else."

"In the Middle East, they live mostly in Iraq today and are a persecuted sect under Islam. They have nine tenets of Faith. They believe in a Supreme and Formless entity, as does Judaism. They believe in a dualistic universe. They believe in a world of ideas as existing in another dimension. They believe in the soul as an exile from the Formless Entity from which it is born. They consider that the planets and stars have great influence over humans and after death humans are detained on various planets. They believe in a Savior Spirit or Spirits that assist the human through a human life into the World of Light. They use a cult communication language of symbol and metaphor where ideas are personified into demons and other personalities and they have sacraments. They also insist upon great secrecy as a requirement of membership."

"Some scholars believe that Jesus was a Nasoraean priest under John the Baptiser who attempted to usurp leadership in his movement. When that failed, he started his own subsect within Judaism. They also believe that "Jesus the Nazarene" is a mistranslation, either intentional or by accident of the phrase, "Jesus the Nasoraean." Both groups spoke Aramaic and the pronunciation of both terms is very close. It is therefore possible that Jesus brought his strange ideas to Judaism from this Gnostic sect which his first cousin John led and in which he was a priest."

"But there are other points of view here and more in the mainstream."

"Perhaps the closest group to what you and I might consider to be traditional Christianity would be Jesus the Savior group. There are three scholars in that specific group who barely move away from ancient conceptions of the Christ. They are not ascendant in the larger group and often find the larger group frustratingly hard to penetrate with their ideas."

"I must admit however, that I find the Jesus as Myth groups compelling. I personally believe that such a man named Jesus lived. But if he did not and the whole thing is a public relations story, it is the finest work of public relations that has ever been foisted on the world. It is a work of genius. It makes the creators of Santa Claus, the Easter Bunny, Uncle Sam and John Bull look like children. If Jesus truly did not exist, whatever geniuses created him were truly some of the cleverest people who ever lived." With that he finished his pasta with relish. O'Bardon did the same. 'Jesus talk' could make one very hungry at this level of intensity.

O'Bardon was intrigued by what Cusack was saying and he was especially intrigued with the Jesus as Myth line of thought. The McGurk was exercising great influence here.

"Tell me more about the Jesus as Myth point of view, if you don't mind." Cusack agreed. He continued. "Well, now be completely aware before I start talking. This is not my line of argument. I do believe that Jesus existed. He is inferred very strongly by things written in the New Testament. In my view it is not reasonable to assume that he did not exist. However, a strong case can be made that he did not exist at all."

"Flavius Josephus reports four subsets of Judaism and they were the Pharisees, Sadducees, Essenes, and Zealots, also known as the Iscarii or perhaps loosely translated, the Dagger Men. The earliest followers of Jesus were known as either the Nazarenes or perhaps the Nasoraeans as previously mentioned, and perhaps later, they were called the Ebionites, but we cannot be exactly sure if that is true. There is not enough evidence that they were the same group. These various subsects form a significant part of the greater whole of Second Temple Jewish groups in Jesus' time."

Cusack continued. "As I mentioned to you earlier, the Ebionite/Nazarene or perhaps Nasoraean movement was peopled by the mostly Jewish/Israelite, followers of John the Baptizer, who we refer to as John the Baptist. It is my professional belief that later Jesus took command of the group with the beheading of the Baptizer. I further believe that upon Jesus' death those marginalized Jews who were concentrated in Palestine and surrounding regions, were led by "James the Just," oldest brother of Jesus, and they were flourishing and significant to Judaism as a whole between the years 30 to about 82 CE. Others believe that Jesus was a literary construct of other messiahs of that time and that he did not exist at all."

"The Nazarenes which were a different group from the Nasoraeans, were aggressively zealous for the Torah, and continued to live in all the mitzvot or commandments as guided by their Rabbi and Teacher. They were accepting of non-Jews into their fellowship on the basis of some version of the Noachide Laws as can be seen in Acts 15 and 21. Now this is important for you to stop here and reflect. If in fact the Nazarenes were open to accepting into their fellowship such people as the Gnostic Nasoraeans, it is quite understandable why the two groups would be confused and seen as one group. They were two different groups who believed very different things, but if there has been confusion over the last two millennia over their relationship, it is understandable."

"The term Ebionite is from the Hebrew *'Evyonim* and it means "The Poor Ones." In my professional opinion it was taken from the teachings of the alleged Jesus. Remember he said "Blessed are you Poor Ones, for yours is the Kingdom of God" based on passages in Isaiah. He also spoke of other related texts that address a remnant group of faithful ones."

"Nazarene comes from the Hebrew word *Netzer*, drawn from Isaiah and means a Branch—so you could say that the Nazarenes were the "Branchites," or followers of the one they believed to be the Branch of the Root of Jesse, very much like the Christmas Carol says in its lyrics. The term Nazarene was likely the one first used for these followers of Jesus, as shown by the words of Acts 24:5 where Paul is called "the ringleader of the sect of the Nazarenes."

"Here we see the word Nazarene used in a very similar way to that of Flavius Josephus in writing of the four streams of thought of Second Temple Judaism: Pharisees; Sadducees; Essenes; and Zealots." So the term Nazarene is probably the clearest and most accurate term for the Jesus movement, while Ebionite or Poor Ones was used as well, along with a whole list of other terms like the Saints, Children of Light, the Way, New Covenanters, and some other terms perhaps. We are not completely sure yet. Research has not been completely exhausted on this issue. And you must not forget the confusion that sets in when considering the Nasoraeans and *their* place in all of this." Cusack took a long sip of iced tea and continued. O'Bardon sat spellbound.

"We also know from the book of Acts that the group itself that we refer to as 'Early Christians' preferred the designation "The Way" as written in Acts 24:14; 22, and some other passages. The term "Christian," first used in Greek speaking areas for the movement, seems to be an attempt to re-translate the term Nazarene, and basically means a "Messianist. It is very interesting to note that in modern Arabic the word for Christian is 'messihee" which essentially means "a messianist." Interesting indeed, isn't it?"

"Now here is where it starts to get a lot more dense and even more confusing. Even scholars who have studied this subject matter for their entire lives can get lost at this point." Cusack took a long drink from his iced tea and continued.

"The Essenes, whose name possibly comes from the Hebrew word *'Ossim* which could be loosely translated as "The Doers of Torah", wrote or collected the manuscripts that we call today The Dead Sea Scrolls. It is crucial that you understand that the Essenes pioneered certain aspects of this "Way," over 150 years before the time most of us consider to be the range of dates for the alleged birth of Jesus. Those dates are roughly 7 B.C. to 2. A.D. And right here is where the whole historical Jesus story can take any one of thousand different directions. This is the departure point for various opinions held by most biblical exegetes engaged in historical Jesus research."

"Based on verses in Isaiah these people lived in the wilderness, practiced baptism as an entrance requirement into their sect, considered that they had made a new covenant with Adonai that superseded the one He had made with the Jews and they were a messianic and apocalyptic group who were expecting either three redemptive figures to appear soon at the end of time like Moses and two other messiahs or they were expecting one messiah who was all three things they were looking for, that is Priest, Prophet and King. There is a difference of opinion on this last point."

"Now it gets even more confusing," Cusack opined. "These Essenes also referred to themselves as the Way, the Poor, the Saints, the New Covenanters, Children of Light, and other appellations that Christians would eventually claim for their own. Perhaps their most common self describer was the Yachad, which literally meant the brotherhood or the community. They would normally refer to each other as brother or sister. They were all bitterly opposed to the corrupt and powerful Priests in Jerusalem whom they saw as willing collaborators with the Romans. They opposed the puppet kings of the Romans who we know as the Herods. They opposed the Pharisees whom they saw as compromising with the Roman occupiers and their puppet kings and they most bitterly opposed the Second Temple establishment who they saw as prostituting themselves in order to get power and influence from the Emperor in Rome."

"They had their own developed Halacha, which as you know is an interpretation of the Torah. And it is clear that some aspects of their Hallacah, the alleged Jesus picks up and openly teaches. Those things would be the ideal of no divorce, not using oaths, and a few other things that were clearly Essenic. They followed one they called the True Teacher or the Teacher of Righteousness whom most scholars believe lived in the 1st century B.C. which of course was long before the alleged Jesus lived. This Teacher was opposed and possibly killed by the Hasmonean King/Priests at the instigation of the Pharisees. John the Baptizer seems to arise out of this context and re-fire the apocalyptic mania of the movement in the early part of the first century A.D."

"So, as you can see the terminology is flexible at best and very confusing at worst because there are a variety of self-designations used by the very early Jesus movement which are clearly either stolen, shared or directly transmitted from the Essenes. No one is really sure which of these it is. The choice of course depends on your point of view. But it is very clear that most of these terms that the early Church either inherited or stole had previously been used by the Essenes. In that sense you might call the early Jesus movement in Jerusalem a further developed messianic "Essenism," modified through the powerful, prophetic influence of the alleged Jesus as Teacher."

"Now the picture gets even messier. When Christianity developed as we understand it, which was mostly in the 3rd and 4th centuries, it gradually lost its Jewish roots and heritage and it almost completely severed its Palestinian connections. Things got distorted, history was forgotten, the major players and major themes were pushed aside for more contemporary needs and theologies. In short, the Jewish Church Fathers in Jerusalem were no longer needed. They were much more of an embarrassment to the Popes and later Christian Church Fathers in North Africa, Asia Minor and Rome than they were in the beginning. They were too Jewish, too messianic in the old sense of that word to be useful any longer to the powers that be of the Church in Rome. They had served their purpose but Christianity was outgrowing them. They had to be pushed aside and their influence and original direction had to be ferociously eradicated. History had to be rewritten. It was as simple as that."

"So, the Gentile, Roman Catholic Church historians began to see the Ebionites and Nazarenes as two separate groups. To be fair by the late 2nd century there might have been a split between these mostly Jewish followers of Jesus. The distinction these Gentile Christian writers make, and remember, they universally *despise* these people and call them "Judaizers", is that the Ebionites reject Paul, and the doctrine of the Virgin Birth or "divinity" of Jesus; they use only the Hebrew Gospel of Matthew, and they are thus more extreme in their Judaism. They describe the Nazarenes more positively as those who accept Paul but with a great amount of caution and these Nazarenes believe in some aspect of the divinity of Jesus such as the virgin birth. What we have to keep in mind in reading these accounts from the Church fathers is that they are strongly prejudiced against

112

this group or these two groups, whatever they may have evolved into at this point. These Church Fathers now claim to have replaced Judaism entirely with the new religion of Christianity, overthrowing the Torah for both Gentile and Jew."

"At this point then, the Jesus Movement is dead. It cannot be reborn. What was eventually to become the Catholic Church has rewritten history and redefined and radically upgraded the Jewish concept of messiah. No one who was with the Apostles at Pentecost, if in fact it is a true event, would recognize this new Christianity. It was not the Faith of the Apostles. It is going in an entirely new direction and it is now called Christianity. That much is clear."

"But it is also true that the alleged Jesus and his followers could have been invented after he allegedly lived. This would be to put forward the agenda of the remnants of the Essenes. That cannot be completely ruled out." He took a long sip of tea and continued. "You have to understand something crucial about biblical exegesis, Liam. *Everyone* has an agenda. There is no such thing as scholarship without an agenda. That is what makes this so very difficult. One can never be sure if he is reporting his findings with academic accuracy or in the light of his own biases. It can be almost impossible to tell at times."

"With this in mind, Some scholars believe that Christianity began with a mythical Christ. They argue that the many streams of religious thought which we today call the Jesus Movement is a philosophical and theological descendant or perhaps a distant relative of Jewish mystical considerations on the scriptures. These would be found in such writings as the Odes of Solomon or the Wisdom of Solomon, and the writings of Philo of Alexandria."

"These would have been well-received by those converts to the Jesus Movement who were schooled to think in the mode of Platonism and Greek ideas of the day. The cosmology of the time saw the heavens as multi-layered and these Greeks and Hellenized Jews would understand the descent of a heavenly Christ. They would further identify with a Christ who was to be sacrificed in the lower spheres of the heavens before being raised to the right hand of the Father. This very thought process is called the "Jerusalem Tradition." It is very apparent in the epistles of Paul, and about seven of these are accepted as authentic. But of course, things are never this simple. Once again, the waters get muddy." Cusack continued. O'Bardon was mesmerized.

"There was yet another tributary to early Christianity. We have the "Galilean Tradition," a separate Kingdom of God preaching movement located in Syrian speaking Palestine. The famous "Q" document that is speculated to have existed as the original proto-Gospel supposedly makes clear that there is no founder! In other words all of the passages that say "Jesus said.." were added years after the supposed proto-Gospel was written. In other words, Jesus was fabricated in this point of view. In this view, the author of the Gospel of Mark who had been brought up in the "Galilean Tradition" devised a brilliant bit of religious syncretism. In this view, the author allegedly identified the fictional Q founder with the exalted Pauline Christ in fashioning the passion story out of whole cloth. That is to say, the writer of Mark's Gospel, the basic and primary Gospel Story that the others borrow heavily from, made the whole thing up!"

"This is not completely implausible. Mark's narrative which was written from 85 to 90 A.D. was the sole basis upon which the later evangelists retold the Jesus story. That is to say, if Mark lied about an historical Jesus, so did the others because his basic story was the matrix they used to tell their own story. Matthew was written about 100 A.D., Luke was written about 125 A.D. and the mercurial John was written about 125 A.D. All points of view, all starting points for history, all basic tenets of the Jesus Story depended ultimately upon the veracity of the author of Mark. In this view the book of Acts is a catholicizing fiction written somewhere around 150 A.D. Although certain second century apologists continued to espouse a purely divine Christ, the Gospel myth eventually came to dominate Christian thought. In this view, the lie won out."

Cusack then continued. He was clearly tired from all of this talking, but O'Bardon was stunned with his command of the facts and the theories. O'Bardon sat there in awe and listened in wide-eyed amazement.

"There is yet another view of the mythical Jesus, the Jesus that did not really exist. It could be reasonably argued that Gnosticism was the original Christianity. In this view what we know as Christianity developed from the Pagan Mysteries with the Jesus story as a Jewish version of the perennial myth of the dying and resurrecting Mystery god-man." This view of the Gospel story would be written like this "The Messiah was expected to be an historical personage of flesh and blood and definitely not a mythical, savior. The Jews expected this and nothing else. Therefore, it was inevitable, that the Jesus story would have to develop a quasi-historical setting."

"And so it did. What had started as a timeless and multi-cultural Middle Eastern myth espousing perennial and universal ancient teachings now appeared to be a historical account of a once-only event in real time. This is the only way that Jews could accept such a belief system as their own. From this point of view, it was unavoidable that sooner or later due to the nuances of the Jewish mind and the Jewish belief system of a personal God who talked to them directly through real prophets who they believed actually existed, this story *must* be interpreted as historical fact. The Jews did not believe in god myths like the Greco-Roman world did. They had real flesh and blood prophets and only real prophets could speak to them for God. They had no appreciation of religious devotion to myths or mythical gods."

"Once the Jesus myth was interpreted as history, a whole new type of religion came into being for the Jew and the Greek. It was a religion based on history not myth. This new Faith was based on blind faith in supposed events rather than on a mystical understanding of mythical metaphors, allegories and rituals. It was a religion of the Outer Mysteries without the Inner Mysteries. It was a religion of form without content. It was belief without Knowledge. In this view there are definite parallels between the mythical Christ of the Gospels and the Osiris-Dionysus myth." Cusack continued, "this is not my view, but it is certainly plausible. I cannot honestly completely rule it out."

"There is one last view of the Jesus Story that I want you to be aware of before I take you to the hotel. You need to understand that all of the rabbis or scholars among the Jews have never completely accepted that Jesus existed. And this goes back to very early days in the common era." He continued slowly that O'Bardon would grab the significance of what he was saying.

"There were many, many messiahs and teachers and healers named Jesus, perhaps dozens in the 150 years or so both preceding and following the life of Jesus Christ. To put this simply, many rabbis in the Middle Ages simply assumed that Jesus of Nazareth was a composite of all of these miracle workers named Jesus. It cannot be proven. But it cannot be disproven either. That is basically the line of thought that I refer to as Jesus the Myth. Any questions?" Both men laughed out loud. It was time to get to the hotel and get some rest. O'Bardon was exhausted from taking in so much information but exhilarated. He had learned more in the last half hour about the historical Jesus than he had learned in his lifetime. Cusack was obviously a genius.

Dom Cusack dropped Father O'Bardon off at the hotel and said as O'Bardon got out of the car.

"What I or anyone else thinks about the historical Jesus is nowhere near as important as what you think about Jesus. Remember that!" O'Bardon thanked him and then said, almost automatically, "God bless you, Father." Cusack chuckled. Old roles and behaviors do not die easily, Cusack thought to himself. O'Bardon took up his bags and entered the front desk of the hotel. He got his room, took a shower and fell asleep. He dreamed.

LIAM AND THE MCGURK

L iam dreamed the confused dreaming of a tired and
troubled young man. He was now in his mid thirties and
was at the point in his priesthood when he questioned
everything. Nothing was certain, Faith often seemed like a fairy
tale for fools and his life was an intellectual and emotional mine
field. All of this weighed heavy on his heart and his mind. His
sleep and his dreams reflected this dissonance.

Liam found himself in front of the altar at Saint Michael's
parish on Second Street in Philadelphia. He had been in that
church many times since it was the first parish that his family had
joined when they came from Ireland so many generations before
his time. He prayed while standing directly in front of the altar.
He was more or less opaque like a ghost, hard for anyone to see.
He looked like smoke in the dream but he was wearing the suit
and clerical collar of a priest in 2006. He slowly realized that *he*
was the incorporeal body in the church, the other worshipers were
solid. And he noticed something else in this lucid dream. They
were Irish and dressed in the rough garb of working people of
the late 19th Century. He was in Saint Michael's parish and it was
somewhere around 1880. That much he could sense.

"Excuse me Faather!" a voice behind him said. He turned. There before him stood a priest of about forty years of age, by the look of his face and his brogue the priest was obviously Irish. "Faather, can I help you?" the priest asked. Even in the dream, Liam realized that he would be hard to spot since he was mostly a shadow, not a solid body. Liam was strangely amused at the physics in this dream. He slowly said to the priest, "Can you see me Father?" and the Irishman laughed, "Of course I can see you Faather! But the bigger and more important question is, can *you* see *me*?" They both laughed. The Irish priest motioned for he and Liam to have a seat in the pew. Both priests walked to the pew and sat down.

Liam was now more or less amazed at this turn of events. He was dreaming and it all so seemed so real. He at one and the same time realized that he was dreaming and yet was fully cooperative with whatever was going on in the dream. He did not fight anything nor did he seek to control anything. He just let the dream play out.

Liam realized that the priest was dressed in the cassock popular with clergyman at that time. It stopped just below his knees and it had wide and open collar, much more like an Anglican clergyman would have had and not the typical Roman cassock of later times. He quickly reflected that this might have been the way immigrant Irish priests dressed. He found it odd but interesting.

"Faather, ya' seem troubled. Can I help?" the Irish priest asked kindly and quietly. Liam replied in genuine pain. "Father I am confused. I have been ordained about eight years and the cardinal archbishop expects me to find answers that I do not believe exist. I am to construct a plan to keep history at bay, to keep research from coming to light, to keep the Jesus Story exactly as it has always been. I do not believe that I can do that. There is too much information available now that will come to light one way or another. I cannot stop it or direct it. I am not sure why I am telling you this, but I fear that my Faith is not adequate to carry this cross."

The Irishman looked at the priest. "Faather, all that matters when one is a priest is that whatever view one takes of Christ and His message, one is faithful to it. It is impossible for any group of human beings to manage thought control over hundreds or thousands of years. What is, is. What was, was. No one can change that."

He continued. He waved his arm slowly in an arc encompassing all of the worshipers quietly praying in the church. The he turned back to Liam and said "Do you think that *they* care about which line of theology you have chosen to guide your life? Do you think that *they* are interested in this or that school of thought concerning whether or not Our Lord was real or unreal or Sephardic or a Greco-Roman myth or a Pauline fantasy? Do you think *they* care?" Liam did not know how to answer that question.

"Well, they do not care, let me make that clear, my priestly friend. They are in too much pain to care about semantics wrapping up a theological argument. Their burden is too heavy for them to give one whit of attention to Jesus theories, ancient or present. They are suffering and they desperately need assistance in carrying their crosses throughout their lives. They need assistance from people like you and me." He stopped talking and looked intensely into the face of Liam O'Bardon. "And that is where you come in, Faather. You see, they love you not because of who *you* are, but because of who *He* was! You don't matter, not one whit. *He* matters. He is the only thing that matters in your life. If you can remember that and live with it, your priesthood will be hard but sweet. I promise you that!"

Liam was humbled and strangely at peace. "Father, what is your name?" The Irishman laughed. "You know may name quite well. I am Jamie McGurk. We know each other quiet well" and the Irishman smiled. "YOU! What is this? How can this be?" Liam almost jumped out of his skin. McGurk laughed. "How can it be? Don't ask me! It's *your* dream, not mine!" and with that they both laughed. The parishioners turned at once and looked at the two priests disturbing their prayer. One old Irishman was saying his rosary under his breath. He shooshed the men loudly and placed his forefinger to his lips, indicating a request for silence from the two priests. "Sorry!" the McGurk intoned to them all.

"Father! I have so many questions to ask you!" Liam said. "Well, lad, ask away!" the Irishman chuckled. And so the two men spent an hour in conversation. It was an incredible experience for Liam.

119

They talked about Bibiana, about Martha, about whether Jesus was real or not, whether the Church was a help or a hindrance to the Faithful and about Liam's priesthood and about Jamie's ministry. At the end, Liam felt refreshed and exalted and purified in a strange way.

He was waking up. Morning was coming. Liam could feel himself about to leave any minute. He told Father McGurk the same. He asked what was it like to die and the McGurk laughed. "Faather, I am not sure. Most of the dead do not completely comprehend that we are dead. It does not work like that. I think that the Jews were probably closest to being correct about death, about sheoul. It is pretty much like that here. We are dead. Some of us know it and some of us don't. But it is pretty much like life here only a lot less intense and there is no real sense of time. Can you understand any of this?" McGurk questioned the younger priest. "I am not sure, but I think so" O'Bardon said.

Then the McGurk continued. "Before you leave me I need to tell you something. Both of our mother's were Haggerty's from home. We are kin Liam. My mother was the sister of your mother's great-grandmother, and they were Haggertys all! That is why you were chosen to receive and read the diaries that I wrote at the end of my life before you give them to the archbishop. And you must give them to archbishop. That is why you were chosen, cousin. God bless you!"

Liam could feel himself being pulled quickly away from the church. He was now half awake. He woke up. It was 2:22 AM. He dropped to his knees at the bedside and prayed. He was sobbing. He felt a weight fall from off his shoulders. He was strangely sad that the dream had ended so abruptly but he was also shaken to his core. This was the most intense dream of his lifetime and it was so incredibly personal. He prayed hard on the meaning of it all. He prayed till morning and then got showered and dressed and took a cab to the airport. He walked to his departure area quietly and almost in a daze. He was still in the dream, at least in spirit.

RABBI KAHN

O'Bardon boarded the plane and took his seat and started to read his breviary. An older man came and sat across from him. O'Bardon noticed that a book he was reading had Hebrew inscription on the cover. The two men smiled and the older man said, "Well hello, Father. I am Rabbi David Kahn. Are you flying to Philly today?"

O'Bardon smiled and said, "Well, yes I am. And you Rabbi?" The Rabbi smiled broadly at the young priest and offered, "Yes, what brought you out here, Father may I ask?"

"It would be very hard to say exactly!" O'Bardon exclaimed almost absentmindedly. "The archbishop sent me here to make our case to biblical scholars that the Jesus Story we tell has merit. It is a very long story and I am quite sure that I would bore you!" O'Bardon said to the older man. "No please! I want to hear. It will pass the time. Please tell me about this mission from the Archbishop to such a young priest."

So, O'Bardon obliged and gave the older man the ten minute version of the situation. He spoke of his situation, what it was, why O'Bardon had flown to California, what the scholars at the

Westar Institute found of the historical Jesus and the confusion that it all left O'Bardon within.

"Confusion?" said the old, white-haired rabbi, "why confusion? Father, if I may be so bold to offer advice?"

O'Bardon smiled, "please, Rabbi, I am all ears!"

"Well, in our business it is best not to have too many answers. Answers have a way of solidifying over time, turning themselves from the sweet honey of salve for wounds into the hard concrete of dogma for theologians. If you are confused over your vision of your covenant with God, that is good! It means that you are struggling to make sense of it all, to put it in the context of your own life, to make it meaningful to yourself as a believer and to your people as a priest. If you were not confused you would be a very good theologian, but perhaps not so good a priest. Your confusion stems not from any misunderstanding of your relationship to the One God but from a need to know how to make it real, for yourself and for your flock. Be happy that you are confused. It is a blessing."

O'Bardon smiled and took the Rabbi's hands. "Thank you rabbi, that was very kind. Can you do me the favor of explaining to me the contemporary Jewish version of Jesus? It would help greatly in my understanding of the whole panorama of contemporary views on Jesus."

The rabbi said, "You may not like it, are you sure?" O'Bardon smiled, "Rabbi, trust me, it cannot be any more startling than what I have already learned. I actually need to have it explained to me. I am going to have to explain it to others very soon I think."

With that, the rabbi sat back, looked out the window and said, "When the plane takes off and we are in the air, I will bore you with my understanding of the contemporary Jewish view of Jesus. Will that do?"

"Thank you Rabbi," said O'Bardon. The men sat back and in minutes the plane was in the air.

"Okay, young man, since you asked me, I shall tell you" the rabbi said with a smile. "The contemporary view of Jesus among educated Jews is a bit scattered I am afraid. There is no one view, as I am sure that you expected me to say. Judaism has no one special or any particular view of Jesus, and very few texts in Judaism directly refer to or take note of Jesus. Judaism is constructed philosophically and theologically in such a way that it is heresy to believe that God is divisible, or that there are intermediaries between God and Man, such as belief in saints or in the power of a priest in confession.

"And it is also true that Jewish eschatology holds that the coming of the Messiah will be associated with a specific series of events that all have not yet occurred, including among other things, the return of all Jews to their homeland and the complete and utter rebuilding of the Temple in Jerusalem, a very specific era of peace as told in Isaiah 2:4 and a complete understanding where "the knowledge of God" fills the earth from Isaiah 11:9 which will lead the nations to "end up recognizing the wrongs they did Israel" as outlined in Isaiah 52:13–53:5."

"Most Talmudic scholars believe that "Yeshu", a common name mentioned in the Talmud, refers to numerous different people at different times and is not likely to refer to Jesus of Nazareth, a man who may or may not have actually existed. This would depend on what school of thought any particular Jew was a student within relative to the existence of Jesus of Nazareth. Yeshu is thought to be a literary device and/or refers to various people who lived at different timeframes that are either too early or too late to fit Jesus of the New Testament. As Jesus plays no role in Judaism, doubting the historical existence of Jesus is not inconsistent with the basic tenets or philosophical underpinnings of Judaism."

"The belief that Jesus is God or the Son of God or the 'Son of Man' as he purportedly called himself or that Jesus is part of a godhead called a Trinity, that he is the long awaited Messiah, or a prophet of God are incompatible with traditional Jewish core beliefs. The idea of the Jewish Messiah is so different from the Christian idea of Christ, or the Anointed One, that it is clear that Jesus did not fulfill Jewish Messianic prophecies that establish the criteria for the coming of the Messiah. Authoritative texts of Judaism reject Jesus as God, Divine Being, intermediary between humans and God, Messiah or saint. In fact many Jews even just a few hundred years after Jesus of Nazareth supposedly lived were already calling into question his supposed existence."

"The belief in the Trinity, as with many other central Christian doctrines, is held to be incompatible with Judaism. They do not make any sense when placed inside a Jewish context of Second Temple Judaism. Let me explain further" the rabbi continued in a low, soft voice.

"In Classic Judaism, the idea of God as a duality or trinity is pure heresy; it is considered a cousin to polytheism. Judaism believes that the Torah rules out a Trinitarian God in Deuteronomy 6:4 when the Torah states: "Hear Israel, the Lord is our God, the Lord is one." The rabbi cleared his throat and continued. "Essentially then, Judaism believes that God, as the creator of time, space, and matter, and all other human measures of existence is ultimately beyond all of them. He is essentially completely unknowable and cannot be born or die. He cannot sire a son, as so many Greek gods seemed to be able to do. Judaism teaches that it is heretical for any man to claim to be God, apart of God, or the literal son of God. The Jerusalem Talmud in Ta'anit 2:1 states explicitly: "if a man claims to be God, he is a liar."

"In the 12th Century of this common era, the Jewish scholar Maimonides elucidated the core principles of Judaism, writing, "God is a unity unlike any other possible unity." There is no way to divide Him.""

"In fairness to all concerned both past and present it must be stated here that some Jewish scholars note that Jesus is said to have used the phrase "my Father in Heaven" as in the famous Christian prayer, The Lord's Prayer. You should know that this common poetic Jewish expression may have been misinterpreted as literal by uneducated peasants in Judah in Second Temple times."

"Judaism's view of the Messiah differs substantially and completely from the Christian idea of the Messiah as it is preached today in the 21st Century. According to Judaism's conception as described by the Prophets Isaiah and Ezekiel, Jesus did not fulfill the predictions associated with the Messiah's coming in any way. The kindest thing that I can say here is that these two ideas of Messiah,

Jewish and Christian, hardly relate to each other at all in either history, culture or theology. They are very different concepts."

"I must also tell you that according to Isaiah, the Messiah will be a paternal descendant of King David per Isaiah 11:1 via King Solomon per 1 Chronicles 22:8-10. He is expected to return the Jews to their homeland and rebuild the Temple. He is expected to reign as King, and he is expected to usher in an era of peace per Isaiah 2:4. The Messiah is to be completely understanding of where "the knowledge of God" fills the Earth per Isaiah 11:9 and most of all, he is expected to engage in leading the nations to "end up recognizing the wrongs they did Israel" per Isaiah 52:13-53:5. Ezekiel states the Messiah will redeem the Jews Ezekiel 16:55 but *only* the Jews. There is no mention of Gentiles here. I believe that this was a problem for the Rabbi Saul of Tarsus whom you know as Paul the Apostle" the rabbi said and O'Bardon continued to listen attentively.

"Jesus lived while The Second Temple was standing, and not while the Jews were exiled. Jesus of Nazareth never reigned as King over Judah let alone a reconstructed Israel, and there was no subsequent era of peace or great knowledge upon his supposed execution and death. Rather than being redeemed, the Jews were subsequently exiled from Israel soon after he supposedly lived. These discrepancies were noted by Jewish scholars who would be contemporaries of Jesus if in fact he lived at all, as later pointed out by Nahmanides, who in 1263 observed that Jesus was rejected as the Messiah by the rabbis of his time."

"Judaism does not believe that salvation or repentance from sin can be achieved through sacrifice on another's behalf, per the Talmud which says "The fathers shall not be put to death for the children, neither shall the children be put to death for the fathers; every man shall be put to death for his own sin." Judaism is instead focused on personal repentance."

"In addition, Judaism focuses on understanding how one may live a sacred life according to God's will in this world. It does not in any way look to the hope of or methods for finding spiritual salvation in a future life. Judaism views Jews' divine obligation to be living as a "holy people" in full accordance with Divine will, as a "light unto the nations," and Judaism does not purport to offer the exclusive path to salvation or "the one path to God." Christianity does so. Accordingly, the implications of the Christian conception of Jesus diverge greatly from the Jewish worldview, either then or now. In many ways it is hard to believe that Jesus was a Jew at all, if in fact he lived and was not a theological construct placed into history deliberately by people with another agenda." The rabbi stopped speaking and looked at O'Bardon. "Shall I go on?" "Please do Rabbi!" the priest said.

"As for the Talmud and Jesus, we have a whole different set of problems," the rabbi said.

"Such as?" O'Bardon asked.

"Well, The name Yeshu " appears in various works of classical Jewish rabbinic literature including the Babylonian Talmud. Hebraic scholars have debated for centuries the meaning of the name, which has been used as an acronym for the Hebrew expression yemach shemo vezichro 'May his name and memory be obliterated'. As you can see" the rabbi continued, "he was not one of Judaism's favorite people."

"The word is similar to Yeshua. This name is believed by most today to be the original Aramaic name of Jesus. Because of this and along with the occurrence in several manuscripts of the Babylonian Talmud of the title Ha-Notzri, meaning the Nazarene, and also some similarities between the stories of the two figures mentioned, some or many of the references to Yeshu have been traditionally understood to refer to the Jesus of Nazareth or the Jesus of Christianity if you prefer. Conversely, others have criticized this view, citing discrepancies between events mentioned in association with Yeshu and the time of Jesus' life, and differences between accounts of the deaths of Yeshu and Jesus. So it is crucial to note that scholars do not agree here on exactly who Yeshua might actually be.. It might be Jesus of Nazareth. It might not. It is impossible at this point to tell."

"Are you sure that you want me to continue" Rabbi Kahn said to the priest.

"I would not stop you now for all the rock candy in the world, Rabbi!" said the priest. They both laughed and the rabbi continued.

"In all cases the references are to individuals who whether they were real or not, are associated with acts that are seen as leading Jews away from Judaism to minuth. This is a term usually translated as "heresy" or "apostasy." Therefore, whether Yeshu equates with "Jesus" has historically been a delicate question at best. This is because of course "Yeshu" is portrayed in a negative light, and negative portrayals of Jesus in Jewish literature might incite, or be used as an excuse for, anti-Semitism among some Christians. It is a very, very difficult tightrope of scholarship to walk upon!" the rabbi said.

"I can see where it would be!" the priest offered. "Please continue Rabbi," the priest asked.

"Now here is the core problem for scholars. Some argue that there is no relationship between Yeshu and the historical Jesus. Other Talmudic scholars argue that Yeshu refers to the historical Jesus. Still other scholars within Judaism argue that Yeshu is a literary device used by the old rabbis to comment on their relationship to and with early Christians and has nothing whatsoever to do with any individual at all. All have elements within them that would support and deny their validity. One can waste a lifetime in this morass of opinion!" that rabbi said with consternation in his voice.

"So, was Jesus of Nazareth real or not? I do not know. Moses Maimonides believed that he was real and existed. Other Talmudic scholars did not. It is obvious that there was no love lost here, so the fact that some Jews of high scholarship accepted his existence is remarkable. That is about all I can say. I am all talked out!" The rabbi smiled and looked at the priest kindly. "Thank you rebbe, I am going to need to think and pray on all of this!" "No Father, thank you, for being so kind and listening so well." With that the two clergymen went back to reading and the priest once again fell asleep until the plane arrived in Philadelphia.

OTHER VIEWS OF JESUS

B ack in Philadelphia, Liam called the convent at the Cathedral parish and asked to speak to Martha. She answered the phone and was breathless when she realized who it was on the other end. He asked to meet with her. She said of course and they made a date for dinner at her next class.

O'Bardon drove to Saint Joe's University as before and waited for Sister Martha on the steps. He was not in clericals this time. Martha was. They walked slowly to the Student Union Building so that they could have as much time as possible with each other. Neither said a word.

They got their meal entrees and O'Bardon paid. They sat at 'their' table and looked at each other as they ate. They had to be careful. Martha was in her habit and O'Bardon had a high profile job in the archdiocese and would be easily recognized on the campus of a Catholic university in Philadelphia. They simply had to be careful.

"I am missing you, I must admit, Martha."

"I know, Liam. I know. What are we going to *do*?" she said.

"I don't know Martha. I do not know," was all he could say.

Liam told his friend all about his trip, what he had learned, and he even mentioned his dream without going into great detail. She listened attentively and said very little as he spoke. He was clearly troubled and had a great weight upon him she thought. "What is *really* wrong, Liam?" Sister Martha said.

"Martha there is just no easy way to say this." Liam cleared his throat, looked into her eyes and said softly, " I am in love with you. A priest is in love with a nun. I feel like Martin Luther...he had the same experience in life. What are *we* going to do? What am *I* going to do?"

Martha blushed and looked at the table. "I know that you are in love with me, Liam. And to be frank, I am in love with you. But you are a priest and I am a nun and I am not sure what to do about all of these emotions!" she said.

"Well, that makes two of us, then!" Liam stammered. "So what do we do?" he said again. "Do we keep our vows or stay true to our love?" The question was rhetorical. Neither one of them knew the answer at the present time. "We need to have time together to sort this out. Real time together, alone and with no one around. When can that happen?" Liam said.

Martha answered, "This Easter I am traveling to see my mother in Chicago. Can you get to Chicago for a few days?"

"Sure" he said, "we will meet in Chicago this Easter and try and work this out." "Good!" she said and she seemed happy with that. "Finally" Liam thought, "we can get this resolved one way or another."

While driving Martha home to the convent he reached over and touched her hand. She held his hand and stroked it the entire drive. They were in love and now they knew it. This was not going to be easy from now on. The Rubicon had been crossed. A decision had been made. The situation would now play itself out, once way or another. This much they both knew now.

IN THE LIBRARY AT SAINT JOSEPH'S UNIVERSITY

Liam had decided to do some research on some other views of Jesus. He traveled back to Saint Joe's University that weekend to do some reading. What did other religions think of Jesus and what was their thinking about him based upon? He found that following facts.

The Hindus of India had a long a complicated series of stories and even literature based on the life of Jesus both before and after the crucifixion. They saw him as an Essenc, a group which they believe is connected to the Brahmin traditions. They accept him as historical.

The Muslims see Jesus as a major prophet in Islam and accepted his virgin birth as fact. They accept him as historical.

The Druze have a belief system about Jesus which is very similar to the Muslims. They accept him as historical.

Buddhists do not generally consider Jesus in any special way. They really do not consider him at all. Whether or not he is historical seems to have no significance to Buddhists.

Within Judaism there are various schools of thought. Most hold that Jesus was historical. Some few others do not see him as historical but as a literary construction of several messiah-like figures within a period of about 300 years. None see him as the promised Messiah with the exception of a small Christian sect called "Jews for Jesus."

All in all , the worlds major religions had staked out their claim to Jesus and most of them at least grudgingly accepted Jesus as an historical figure. But was that really central to the idea of an historical Jesus? Did that really matter in the end? Hundreds of millions of children believed in Santa Claus. Their belief did not make him real.

O'Bardon did not know where to go from this point forward. Where he should turn to find an answer in controlling the war of ideas about the historicity and personality of Jesus was something that evaded him completely. He had followed his bishop's orders and took materials out of the personnel files of priests that were incriminating. In doing this, he covered up a great deal of controversy relative to child abuse by priests and essentially broke the law. He was in love with a nun. He was dreaming about a long dead priest and having conversations with him in his sleep. He was confused relative to the central historical issue of his Faith. He was approaching nine years as a priest and not sure that he wanted to continue on with his calling. And more or less he was just dumbfounded with the total situation he was now dealing with on a daily basis. He was afloat on a sea of confusion. And he was exhausted from it all. He needed a rest. There was no respite in sight. And he was not the only one in trouble.

THE CARDINAL AND THE MONSIGNOR—A NEW ASSIGNMENT

"Come in, Bill" Cardinal Renatto said to Monsignor Glenn. This was not good and the Monsignor knew it. In the five months that they had worked together at the Chancery, the new Cardinal Archbishop had never once referred to him as Bill. This was never a good sign. Informality from an archbishop to a monsignor usually meant that the junior member was going to be in for a rough day.

Monsignor Glenn walked into the Cardinal's Office Suite and sat down in front of the Cardinal's desk. "No, no. Sit over on the couch. We are going to be here a very long time this morning" the Cardinal said. Glenn complied. "What in the hell is this all about?" Glenn thought. He sat down and looked very attentively toward his bishop.

Bill Glenn had been ordained in 1975. He was 58 years old now, 40 pounds overweight, in relatively good health in spite of that and he had a reputation as a fiercely loyal company man who was all about discretion. He was not given to small talk. He was the perfect second banana at the chancery level for any bishop. He could be trusted at all times to keep his mouth shut.

The Cardinal was fully dressed in his episcopal cassock and was every inch the archbishop. He started in immediately when Glenn sat down. "How is the assignment coming with the media hounds and the Jesus Seminar people?" he asked Glenn. "As best I can determine, Eminence, it is going well. Father O'Bardon has been to the Westar Institute in California and spoken at length to at least one of the scholars and he has a written summary of the various points of view that come out of the Seminar. He has apparently started something of a professional rapport with the former Dominican Friar, John D. Cusack, who is one of their leading exegetes. They are in contact on an almost daily basis via email. Cusack has proven surprisingly helpful in encapsulating the problem for us. He has been very generous in offering us his opinion relative to the various points of view espoused out there." The Cardinal listened attentively.

"So Bill, you are telling me that a plan that can be realistically implemented to keep the Gospel version of Our Lord in the forefront of people's minds will be ready and on my desk prior to Christmas? This is important. The papal nuncio expects it from me in time to present to the Holy Father on Christmas day. Are we going to make that deadline?"

Monsignor Glenn had no idea. He lied to the cardinal. "Absolutely we are going to make it, Eminence. There is no reason why we should not make that deadline." Glenn made a mental note to ensure that O'Bardon was completely aware that failure to meet the deadline was out of the question. He would tell him so that day.

"Good!" the Cardinal said. "Now on to the business at hand!" the cardinal archbishop said emphatically, almost shouting. Glenn was now curious enough to sit up straighter in his chair and reach for pen and notepad in his pocket. "No notes!" the Cardinal almost screamed. "What we are going to be talking about today must never be written about or noted or recorded in any way. Not ever. We have learned that lesson the hard way with the sex abuse law suits. Records only make us more liable for damages. Do you understand what I am telling you?" the Cardinal asked the Monsignor sternly.

"I do, Eminence" Glenn replied. "Very, very good! Now, let me begin at the beginning" the Cardinal intoned quietly.

What Glenn was about to hear shook him to his very core. He was to be given a new assignment that he could tell no one about. He could have no assistant. He could write no notes. He must report orally to the Cardinal Archbishop when the assignment was ongoing every two weeks. The report must be in person. It must not be given on the phone or over email.

This was to be a face to face meeting per assignment requirements with the Cardinal at all times. Glenn was to investigate Satanic adherence and Satanic Ritual Abuse among the hierarchy of the American Catholic Church and report directly to the Cardinal Archbishop of Philadelphia who would in turn report directly and face to face with the Holy Father. The implications here were startling. Glenn could hardly catch his breath as the Cardinal Archbishop started to brief him on the extent and depth of the problem.

According to the Cardinal Archbishop, American bishops and high-ranking clergy within American Catholicism had been Satanists since the beginning of the Republic. Glenn's assignment was to find out how extensive the problem was, who the main players are or were and what can be done to stem the tide of Satanist practices among the participating bishops and priests of influence under the pastoral care. The cardinal archbishop was quite specific; he wanted Monsignor Glenn to do everything he could to find names, dates, places, any specifics that could be verified.

Glenn was on his own. There would be no staff, no break and there must be absolutely no talk to anyone about what he was doing. If queried, he was to state that he was looking into accounting practices of the various dioceses for the Catholic Conference of Bishops. That would give him cover, especially since in late 2005 over 85% of American Catholic Dioceses reported embezzlement of financial mismanagement at the parish level for amounts of money that are significant. They had been surveyed by a group at Villanova University located just outside of Philadelphia that was concerned about the problem. His cover story would be believable and accepted by anyone who asked. To further give him credibility he was to meet with all of the accounting officers of all the various dioceses that he would be investigating and get a written report from them concerning corrective measures taken.

The Cardinal Archbishop told Monsignor Glenn a story that defied belief. If the Cardinal himself was not the person giving him the information, Glenn would have dismissed it out of hand as a fairy tale. But the Cardinal knew what he was talking about. The story was very, very ugly. Satanic worship among the bishops and clergy and a fair amount of Satanic ritual abuse had been a problem of undetermined size for a very long time in the American church, probably since the beginning of the American Church.

The tale that the Cardinal Archbishop of Philadelphia told the Monsignor was disturbing. The basic storyline of Satanist practices in America and the church as told to the monsignor was sobering and horrific.

According to facts determined by hundreds of Vatican insiders, researchers, exorcists and other parties who over hundreds of years came in contact with Satanists and reported to the Vatican, Religious Satanism is something of a misnomer. To accuse someone of being a Satanist is akin to accusing someone of being a libertine. The term is very broad and includes so many different groups and dogmas as to almost defy description. If one were to look for witches' covens, Black Mass participants and ritualistic murders committed in the name of Satan it would return only a small number of actual cases. Certainly they did and do occur, anecdotal evidence was too great for that possibility to be ignored. But the majority of modern day First World Satanists belong to groups like the Church of Satan. This group does not believe in the existence of Satan as a deity. They see Satan as more or less a symbol for license to live a libertine life free of social constraints. They "use" the idea of Satan and satanic ritual to indulge in sexual perversion and sometimes ritual sacrifice. To them, Satanism is merely a vehicle to give their twisted psyches some sort of framework to work their perversions out.

In the Second and Third Worlds, Satanism tends to be much more ritualistic with blood sacrifice of animals and apparently, sometimes humans. Human sacrifice has been reported in the First World also, but not as much, and is usually reported as involving infants. So the term "Satanism" is so broad that it is difficult to describe in specific terms exactly what it totally encompasses. Many of the adherents in the First World are highly educated, powerful, wealthy and most important of all, bored with their lives. They seek the excitement of the bizarre and most importantly of all, they seek the rush that illegal and socially improper activities give them. They are twisted people, but usually they are very well connected to the local, state and national social infrastructure. This makes them very dangerous and almost impossible to arrest, control or even suspect. These people are literally above suspicion. And they occupy professions that would never lend themselves to such suspicion. Doctors, clergymen, police commissioners, judges, politicians, and all sorts of well-connected people can find unconventional thrills in leading such a twisted double life and often do so.

Although Satanism is a term which casts a wide net, the Church's view of it does include some specific characteristics which the church sees as opposing a Christian lifestyle. One social characteristic of Satanism is the belief in extreme individual self-determinism, often to the exclusion of the right for safety and protection of the larger group. That is to say, the rights of the individual rule supreme at all times. For most Satanists the idea of Satan serves more as a symbol of individual liberty and freedom, but "freedom" here means license. In addition, most Satanists believe that Christianity is flawed, that there is no absolute morality, and that individuals are solely responsible for their actions. They have a fascination with death. They are the ultimate practitioners of amoral human behavior.

It is known by the Church that only a very small number of Satanists worship Satan as a God, and this form of Satanism is usually referred to in the Church as "Luciferian" Satanism. Lucifer of course is the angel of light who we commonly refer to as the Devil. According to Jewish and Christian folklore, he led the Fallen Angels in a revolt against God. These believers worship Lucifer and look upon him as a liberator who frees his worshipers from oppression. In their view, God the Father is an Oppressor who must be opposed. In this view, Lucifer is not particularly seen as an enemy of God, but as a counterbalance to the power and influence of God. Some members of this group believe that Lucifer was banished by the Abrahamic God because he saw many flaws in creation and traced the responsibility of these flaws back to the Creator Himself. In other words, he is a theological rival of God, in their view. This group sees their role in the Cosmic as counterbalancing the power of God through their service to Satan. They see themselves as necessary and serving the interests of mankind. They see the concept of evil as a worthy counterbalance to all things that Western society would consider sacred.

In the United States, a republic founded specifically on individual rights and whose creation had remarkable input from a circle of Masonic brothers within the founding fathers, the Vatican legitimately feared that anti-Catholicism was woven into the fabric of the Nation from the beginning. Much of American history supported the Vatican's view of the U.S. as an anti-Papal republic. However, Satanism in the church was a cancer from within the Church itself. Although by no means was the American arm of Catholicism the only national branch of Catholicism to have a problem with Satanism, by the 20th Century it was the richest, the most influential and one of the hardest to control because Americans had no national church to offset the influence of Satanism.

There was a cardinal archbishop of Philadelphia who was allegedly a high level American Satanist and he was suspected by many bishops and senior clergy both in America and in the Vatican of being a Satanist who practiced Satanic ritual both in Rome and in the seminary basement in Philadelphia. There was a cardinal archbishop of Chicago in the latter part of the twentieth century who was supposedly a dedicated Satanist since his days as a young priest in the Diocese of Charleston, South Carolina. Supposedly he raped a young eleven-year-old girl named Agnes in Greenville, S.C. when he was a young priest in a satanic ritual in 1957. As an old woman, she eventually came forward to speak openly of the incident. Other priests and a few bishops had secretly implicated an

Archbishop of Los Angeles in this ring of high level Satanists when they spoke personally to the Pope of the problem of Satanism in America. A well known sociologist and novelist who was a priest in Chicago openly stated on several occasions that he personally knew of a ring of pedophile priests in that city who routinely had committed group sodomy on children, and on one occasion, he claimed that they committed a murder. He suspected that they had satanic ties.

Pedophilia was a marker of great interest for those following Satanism and its influence because it is believed to be a Satanic sacrament. Wherever there is mass pedophilia, the police suspect satanic ritual may be involved. It is for this reason alone that priestly pedophilia raises so many eyebrows among those that are acquainted with Satanism. It is almost a calling card of Satanism. And pedophilia had been proven to be an immense problem in the American Catholic church. The Vatican was fearful therefore of even greater problems with the Americans. All indications were that the Vatican's fears were well founded. The Catholic clergy of America may very well have been long past schism with Rome; they may actually be in the process of switching sides in the Cosmic battle against evil. Their libertine tendencies were apparent enough to merit such a discussion in the Vatican. Because of their economic power, their upbringing in a pluralist and secular society and their ability to amass large sums of donated money with very little effort, the American bishops were always suspect in Rome but now even more. The Vatican never really knew where it stood with this group of men and vice versa. It was a marriage of convenience in many ways.

Glenn's assignment was to garner an update on the problem as best he could, however he could, using whatever means he could and report on the actual state of Satanism within the Church in America and stay as close to the facts as he could possibly get. He was to do this quickly. The Pope was nervous, especially considering the fiasco concerning the "marriage" and ordination of married bishops by Archbishop Milingo of Africa, who had a large and affectionate following due to his charismatic healing services. He eventually broke away and formed a rival pseudo-

Catholic sect with married priests and four bishops that Milingo himself ordained.

And there were several African bishops who openly took part in genocide in Rwanda, cult murders in Uganda and ritual Satanism in other parts of Africa. It was feared that these African bishops had strong and organized Satanist ties around the globe. How strong and prevalent were Satanist ties among American bishops? The Pope wanted to know. He wanted no more surprises. The worldwide sexual abuse scandal had been almost more than the papacy could handle. Another scandal could set the church back a thousand years relative to international influence and organizational credibility, to say nothing of what it would do to its moral authority. And the fact that English speaking American bishops appeared to be involved in Satanism in a big way was even more disturbing since English was now the language of the global economy. These men could not only be Satanists, but rich, powerful, connected, clerical and Catholic Satanists. A scarier scenario could hardly have been drawn up by Rome if it set out to ruin its own reputation. Much was at stake and Rome wanted to know what cards it should play in this very serious game of power poker.

This was all overlaid with related problems. American priests and many women religious superiors had reported to Rome growing and widespread abuse of nuns by priests and a few bishops especially in Africa where AIDS and HIV are a problem and nuns are seen as a safe object for sex. In the United States, a highly publicized murder of a nun by a priest in the 1970's was prosecuted in 2005 and the priest was found guilty of murder. The crime had satanic ritualistic elements to it. The Reverend Gerald Robinson was found guilty in the murder of Sister Margaret Pahl in Toledo, Ohio in 2006. She was murdered on her 72nd birthday. Details of the murder were all over the internet within a day or two of the priest's arrest. After the murder of the nun, at least one other woman came forward with allegations that Father Robinson had ritually abused her in the presence of other priests in a satanic ritual. This sort of allegation was surfacing more and more in police investigations of clerical sexual abuse within the Catholic Church. Rome was taking very intense notice of all of this.

And there were even more factors at play that bothered the Vatican. In short, due to the availability of this sort of information on the internet, the crisis of faith in the church and its abilities to remain above stain of immorality was now virtually impossible. The damage control for which the church had worked so hard after the sex abuse scandal broke in Boston was now unraveling. If large scale accounts of satanic worship in the Catholic Church should become public knowledge and break into the media in the same manner as the sex abuse scandal did, it would mean the end of the Catholic Church in America. That much was certain. The Church simply would not be able to withstand another full-scale public relations meltdown like the sex abuse scandal. The lawsuits that would result from victims of clerical Satanism would effectively end participatory Catholic presence in America.

Monsignor Glenn was aware that the Church, like any other human organization, was not above scandal. Scandal of practically any type could infect the Church as well as any other human group. Certainly Satanism was not the only scandal the modern church had to deal with in the world.

In January 2006 a priest in Poland named Father Tadeusz Isakowicz-Zaleski announced that he planned to publish a book naming names of priests who collaborated with the Polish Secret Police against other priests and churchmen during the Communist Regime. The list had thirty-nine priests on it and included three active bishops. In fact, Father Zaleski forced the resignation of the designated archbishop of Warsaw in that same month of January 2006, a former priest collaborator named Stanislaw Wielgus. Apparently the Pope knew of the collaboration prior to the appointment. In fact, the Pope himself had served in the Nazi Luftwaffe in an anti-aircraft battery during the Second World War. The past always has a way of coming around to bite the present in the neck.

In that same month a Catholic priest serving in the Diocese of Richmond in the U.S. named The Rev. Rodney L. Rodis who was pastor of two Virginia Catholic Churches over ten years was arrested for allegedly embezzling over $990K from the church coffers. Upon further investigation, it was found that Rodis, a citizen of the Philippines, had a 'wife' and three children. In February 2007 in Florida, it was discovered and disclosed that two Irish priests had allegedly embezzled over $8.7 million dollars from a parish over a period of several decades. The blowback to church finances and donations was huge. A Villanova University study in 2005 found that 85% of Catholic Church parishes suffered embezzlement of some kind, apparently on a semi-routine basis. Scandal was everywhere. And priests, bishops, nuns and lay brothers were right in the middle of all of it.

But clerical involvement in Satanism was different, for after all, Satan was the supposed Principal Enemy of the Church of Rome and some of her bishops were allegedly worshiping him? The Pope had to know the extent of the damage and come up with a plan to counter it quickly. That was Monsignor Glenn's assignment, simply put. The job was overwhelming, the ultimate task monumental, the assistance from the hierarchy was non-existent and the loneliness in the assignment was ever present. This was the kind of thing that could crush a priest.

Monsignor Glenn accepted the assignment from the Cardinal Archbishop in absolute and stunned silence. He was literally speechless and said not a word when the Cardinal asked him if he had any questions. He had none. He simply shook his head, "no." The Cardinal got up and walked out of the office suite, a signal for the Monsignor to leave. Glenn did so. He left the building immediately. It was 10:30 in the morning. He took the train home to Glenside and walked the mile and a half to the rectory in Ardsley at Queen of Peace parish. He went directly to his room, took off his clerical collar and jacket and fell directly to his knees. He prayed for three solid hours. He did not come down to dinner that night. The housekeeper kept his dinner plate wrapped and near the microwave in the kitchen. He ate dinner alone that night at about 9:00 PM. in the rectory kitchen. He was crying. He was terrified. He was alone.

The next morning Monsignor Glenn went to the Chancery and picked up the list of all the accounting officers in the various selected dioceses that he would visit in the next two weeks. He left immediately for Villanova. He asked O'Bardon to drive him there and the two of them talked on the way to the college. O'Bardon could see that Glenn was highly agitated. He said nothing about it. O'Bardon walked around the campus as Glenn had a meeting with the survey staff in the 2005 survey of accounting practices for American dioceses. They both drove back to the chancery after eating in the student union building at Villanova for lunch. Monsignor Glenn said very little. Father O'Bardon let him keep his silence. Both priests had a great deal to think about now.

THE DEVIL IN CHICAGO

Chicago was the first stop on Monsignor Glenn's research in American Satanism in the Catholic Church. He immediately visited the chancery and talked to the fiscal people and then sent an alleged email report on finances to the Cardinal's Secretary, Monsignor Allen, in Philadelphia. That provided cover for why he was there. He then left the chancery, went back to his hotel room and called the priest-sociologist who had made the claim of a ring of pedophile priests in the archdiocese. They made arrangements to meet for dinner in the hotel where Glenn was staying.

The two priests met that night at 6:00, had dinner with a glass of wine and a beer each and talked for five hours straight. The sociologist was a treasure trove of information on devilry in Chicago among Catholic clerics and nuns. No hard evidence could be found but anecdotal evidence that strongly suggested Satanist activities among clerics in Chicago, New England and South Carolina seemed to have a connection here. It seems that seminary classmates all seemed to keep the Satanist influence going in all three locations. Several of the same seminaries served these three locations and had great influence as a result. Monsignor Glenn was starting to get the picture. The Satanist connection among American bishops had a seminary connection that went back to some sort of informal 'brotherhood' that started in seminary days, usually wound up with these men practicing Satanism while taking advanced studies in Rome and later figured into the politics of who got elevated to bishop within the country. Simply put, these men lobbied for each other to become bishops. They were a dark brotherhood within the hierarchy and they kept the dark circle extant by constantly placing each other in positions of high importance within the American Church.

Even those who knew very little about the specifics knew that the Satanist influence among Catholic bishops was centered in their early years as seminarians. When they would speak to Monsignor Glenn about what they knew they would be very clear that it was obvious that influence simply followed these Satanist bishops through the priesthood and as they advanced through the ranks, sometimes to a bishop' appointment or even cardinal, they brought their Satanist colleagues from seminary days with them to their new assignments or covered for their activities wherever they might be assigned throughout the country. This all seemed to be a very common and badly kept secret. These Satanist bishops either largely kept the Conference of Catholic Bishops in the blind or they were so powerful that the Conference looked the other way relative to their activities. In one instance that was later widely reported to Monsignor Glenn by several priests who sought him out in secret at the request of the sociologist he had met, there was the ultimate blasphemy. It seems that in a small wooded area outside of Chicago these bishops and priests had apparently taken part in a ritual murder and then held pseudo-Catholic rituals interspersed with Satanist rituals over the body. Although the whole situation was ugly it was impossible to pin down. Facts were few and far between but broken lives, child abuse, forced abortions, homosexual rape and group perversion showed up time and again in rumor after rumor. Anecdotal evidence was everywhere to be found and it had been extant for years, even decades. Something was tragically wrong. And to make matters worse, the code of silence among priests made the Mafia look like amateurs. This evil was going to be very difficult to penetrate or control. According to the sociologist, even the Catholic policemen and policewomen who knew something about this situation were very reluctant to say what they knew. Everyone involved in this was afraid for his life. That much would become apparent to Monsignor Glenn as the months wore on and he talked to more and more people.

But as for the meeting with the sociologist-priest, Glenn's eyes were opened wider than he ever would have wanted. At about 11 p.m. the men bade each other good night and Glenn retired for the evening. The night had been long and numbing, even frightening. There was no lack of anecdotal evidence to implicate any number of American bishops and high placed clerics, both past and present. And how many Satanists were being trained in secret in American seminaries? It was impossible to know. Glenn prayed on his knees by his bedside for a half hour before retiring. He was exhausted and stunned. He never expected his priesthood to take a turn like this. Who would?

Monsignor Glenn had been a faithful soldier of the church and a fine and loyal lieutenant to Cardinal Kraske, then Cardinal Bertelli and now to Cardinal Renatto. He had served as a seminarian or priest under three Cardinal Archbishops and as a personal assistant under two of the three and he had never questioned any order he was ever given by any one of them. Now he had lots of questions. In fact at least one of these men might have been involved in Satanist practices for all he knew. He was stunned and did not know what to think. So he prayed. He received no answers to his prayers.

THE MCGURK AND
MONSIGNOR GLENN

Glenn fell asleep after only a moment upon laying down in his hotel room bed and he began to dream almost immediately. His dreams were fitful at first but eventually he found himself in a dreamlike state in front of the altar at Saint Michael's Parish on Second Street in Philadelphia. The dream felt so real, he thought to himself within the dream.

"May I help you Faather?" a voice said to him from behind him. Glenn turned. The dream seemed so remarkably real!

"Why yes, Father!" he said to the priest standing behind him. It occurred to Glenn that the priest spoke with a brogue.

"Father, your name is....?" Glenn inquired.

"Oh, I am sorry!" the priest chuckled and stuck out his hand and shook the hand of the American priest. "I am Father McGurk. Jamie McGurk is what I am called by friends and fellow priests."

Glenn shook his hand. "I am Monsignor Bill Glenn from Queen of Peace Parish in Ardsley." McGurk laughed. "I am not sure that I know where Ardsley is, Faather! And I have never heard of Queen of Peace parish! But no matter."

Glenn looked puzzled. How could this Philadelphia cleric not know where Ardsley was? It was then that he noticed that the priest before him was wearing a cassock that had gone out of style over a hundred years previously. It was a sort of Anglican cassock that ended just below the knees that was popular with Catholic priests from Ireland before the turn of the 20th Century.

"Father" Glenn said very slowly, "What year is it?" McGurk laughed loudly, "Why its 1885. Why do ya' ask?"

Glenn stood there dumbfounded. "Oh, no reason, Father, no reason at all", Glenn said. McGurk motioned for Glenn to sit down with him in the pews.

The two priests sat. McGurk started in. "So, Faather, why have ya' come to Saint Michael's today?" He waited for a reply.

"Well, to tell you the truth, Father, I am not sure that I *am* at Saint Michael's. I think I might be dreaming." McGurk laughed, "We're *all* dreaming, Faather! What can I help ya' with?" McGurk said with a wide smile. Without completely understanding why, Glenn simply decided that in fact he *was* there to be helped by The McGurk!

"Well, the truth be told, Father, I am on assignment from the Cardinal Archbishop to see if I can find Satanists within the ranks of the Hierarchy here in America." At the sound of the word 'cardinal' McGurk raised an eyebrow.

"*Cardinal* Archbishop is it now?" McGurk chuckled. "And Philadelphia is that important to Rome in your time, is it Faather?"

"Yes, I suppose it is" Glenn said almost absentmindedly. "What am I to do, Father? I don't know where to look for pertinent information and I certainly don't know what to do with it once I get it. Most of what I have gathered is possibly believable rumor and anecdote, mostly stories told by marginalized priests, nuns and former clerics and seminarians. Is it all true? Is it all revenge taken on a church that is unbending and vicious with reformers? Is it to be believed or is it to be pushed aside as hogwash? I simply do not know what to do, Father!" Glenn sat there and looked at the Irishman. Neither spoke.

After a moment McGurk spoke. "Certainly you hear that I am from Ireland, from a different time and a different Catholicism than the one you must live within, I suppose. In this day and age, Catholicism is a salve on the open wounds of poverty, oppression and discontent for the many European immigrants that have come here to escape the horrible dissipation that life under the thumb of an overlord produces. They've brought their European Catholicism with them and slowly, they become Americans and they make their own brand of Catholicism work here. It is more pragmatic, more direct, more progressive and even more sacred in a working class sort of way than European Catholicism ever could be. But in your day, in your time, for your type of Catholic, I am not so sure that simple piety works anymore. You must live in an age of science when the magic of the sacred no longer matters, when it is all seen as foolhardy and childish nonsense. If that is so, then it is no wonder that Satanism should infect the Church and especially the hierarchy, for I am sure that in your day as well as this, the bishops still take themselves much too seriously!"

At that comment both men laughed out loud. Immediately the people praying in the pews looked sternly at both priests. "Sorry!" Father McGurk whispered in a stage whisper to the penitents in the church. "I do that all the time, now! I think that they are always wishing that I would just sit here quietly when I get a visitor."

"Listen to me Faather Glenn, excuse me, I mean *Monsignor* Glenn," McGurk said with a smile. "No matter what you find, or do not find, it is highly doubtful that you and or anyone else can intervene to change the evil of the times you live within. Evil does not work like that, it is not there to be changed, only recognized and challenged at every turn. For Catholic priests, it is a constant and daily struggle for supremacy within ourselves so that we can remain faithful without. Whether it is Satanism, or some other sort of abuse, is to some extent and in some regards completely off the point. The fact is that your time has its own strengths and miracles and its own evils and weaknesses. It is up to you and your fellow priests to find a way to make the miracles outweigh the evils in such a way as to give the people hope. Your job is not to discover evil. Believe me, Faather, it is there. It always is. Your job is to help the People of God live with evil in such a way as to not be drowned by it. Do you understand me, Faather? Can you do that in this assignment from the cardinal archbishop?" Glenn looked at the Irishman with an affection and warmth that he could not hold back. "I can certainly try Father. I can certainly try." The two priests shook hands. Glenn woke up with a start.

The dream had been so real. It was the most realistic dream he had ever experienced. Glenn was weeping. He dropped to his knees at the bedside and prayed. He had been given his assignment again, but this time, he knew how to handle it.

LIAM AND THE MCGURK—
THEIR LOVES

L iam was resolved to pray and discern what he must do relative to his love for Martha. So far, they had done nothing physical to seal their relationship except hold hands and declare themselves in love. Liam was leaving for a long weekend in Chicago the next day. Easter had come. It was time to spend some time with Martha alone and find out what they wanted to do.

The night before he took the flight to Chicago, he spent alone in his room. He prayed and meditated on what the trip might bring into his life and then he reached for the third diary journal. He had yet to finish it all. He started to read.

"I state again that I could not have lived the life of a Catholic priest without the love of a woman, Bibiana by name. Although it is true that we were never one in body, that is completely off the point. I could not ask her to take the body of a dead man, for that is what a priest is, dead to the world. The world that he lives within is all spirit and emotions and dreams and aspirations. It is absolutely true that his life is not his own, he is on borrowed time and his life belongs to his people. He is truly "alter Christus" and he must understand and accept the crucifixion that comes with that designation.

"But I must also state that a priest is only a man, and without some type of love and cherishing in his life, he cannot be truly human. My love came in the form of one of the most beautiful women I was ever privileged to behold. But it could have come from other quarters I suppose. Bibiana never asked anything of me, and she took my quiet and determined admiration as the gracious woman that she was. She knew of it, acknowledged it quietly and never made me pay a price for my emotional indiscretion. She allowed me my dream of her love and she returned it to me by never making me declare myself. When I finally mouthed the words to her, when I finally told her that I loved her, it was on her deathbed. Even then she took my indiscretion with great grace. I owe her so much.

"She was always present for me when I needed help with money for the poor of the parish. She funded more church aid than anyone in the parish and in truth, Bibiana was not from my parish but rather Saint Mary Magdalene's. She was truly a saint in her own way. I have stated before that she had many lovers, and that is true. It was not my place to challenge her on her needs as a woman. In that regard, we were never lovers. But I held her heart in my hands and we both were aware of that. In return I never chastised her for anything that she might have been accused of by her less capable peers. She gave freely of what she had to those who had nothing. To me, that was all that mattered. Anything else was minutiae that any just man would be willing to overlook.

"I have often wondered why the priest of the Church of Rome cannot marry. The story is that we are living as Christ lived. I do not believe that. I never did. The Christ could not have been as fully human as he was, he could not have been the savior that he was, without an intimate knowledge of that which makes human beings godly and godlike. If there ever was such a man, He must have known some sort of human love. I have always believed that and I will always believe that. It is my considered opinion, now at the end of my priesthood and the end of my life, that the church has overplayed its hand in the story that it has foisted upon us concerning the loveless life of Jesus. It is simply not possible that a man could live like that and make a difference. Therefore, either there was no Jesus in the flesh, or if there was and I am wrong, then he loved. It is truly that simple.

"As for my precious Bibiana, she died young, at the age of 42. I loved her so very much and was lost when she passed away. I was lost for many years. I think now that I reflect upon our love as an old man, I would have left the priesthood for her and married her if she had asked me to do so. I loved her that much and she made me so much the better man by her love. Even now, all these years later, I miss her so. As my life is quickly ending now with this sickness, with these miseries I am presently undergoing, I think most often of her and the life we could have had together. It is my one comfort in the pain. I often wonder what our children would have looked like. May her soul rest in peace.

"When my mother died I was with her. She asked me to hear her confession and I refused and I brought in the parish priest to hear her confession. Whatever she may have done, whatever sins she may have committed, she was still my mother. It was not my place to stand in judgment of her. She wanted badly I believe to tell me of some indiscretion which to her must have weighed heavily upon her heart. I would not hear of it. It was not for me to judge her or to place her in that position. Although I had suspicions over the years as to what may have troubled her in this regard, I shall never speak of it to anyone or even write it down in this diary. She was my mother. And the finest of all mothers was she. I owe her so very much. May her soul rest in peace. I will die knowing that when I lived, I had the finest mother that ever breathed.

"My father I never knew, he died before I was born. My mother always told me of his great physical strength, his handsome looks and his kindness to all. That is enough for any boy to know of a father. May his soul rest in peace.

"I have known many priests and a few bishops in my lifetime. Some were very good men. Some were not. In truth, some of the most wicked, narrow and devious men I have ever known have worn a cassock. This is not true for all or even for most, but it is powerfully true for some, and this is scandal and horror enough to send a chill down the spine of any good Catholic and any committed Christian.

"Some priests that I have known have taken liberties with children. Because of the nature of what we do, it is easy enough to carry through on this heinous evil. And due to the fear of scandal, it is always hidden away. The bishops will never openly reveal this evil, they do not discuss it even among themselves. I have never actually seen this but I have been involved in its aftermath and the terrible pain that it brings many times. The children are simply not believed and are often beaten by the parents for "lying" about the priest. The truth is, they are not always lying. Sometimes the priest is a demon. Some of these demons have I lived with in rectories. May God have mercy on their souls. And may God have mercy on mine for overlooking this evil. My only defense is that canon law forbids a priest to openly speak ill of another priest.

"Other priests are womanizers, some are thieves for they take money from the poor box and Sunday collection, others burn for boys and young men and act upon their fleshly instincts, others use their position as priests to garner favor with all sorts of powerful people and thus protect themselves unjustly when other men would be crushed by the weight of their sinful actions. None of these things are Christ-like. All of them I have seen. Certainly priests are men and like all men, subject to sin. But when a priest sins against the very people to whom salvation has been entrusted, the Devil himself is about and above ground! I have lived with a few demons wearing Roman cassocks. I have known many more.

"If I had my wish for any sort of heaven that I would want, I think that I would want to be a young priest again administering in Saint Michael's Parish, my first assignment out of seminary. I would want especially to administer to troubled priests. We have no such "priest caring for priests" structure in the Church. I would want to be a priest to other priests. I would want to counsel them, tell them of their strong points, allow them to bear up under their obvious and painful weaknesses and to continue on their journey in Christian witness to their final resting place. Yes, that is my idea of a well-spent eternity.

"Catholics are right to expect their priests to be Christ-like but they are wrong to expect their priests to be anything other than men. Priests are men in all the honor and evil of men. They can be kind and compassionate as well as being narrow and unbending and uncaring. Priests can easily get lost in the trappings of a magical thought process filled with pretend powers and impossible schemes to mount the heights of glory with supposed graces "given" to them by God. No such things exist. A priest is only a priest when he lives like a priest, acts like a priest, dies like a priest. There are no shortcuts to holiness, there is no respite. To live the life of a priest is to climb to a personal Golgotha and watch oneself be crucified. There is no escape. The life of witness to Christ is a life of self-sacrifice and death to the things of the world. There is no other way to be a priest.

"As I ready myself to die, I rest assured in the belief that God is merciful. For I have sinned greatly, more by omission than by commission. I have watched great evil prevail in my church and I have kept silent because I was ordered to do so by the very Canon Law which governs her. I have cherished obedience over justice. May God have mercy on me. May God be just to me but mostly may He be merciful, for if there was ever a priest who sought mercy in God's judgment, it is me.

"I go to my death knowing that I have been a fully human soul. I have not always done what I should have done. I have sometimes done what I knew full well I should not have done. For that I beg forgiveness of those whom I have injured and of my God. I will seal these books with string and bound the string with the waxed seal of the parish. I will place a handwritten note on them to have them delivered to the bishop if they are ever found intact. I will hide them in the high altar of this parish I have founded in my middle years as a priest, St. Kevin's, and the parish in which I will have died as its pastor. It is my crowning glory as a man and a priest. I founded a parish. People were baptized here, married here and were buried here. Children received their First Communion here. No greater gift could I have given to my church. I die happy and content knowing full well that I did what I could to remain faithful to my calling. I was a priest. For that, I am truly grateful.

"I have only one regret, more of a wish really than a regret. If a way could have been found that I could have remained a priest and married my beloved Bibiana, had my children by her and slept with her every night by my side I would have been a more complete man, a holier human being and a stronger and finer priest. Her love would have made me completely whole. If that way could have been found, I would have been fully alive. I would have been a complete man.

"When the moment of my death comes, and that will be quite soon, I hope that Bibiana will come for me to take me home. For if I ever had a guardian angel at my side, it was Bibiana.

"Tonight, in the darkness of the empty church, with no other light than a candle, I will remove one panel from the high altar and place these diaries and a personal note into the altar. I will die very soon now. The doctor has warned me.

"I praise God and thank him for the life He gave me. I gave my full measure as best I could. I saw my duty as God gave me the light to see it. I ask now for the mercy of God to be showered upon me and in some way, I ask that He allow me to serve Him as a priest in my eternal life to come. Amen.

Signed,
James McGurk, Priest of Jesus Christ and of His Catholic Church
August 15th, 1911
Philadelphia, Pennsylvania"

Liam openly wept. He had checked the archdiocesan records. Father James McGurk, founding pastor of Saint Kevin's parish, died of cancer on August 29th, 1911. He was unconscious the last three days of his life. He had therefore sealed these books within the high altar of his church a scant eleven days before he was lost to the world for good. He had fought the good fight. He had run the good race. He had died a good priest. Not much more can be asked of a man. Nothing more can be asked of a priest.

SATANISM'S
DARK LEGACY FOR ROME

Monsignor Glenn had now reported twice to the Cardinal Archbishop about what he had found. The hierarch sat motionless, expressionless and gave absolutely no hint of what he was thinking. The archbishop never spoke to Glenn when he was finished giving his oral report. He said "thank you", dismissed the priest and turned back to reading his paper on both occasions. Glenn was beginning to suspect that there was another agenda here altogether. Why would the cardinal archbishop send this man all throughout the country to find Satanist activities without so much as a single lead on where to go or what to do, or even to whom he should speak? The whole assignment seemed odd right from the start. There was more going on here than met the eye, Glenn was sure of that. This was an assignment whose real agenda was a hidden agenda.

Glenn flew to the West and went to several dioceses that had long histories of abuse by high-ranking priests and bishops. There were stories of bishops blackmailing priests into being their lovers, some were substantiated. There were stories of clerical witchcraft, coven meetings, homosexual priests meeting at night dressed as nuns, priests taking long vacations out of the country to indulge in perversion overseas. Some of these stories were substantiated and the priest was sometimes removed. The sad thing was this: no bishops were being punished or removed except for illegalities uncovered by the police that could not be hidden by the church itself. And that was only a handful of cases at most. The bishops were not being held accountable; not by anyone and not anywhere. The bishops, as always throughout Catholic history, were getting a pass. This rankled even Glenn, the consummate company man. This could not go on forever he thought.

Something was very wrong with the system. There was essentially no way to control an out-of-control bishop unless local law enforcement stepped in with criminal charges. Governor Keating of Oklahoma, a Catholic himself, was absolutely correct. He had been the first chairman of the bishop's conference investigating committee on sexual abuse of children. He stated upon his angry resignation after only about a year on the Board that the bishops were more darkly organized and in many ways more criminal than the Mafia. This was becoming more and more clear to Monsignor Glenn the further he dug into satanic abuse in the church. The bishops were intimately involved in it, if not in the actual acts at least in the cover up. That much was clear to Monsignor Glenn. What was not clear, what was infinitely hard to discern and uncover were the actual facts of the abuse and perversion. Anecdotal evidence was everywhere. Verifiable evidence was as scarce as hen's teeth.

Monsignor Glenn was beginning to suspect that the real reason for his assignment was different than the one the Cardinal Archbishop had given to him. This would explain why the Cardinal Archbishop was not all that interested in what he had to say, why his reactions when briefed were more coldly polite than interested. Many of the bishops and high-ranking priests that Monsignor Glenn was reporting on were lifelong friends and some were seminary classmates of the Cardinal Archbishop in Philadelphia. Then one evening upon retiring the truth hit him like a bomb blast. Glenn was not being sent out to uncover information about Satanism. Glenn was being sent across America by the Cardinal

Archbishop of Philadelphia to see what an insider could find out. That was now clear to Monsignor Glenn.

His assignment was to see what could be uncovered and what could not. Monsignor Glenn was a pawn in the chess game that the Vatican was playing with the media and the authorities. The Cardinal Archbishop was the chess master and he was also intimately familiar with Satanism in the church. Glenn's role was to confirm to the archbishop just how secure this evil was from prying eyes. Monsignor Glenn was a dupe with the false assignment of discovering facts about clerical Satanism while being covered by yet another false assignment, embezzlement within the church. The realization hit Monsignor Glenn like a hammer in the chest. He had been duped.

The Cardinal Archbishop may or may not be a participant in Satanism. But he was most certainly a participant in the cover up of the same. Glenn's loyalty to the institutional church was being turned against him, he was now sure. He was not sure how to react. He was not sure what to think. He was not sure what it meant to be a "priest" anymore. Monsignor Glenn was numb with fear, loathing and self-hatred. He was raging inside, raging against his false sense of loyalty, raging against his Cardinal, raging against his own gullibility. What had he done? What bargain had he made with the Devil by being so "loyal" to the "church"? Weren't the people the church? What about the People of God, where did they fit into all of this subterfuge?

His flight home from Denver to Philadelphia was uneventful. Glenn tried to sleep but he could not. He was going to have to confront the Cardinal with his fears. Would he have the courage to do it? He did not know. He openly wept on the airplane during the flight back to Philadelphia, his shame was that great.

The next morning, he gave his briefing to the Cardinal Archbishop as usual. The cardinal listened politely and with very little interest as he had on many occasions before. When Monsignor Glenn was finished and before the Cardinal had a chance to dismiss him perfunctorily, Glenn asked, "Eminence, is my impression correct that you are already aware of everything I have reported to you since I started this assignment of discovery?"

The Cardinal looked a bit startled but recovered quickly. "Well, I would know more than most. After all, a Cardinal moves in the highest circles of the church."

"No, Eminence." Glenn responded quickly, "that is not what I mean. It is my definite impression that you, the Cardinal Archbishop of Philadelphia, have sent me around the country on a fact finding mission in order to find out *if* I could find out something, not *what* I could find out. To be frank, Eminence, I am sure now that my true assignment was to see what an insider could learn from talking to anyone he wanted. In other words, the assignment itself is something other than I was led to believe. I believe that the real point of my assignment is for you to find out what can be found by an investigator who is allowed to follow any lead. Is this true?" Monsignor Glenn himself was startled by his own courage. In his entire priesthood, he had never spoken out like this before. The Cardinal Archbishop of Philadelphia said nothing. He did not even move. He sat expressionless. The two men sat that way, neither moving nor giving an expression, for over twenty seconds.

Finally the Cardinal said, "You have done well Monsignor and I can see that your duties are too taxing for you to continue with this heavy assignment. I am relieving you of this assignment immediately and you can continue on with what you were doing previous to this assignment. Thank you so much. You have been a great help to me."

Glenn sat there. He did not move. "Is there something else, Monsignor?" the Cardinal said dryly. "Only this your Eminence; I will be taking a vacation immediately. I need to pray and meditate on whether or not I can continue in my vocation as a priest. Does His Eminence have any problem with this?" The Cardinal Archbishop opened his arms widely and said, "Go my son. Take what time you need. We will fill out the paperwork while you are gone. You can leave immediately."

Monsignor Glenn then left the office and took the train home out of the city and into Ardsley. He packed his bags in silence, left a note for the pastor at Queen of Peace parish, in whose rectory he resided, and took the train back to Center City and then to

Pottstown where he was raised. He knocked on his brother's door and was received by his wife. He needed a place to stay for a couple of days and asked if he could stay there. His sister in law said "of course." He went to the extra bedroom and lay down on the bed. He cried bitterly. Then he fell asleep. At 59 years old his life as a priest was over. He could no longer serve in a church that rewarded organizational loyalty and personal obedience with treachery and deceit. He was dead inside. He would have to be reborn, but how? He did not know. Who ever does?

He awoke the next morning, put on a pair of chinos and a denim shirt that he had packed, and placed white socks and sneakers on his feet. He came out of the bedroom to see his brother sitting at the breakfast table in his pajamas. It was after eight o'clock.

"Bob, what are you doing home? I thought work started at 7:30 for you?" His brother, two years older than him, looked at him with concern. 'What's wrong Billy? What happened yesterday? I am not going to work today. I am spending the day with you. What's wrong?"

Bill Glenn poured himself a cup of coffee, and sat down at the kitchen table. His older brother was a policeman and a sergeant. Taking a day off was not easy. He had to pull some strings to do that. Bill Glenn knew that. "Bob, I do not know what to say. I have been used as a dupe in some scheme that I cannot quite place together in my head. It involves a special assignment from the Cardinal that I have carried out faithfully. The whole thing was a sham. They were using me to find out what *could* be found out. They already knew what I would uncover. What bothers me is this. What did I *not* uncover that they already know? "

"What is this all about?" his brother asked.

"It's about Satanism in the church" Glenn replied. He took a long drink of coffee. His brother, the policeman, did not move.

"Satanism?" he asked slowly with incredulity in his voice.

"Yeah, why do you look so startled?" Glenn asked his brother.

"Why? Because this is Pennsylvania. We are living in what is probably the number one hotspot of Satanism in America. Didn't you know that?" the cop asked of his brother.

"No, I did not" the priest answered. Bill Glenn had no idea that his own brother was so in tune with Satanist practices.

"Look, we get a lot of this sort of thing around here. Don't you remember the rumors from when we were in high school?" the cop asked.

"No, what rumors?" Bill Glenn asked.

"Man oh man, no wonder you became a priest! What! Were you unconscious when we were growing up around here?" his brother asked with real surprise in his voice.

"Bill, any farmer, yokel or bored city slicker who has nothing to do and can read a book can fancy himself a Satanist, witch, wiccan, devil worshiper, moon dancer or any number of other things. He can take a group of people with him and go back into the woods on a moonlit night and dance, howl, drink and drug, have an orgy or sometimes commit animal sacrifice to the 'gods' of nature, lords of lust, barons of blasphemy or anything else he fancies himself involved with. The state penitentiary is filled with nuts and whack jobs that fancy themselves any or all of these things. The problem is proving that this stuff exists on a plane higher than a bunch of bored drunks looking for something spooky to do in the woods at night. Anyone can claim they saw or heard or read about such a thing happening or about to happen. But *proving* it is another matter." "I know, I know" Bill Glenn said slowly to his brother. "Believe me I know what you are saying! Proving it is damn near impossible!"

"Look, I got an assignment from the Cardinal to investigate Satanism among the hierarchy and high ranking priests in the church around the country" Bill Glenn told his brother.

"And what did you find?" his brother asked?

"Nothing" Glenn said, "nothing that I could prove. I collected hundreds of anecdotes, rumors and bits of gossip from high ranking and knowledgeable people. But nobody, and I mean *nobody*, had any proof to offer."

"And this *surprises* you?" his brother asked. "Where is your head? Look, listen to me" the cop said. "I have been in the cop business since after I got out of the Army. You were a young

162

seminarian when I started. I have heard all the rumors, I have even been involved in some distasteful investigations where satanic ritual abuse was almost certainly involved in the crime. The problem is that in our society, this stuff has to be proven and a crime has to be committed in order to be prosecuted by the District Attorney's Office. In my experience proof is very hard to come by in these cases for one of two reasons. Either nothing really happened, no crime was committed, and so the rumors are just adolescent gossip meant to scare friends over a couple of bottles of beer on a Friday night up on Romance Hill. Or maybe a crime was committed and it was so heinous and the perps were so disciplined that talking about the satanic connection would mean harm or death to the snitch. Either way, there is almost always no proof."

"Cops tend to laugh at satanic ritual crime stories because they are so hard to prove. To be frank, I have taken some classes in folklore up at the community college in the past few years and satanic stories always figure large in any community's local folklore, it seems to be a human thing that goes all the way back into the very beginning of human story-telling. The truth seems to be that we like to scare ourselves. It serves some sort of psychological purpose. World folklore is full of this stuff and it goes back thousands of years!" The cop took a long a drink of coffee as he sat at the breakfast table in his bathrobe with his priest brother.

"So, what are you going to do?" the cop asked the priest.

"I don't know" Bill Glenn said. "I just feel so deceived by the Cardinal. First I helped clean out clerical personnel records so that the Archdiocese could protect itself from lawsuits. I broke the law to serve my bishop and my church. We ultimately got away with it due to statute of limitations but Lynn Abramson and her DA's office knew what we were doing. We did not fool them."

" Then I helped to investigate satanic ritual abuse in the church and found some hard-to-deny evidence of Satanism among the hierarchy and told that information to a completely disinterested bishop who happens to be my boss and got dismissed for my efforts. I think I've lost my Faith. At least I have lost my faith in the church as an organization. I just don't think I can go on!" Bill

Glenn told his brother. He placed his head in his hands. He was ashamed, he was exhausted and he felt that he had no options.

Neither man said anything for a long time. Finally Bob Glenn said to his brother, "You could enter a monastery. You could leave the priesthood. You could do anything in between. Why don't you stay here and think about it awhile?"

The priest finally answered, "I think I might take a trip to Ireland. You know, see Grand Dad's grave and where Dad was born; that sort of thing. Maybe when I am over there I can pull myself together and come up with a plan. I never thought at 59 years old and a priest for thirty-three years, that I would question my commitment to priesthood like this. I just cannot seem to believe in it anymore."

"Well if it is any help to you, I have been a cop since I was twenty three and I lost my faith in the American justice system after I had the first judge throw out my first rape bust almost forty years ago on a legal technicality. The young girl got raped and damned near got her brains beat in, spent three weeks in the hospital and the judge threw out the case because the indictment paperwork was wrong. When the "system" lets you down, you don't always get back up. Sometimes you have to fake it for a while until you can believe again. And sometimes you can never make yourself believe again."

"How long have you been faking it Bob?" Bill Glenn asked his brother the cop.

"Oh, probably thirty-five years."

"You've been faking it all that time?" the priest asked.

"Yeah, but I get a pension next year, a real hefty one. The faking was worth it. You might remember that! There is something to be said for "fake it 'till you make it" you know! You get a pension from the Archdiocese in a few years. You can take your trip to Ireland, go on a sabbatical for a year or maybe six months and then ask for another assignment someplace other than down at the Chancery Building. You could teach high school in one of the Catholic schools, maybe at Bishop McDevitt over in Wyncote, it's over by Queen of Peace, right?" The priest nodded 'yes' to his brother's question.

"Well, why screw up a pension after a life served well as a priest because the Cardinal Archbishop may or may not be a Satanist and his bishop friends may or may not be involved in this debacle? You have got a lot of anecdotal evidence to support your hunches and none of them would stand up in court. You are probably correct in at least some of your assumptions, but so what? The law does not operate on assumptions, hunches and insights. It operates on reasoned judgments about what can be proven and what cannot be proven. That is its strength. That is its weakness. And we are all stuck with that."

Bill Glenn seemed unmoved by his brother's statement. "You are not listening! I have already told you that I manipulated records to protect molester priests and I was more worried about being obedient to the bishop than to seeking justice in this whole demon worshiping thing and before that, I was more worried about the how the church looked to the media than as to how it acted towards its own abused children who had been abused by priests and nuns. Why are not listening to me?" the priest pleaded with his brother.

Bill Glenn's brother responded slowly in kindness, but firmly. "I *am* listening to you. *You* are not listening to *me*. You want a perfect world. You want a perfect church. You want perfect justice. You want the Cardinal Archbishop to turn on fellow priests and bishops based on stories which may or may not be true. You are talking about dozens of old friends or acquaintances that he may have that have been implicated in heinous things by force of rumor and inference and old stories that have been floating around for years. Maybe some of them are even true. Some of these stories probably *are* true. What can he do now? How can he change things now by forcing these old men to come forward and take the chance on suicide or murder to cover up their past sins which might range from immature ritual goofiness to perverse ritual sexual abuse of children and disturbed adults to outright murder, but no one knows for sure. And besides, if murder was involved, that is a matter for the police, not the chancery office. The burden lies on their shoulders, not his. I don't enjoy playing Devil's Advocate with my little brother, but it has to be done. You are probably at least partially correct in what you suspect about the bishops and their minions, but you cannot prove a damned thing. We both know that. Every cop in America has to live with his strong suspicions about the dark activities of some criminal that he knows he cannot ever prove. It is part and parcel of being an investigator. Sometimes, the bad guys get away for lack of proof. So you have a choice to make. You can live with your dark secrets, just like the rest of us have to do, or you can let them destroy you. Now what do you want to do?"

Bill Glenn's brother continued. "When you live the life of a cop you spend your entire day with whores, burglars, liars and cheats, thieves, con men and every sort of unsavory guy you can imagine. They make their living on the weak, the unsuspecting, the lonely and the unbalanced. They are cunning, clever and ruthless. They *have to be* in order to survive in the kind of work they do. Some of that rubs off on the cop. No matter how he might fight it, he becomes hardened, cynical and jaded. It just comes with the job. When you deal with the dregs of society all day long; year in and year out, it starts to affect your psyche. Could it be the same with priests and bishops?" Bill Glenn looked at the cop sitting at the table with him and thought about what he was saying. "Father, I rest my case. Lets go fishing. What do you say?" And with that the two men spent the day fishing in silence.

O'BARDON IN CHICAGO AND GLENN IN IRELAND

It was Easter Sunday and Liam was celebrating the early Mass at St. Luke's Parish. He would be catching a 9:30 flight that morning to Chicago to see Martha. Finally, they would have some private time to work out their relationship parameters without the prying eyes of people in the student union building at Saint Joseph's University.

His homily was short, his attention span shorter and he did not even stop to eat breakfast after Mass. His bags were already packed, he changed into jeans and a jacket, took a train to center city and then a cab to the airport and caught his flight. He landed in Chicago on time, took a cab to his hotel and called Martha at her mother's home. Martha had given him the number about a week prior to his departure.

"Hello?" Martha asked hesitantly; it was Liam on the other end of the phone. "Hi! I'm here!" Liam said. "My mother is sleeping and so is my sister. I will leave a note for them that I went out for the day and I will be there as soon as possible" she whispered. Her mother and sister were napping in the early afternoon.

The whole situation would have been strained except that they had waited so long for this time to happen and had been so upfront with each other from the beginning that there was no tension or apprehension. These two thirtyish virgins wanted each other. It was that simple. Martha put on her overcoat and left her mother's house quietly. She took a cab to the airport hotel where Liam was staying. She was excited to have a chance to see him.

When she arrived, she called from the hotel lobby and Liam came down to meet her. They had lunch in the hotel restaurant and then went up to his room. Liam sat down on the bed and Martha placed her overcoat on the hotel room chair, sat down next to him, and took his hand silently.

They wasted no time. Within minutes they were embracing and minutes after that, their clothes strewn all over the floor, they were naked in the hotel bed and they were making love. They were neophytes at this, and certainly not as accomplished in technique as perhaps a paratrooper would have been with a prostitute, but their inexperience was not apparent to either one of them. Inexperience in these matters is not important when that lack of experience is shared equally by both partners. That being the case, the two of them took no precautions. Liam climaxed inside of Martha twice in less than ten minutes. Martha reciprocated with three orgasms. Martha took Liam's seed willingly and with full knowledge of the implications. Neither of them were experienced enough in sexual matters to fully understand the true implications of their impetuousness. For all practical purposes, this was the very first time either one of them had any significant sexual experience at all. Sex can be unforgiving, if wonderful. They would soon learn this.

They lay in each other's arms quietly without speaking. Martha was crying softly, the emotions of the last hour completely overwhelming her. Liam was continually kissing her face and head and arms, slowly drifting into sleep. He never realized how draining sexual activity could be. He realized it now.

After a few minutes more, Liam entered Martha again. These two young lovers were taking to lovemaking. There was no stopping them. It was midday and there were no occupants in the rooms adjoining theirs. And that was a good thing because these two newly initiated lovers were making more noise than two alley cats. It did not occur to either one of them that this sort of carnal cacophony was more or less universal and anyone in the hallway over the age of about 14 would clearly understand what was happening behind their door. It was only a matter of time when they were overheard by one of the chambermaids and she gently knocked on the door. "Please keep it down!" she said in a low voice. The two of them visibly reddened upon realizing that their newfound wild passion had been overheard in the hallway and they started to laugh. So far, sex was fun. It is not always like that.

They napped and made love for the next two hours and then Martha whispered to a groggy and drained Liam that she had to leave and get back to her mother's apartment across town. Liam grabbed her and held her tight.

"I am not going to let you go, Martha. I am not letting you go. Not ever." Martha smiled and kissed him.

"Okay honey. We will talk tomorrow. I will come back." Liam fell asleep. Martha got up and left and took a cab back to her mother's apartment. Tomorrow could not come soon enough for either of them.

Martha's sister and mother were a little surprised that she had been gone so long and she was evasive when they asked her of her whereabouts that day. They looked at each other in mild surprise and finally her mother said, "Now Sister Martha, where ever have you been all day?" Her mother always called her Sister Martha when she was holding her up for mild amusement among family members.

Martha smiled and said, "I spent the day with my lover" and all three women howled in laughter. Her mother and sister were laughing because they did not believe it. Martha was laughing because she knew that at this point, she would not be believed. It was a wonderful time for her to "come out" in a fashion that could not possibly hurt her. She really enjoyed the fact that she had told the truth and was not believed. It was quite a twist on the usual.

Later that evening she realized upon showering that Liam was spilling out of her all day and that his sperm had a smell like bleach. Her sister would be aware of what the smell was and so Martha had to be fastidious about cleanliness for the next day or so, while Liam was in town. When her mother and sister asked her if she wanted to go out for dinner with them, she declined.

As soon as they left, she quickly washed her underpants and other under garments to clean them of sperm. She wanted to take no chances on giving herself away at this early stage. She went to bed early and slept till the morning. Her mother and sister and she went to breakfast and then went window shopping until her sister left for her apartment across town at lunchtime. Martha and her mother came home to her mother's apartment and her mother took a nap. Martha quietly left the apartment and traveled the ten blocks to Liam's hotel by cab. They spent three hours making love when she arrived. Sex was wonderful, they thought.

Liam climaxed twice in Martha. Martha reciprocated with her own orgasms twice. They clutched each other tightly. Liam finally asked, "What do we do if you get pregnant?" and Martha laughed.

"We are Catholics, Liam! We have the baby of course!" Martha said with a smile on her face

"Of course!" he said, and made love to Martha again. She got up and got dressed and went home to her mother. Liam flew home to Philadelphia that evening. They were too much in love to realize the impact of their actions. That would come later.

BILL GLENN AND IRELAND

Monsignor Glenn boarded the Aer Lingus airliner for Shannon Airport at the Philadelphia International Airport just south of the city. He sat in silence. He fell asleep while the plane was still waiting to depart and he awoke two hours later while flying over the ocean. Across from him sat a well-dressed man in an expensive tweed suit. The two men introduced themselves. Since Monsignor Glenn was not in clericals, he did not immediately say that he was a priest, he only gave his name. The other man turned out to be a professor at Trinity College in Dublin.

After a few pleasantries and realizing that they would be spending hours together on the flight, the two men exchanged deeper information than the superficial stuff one gives to a stranger upon meeting him in a plane.

Glenn explained that he was a Catholic priest and the man turned out to be the son of a minister, Church of Ireland. The two men laughed at this, one just could not get away from religion if one was Irish! After a little while it was apparent that the other man, a Doctor James McDougle, had a Ph.D. in Business Management and taught organizational development at Trinity. He had a lot of experience in working with non-profits, especially national church organizations. He had spent much of his professional life traveling around the world posing management fixes for church organizational problems. Monsignor Glenn was fascinated by that and since he had some questions about the organizational make up of his own church, he plowed right in to the professor's brain, hoping for some answers.

Upon receiving an amicable grilling on the subject of non-profit organizational structure, Professor McDougle the college professor was now completely intrigued.

"Where are you going with this line of questioning, Father?" he asked Glenn.

"Please, just Bill. Okay?" the priest asked.

"Okay, Bill, why all the interest in how a religious non-profit should be optimally structured?" Monsignor Glenn swallowed hard, looked out the window, thought for a minute and finally said, "I am struggling with a personal decision. I need to know if my lifetime spent as a priest is any way reflective of the structure of the organization itself. I am asking myself questions like, what did I do wrong? Could I have done better? Why did I do what I did? Why did I not do things I should have done? Did I spend my life supporting an organization that was not worth my support? Did I keep silent when I should have said something?" Bill Glenn then paused. He then said "I need to know how guilty I am personally for the shortcomings of my church."

The professor looked genuinely surprised, smiled and said in a kind voice, "Father, ultimately we all fail. No matter what we do for a living. We are just humans, we are not gods. Try and remember that. The most that we can hope for is that what we did was the best we could do, and we did it with all our talents and abilities. To put this in American terms, if we are only capable of playing minor league ball than we play the best minor league ball we can. It is pretty much that simple."

The professor continued. "But I can see that your distress is real, so I will tell you my small insights into how a healthy non-profit like a Church should be run for maximum ethical conduct of the organization." Bill Glenn was eager to listen. "First, the Board of Trustees, or in the Catholic sense the Bishops and the curia, must be absolutely certain at all times that they are establishing, clarifying and protecting the ability to maintain a line of open and honest communication with the owners, in this case, the Catholic people. They are the church, the Board is not. That must be foremost in the Board's mind at all times and must be openly stated at all meetings to keep the Board honest and above-board in all its deliberations."

The professor continued. "The Board speaks with one voice or it does not speak at all. There are no minority decisions. There are no 'leaks' to the press by Board members when decisions do not go the way they wanted. There is one voice always and only."

"The Board or the bishops in your case, determine the ends to be met, the means to achieve those ends, the professional executive limitations within which the Board members and staff members may act within the organization, how it delegates authority to staff and the organizational philosophy and specifics of its own authority and power. This is the delicate part because at all times the Board must be subservient to the needs and will of the owners, that would be the Catholic people. This is not easy to do."

"I know!" Glenn said loudly.

The professor laughed, "I think we all know!" he said. "The Board or bishops then define policy by going from the broadest policy to the narrowest in that order. They then define delegation of their power to staff and do not react to outside influences or ratify any agenda at this point. They define policy based only on the mission statement of the organization. In the case of the Catholic Church, that would be spreading the Gospel of Jesus Christ. The Board or bishops must always remember that the "end determination" of the mission is the principle duty of governing, that the bishops set boundaries for the staff's professional conduct and the bishops are responsible to design measurement techniques for their own conduct and processes. The bishops forge a link with staff and management that is empowering and safe while at the same time remaining faithful to the owners, who are rank and file Catholics. Finally performance of all members must be monitored rigorously but only against international policy criteria. It must not be arbitrarily set locally. In other words, the conduct of a nun or priest or bishop in Ireland must be measured exactly the same as a nun or a priest or bishop in America or Argentina or Italy or Asia or anywhere else."

"Now that I have bored you with all of this, does any of this make any sense to you?" the professor asked.

"So, if I have this straight, the Board or bishops are to govern at all times with the idea that they are trustees of the people who actually own the non-profit organization in the first place? Do I have that right?" Monsignor Glenn asked.

"Simply put, yes" the professor stated. Glenn looked out the window. After a few seconds he stared at the professor and said, "The bishops forgot that they do not own the church, that the people own the church. They forgot that the people *are* the church. They just forgot."

The professor said nothing for a while and then he said, "Bill, most boards forget. It is the nature of managing organizations. It is very easy for the people at the top to forget that the organization is not them. They only direct it. It is very easy to forget that! It happens all the time in virtually every non-profit that I have ever worked for…people in power seem to always forget that the power they wield ultimately comes from the people who they wield it over…it happens everywhere."

"Remember one last thing, because it is very important. The number one priority of any human organization is to survive. The organization can do nothing if it no longer exists. The very essence of organizations changes all the time. Superficially they appear to be the same organization that they were upon their inception, but in fact they are not. Let me give you an example. What business are American car dealerships in?" the professor asked and then waited for Monsignor Glenn to answer.

"I guess selling cars!" Glenn said a little hesitantly.

The professor continued. "That would have been true up to about 1985 or so. But today, American car dealerships are in the loan business. They make much of their profit by offering car loans to people who come into the showroom to buy a new car. The automobile itself it simply the physical financial "vehicle" if you will, no pun intended, to get the buyer to take out a loan with the car manufacturer and thereby increase their profit margin. Very few buyers actually finance a new car from a source outside the dealership. The overwhelming majority of new car buyers use the dealership to obtain the loan. So actually, new car dealerships are primarily in the loan business relative to realizing a profit, and only secondarily in the car business."

"And your point is what exactly?" Monsignor Glenn asked.

"Well" the professor continued, "car dealerships are no different than any other kind of human organization at their very center. They see an opportunity to market something and they exploit it. So, when it became clear to the carmakers in the 1980s that they could significantly increase profit by offering car loans to people than by allowing people to buy their cars using money from another source, they went into the car loan business. Churches are no different. They market what they are selling by changing themselves to fit the market. Do you understand the full implication of what I am saying?" the professor asked the priest.

"How do you mean that?" the priest asked.

The professor continued. "Well, in the beginning the 'product' that the Christian Church was selling was belief in Jesus Christ, the healer and holy man from Nazareth. For a very short period of time, within the small and local context of the Jerusalem Church, that was enough of a product to keep the church a going concern. But then the Jews as a people completely rejected James and his church, based on his brother Jesus' teachings."

Monsignor Glenn was impressed. "You know an awful lot about church history for a business professor!" Glenn said.

"My Da' was a minister in the Church of Ireland, remember? I had to know this stuff!" McDougle said with a smile. Both men laughed.

The professor continued. "When the church moved out into the world of the Hellenized Roman Empire and away from its Jewish roots, it had to have a new vehicle, a better storyline if you will, with which to spread the Faith. In the parlance of a car dealership, the old model just wasn't selling. So, Paul Hellenized their Faith, he made it Greek and acceptable to the mind of the non-Jewish Roman Empire. He had to do this so that the church could survive. This was essentially the role that Paul of Tarsus played for the church. Paul came out with the new model, the Hellenized church, and he quite frankly saved the church from certain extinction as an obscure and small and insignificant Jewish sect. He added some Greek touches and some Roman ideas and before you know it, a Jewish sect that had originally talked about a Jewish Jesus being the awaited messiah of the Jews, the priest-prophet-king that they were awaiting for centuries, turned into a very Greco-Roman god-man."

The priest said nothing and listened closely. " Following this line of argument then, Jesus was made into the Son of God, just like Mithras or Apollo or Hercules or the Roman Emperor, whomever the local god-man might be at the moment at that locality. Many of the miracle stories that were attributed to a plethora of pagan gods were attributed to him and frankly, he was now "marketable" to a pagan mind. In Hellenizing Jesus, he was changed utterly from a Jewish messiah into a Greco-Roman god-man. This was not the original intention of the Jews that initially followed him but the church survived by changing its organizational thrust. In essence, it changed the 'product'. The church, through Paul of Tarsus, changed the Jesus that it was marketing to fit the market within which Jesus was being "sold." The fact that Jesus' identity was totally changed and radicalized and paganized into a god-man was beside the point because the organization itself found a way to survive. Do you understand?" the professor asked the priest.

"I am not sure what your ultimate point is" Monsignor Glenn said.

The professor explained further. "Well my point is simply this. Jesus was totally reinvented so that the church could survive. It was becoming very apparent to the Jerusalem Church that the Jesus that they were "marketing" had very little interest for the Hellenized world and it had only local appeal. Even the Diaspora Jews throughout the Roman Empire to whom Paul of Tarsus was "marketing" Jesus showed very little interest in the Jesus outlined and preached by the Jerusalem Church. He had no cosmopolitan appeal to them. He wasn't Greek enough. So, Paul changed him. He reinvented him so that the Church could continue to grow and exist outside of Jerusalem, even outside of a Jewish context. How about now, get it? Paul changed the very essence of Jesus to give him appeal to the Greco-Roman world. In effect, because Paul was a Diaspora Jew himself and because he was in tune enough with the Greco-Roman world and he was bright enough to see that the "old model" of Jesus was not selling well, then he was astute enough to bring out a new "model" of Jesus. Because he reinvented Jesus the Christian movement survives to this day. All of the Christian works, Christian identity and Christian fellowship survived because Paul placed the 'Jesus Story' into a Greek context that non-Jews could accept. He reinvented Jesus to save the church. It worked."

"I think I see what you are saying. I am not sure that many Christian theologians would agree with your theology, but your basic business intuition is correct here, I must admit that!" the priest said with a laugh.

The professor went on. "Well, it is no different today. The church, like any human organization, morphs itself constantly to appeal to the world to which it is marketing. The Christian Church has changed dozens of times throughout the last two thousand years to ensure its survival. It initially saw itself as a Jewish movement and only Jews could participate within it.

When that did not work anymore it saw itself as the suffering and politically oppressed masses under the Roman thumb. Then later it became an acceptable Roman religion under Constantine, mostly because so many Christians were Roman bureaucrats and Roman soldiers that to continue to persecute Christians would be to commit demographic and political suicide for the Empire. Next the Christian Churches split into warring factions of Gnostic and Orthodox and later on down the road the Western Christians then split further into warring factions of Catholic and Protestant and then later on they split again into mainline Protestant and Evangelical and so on and so forth. The Catholic Church is presently dealing with its own problem with radical fundamentalism within its ranks. Each time a Christian group splits off from the tree, another "Jesus" model goes on display in the showroom of the "Jesus Story", like in the car dealerships we were talking about."

"At present, there are about 235 to 245 Christian groups in the world. That is a major split from the original Church in Jerusalem. And from my point of view, from a purely business management perspective, it is because there are so many people who are willing to "buy" differing models of the "Jesus Story", a particular model that suits their psychological and emotional needs. In a very real sense, it is no different than buying a car. You take a look at what is being offered, you look at what you want and what you can afford to "pay" in an emotional sense and then you buy the model that best suits your comfort level. From a marketing point of view, choosing any belief system is essentially no different that choosing a car."

"That is a very interesting point of view!" Bill Glenn laughed. McDougle laughed too, both of them realizing that the whole conversation was unique to say the least.

But finally McDougle said, "I hope this helps you in your search for meaning in what you have done within the church. Remember, you did what you could do. That is all that can be asked of any man."

Monsignor Glenn looked at the professor and said, "Thanks. You are right of course. I did what I could do. That is all I can do." Bill Glenn had some thinking, some praying and some more thinking to do. He realized that now.

The plane landed at Shannon Airport and Glenn stood. McDougle stayed aboard bound for Dublin. The two men shook hands. "Thank you Doctor. You have given me more than you will ever know."

McDougle smiled and said, "All in a day's work, Father. Good luck to you. And enjoy Ireland!" Glenn took a cab to his hotel. His rest in Ireland had finally begun.

IRELAND, LAND OF DREAMS

Bill Glenn decided he would not travel through Ireland on a set schedule. He was a man adrift and he just needed to float; so he would. He decided only that he would travel throughout the island and see the countryside in a week or two or maybe even three. He took a bus to Galway and rented a room in a bed and breakfast. He stayed three days, walking and looking at the bay and taking in the people. He attended daily Mass while in Ireland and usually would talk to the priest after Mass, nothing deep or indicative of his state of mind, just superficial conversation with another priest. After a few days in Galway he then took a bus closer to the center of the country toward Blarney Castle and then from there, he went to Belfast and from there back to Dublin. He simply traveled and thought and prayed.

He found himself soon enough at the Seminary at Maynooth. He had not planned to see the place but somehow or other he stumbled across it. He entered the buildings and spent some time in the library and talked to a few priests, exchanging a few pleasantries along the way. He took a room in town, had an early dinner and turned in for the night before 8:00 PM. He was soon fast asleep since his travels had tired him out, straight to the bone.

Soon he was dreaming. He was again at the library at Maynooth and watching all the seminarians come and go. It was strange. It was not the present day, but seemed to be about 1860 or 1870 judging from the way that these young men were dressed. A seminarian approached him. He vaguely recognized the man. It was McGurk! It was a younger version of the priest to be sure; but still, it was him nonetheless.

"James McGurk, do you remember me?" Monsignor Glenn asked the young seminarian in his dream with surprise in his voice. The young man stopped walking and turned and looked at Bill Glenn. He smiled and opened his arms.

"I never forget a friend, especially one in need. Of course I recognize you. You are Bill Glenn" McGurk said. He then added, "We've met in your dreams."

"Now I am really confused!" Glenn said to the much younger McGurk. "I am not supposed to meet you until you are very much older and a priest in Philadelphia!" Monsignor Glenn said with a chuckle.

"Bill, we've been over this before!" the seminarian said. "I am dead and you are dreaming. Anything can happen, and it usually does in a dream. But you called me back into your mind, into your dream life, for a reason. What is it?" the McGurk asked kindly.

"I am not sure exactly. I am in Ireland and I am thinking of leaving the priesthood." McGurk laughed heartily. The McGurk motioned to Bill Glenn that they should both sit down at a table in the library and talk. They took two chairs at a table and did just that.

"Bill, I think of leaving the priesthood every day of my life! What is so unusual about that? The priesthood is a heavy cross to bear at times. Anyone who carries this cross is aware of how heavy it can sometimes be; why would you be any different from the rest of us?" McGurk said to his friend smiling all the while.

"You always know what to say to me!" Monsignor Glenn said to the dream friend. "How did you get so smart?"

The young seminarian McGurk laughed again, "It is one of the benefits of being dead, don't ya' know? One can see things one could never have seen when one was alive. It is a sort of trade-off. Being dead gives a human personality a certain seasoning. It bestows a certain clarity on the human condition. One can actually learn to like it, believe it or not!" They both laughed

"I must tell you something that not everyone can accept. "Just between you and me" the young seminarian told the older priest. " The theologians of the Middle Ages were half right, there really *is* such a place that more or less resembles Purgatory. Believe it or not, you are in it right now talking to me! It is not hellfire and it is not suffering as they thought, so much as it is *searching.*"

"In your death you can choose your conditions, your pleasures, your burdens, your mentors, your tormentors and your way back to Life. Some of us use our time in death to relearn old lessons that we either never grasped or would not learn on your side of the Divide. Once here, we can decide how, when, where, with whom and why we should or should not proceed with the learning process, a process that eventually leads to the soul's reintegration into the Cosmic, into the Godhead, into all that is and ever will be.

To use an analogy from your time, Life is a university, but death is Graduate School. You can go back if you wish under any number of conditions. You can relive your last life or any life you wish or move on to the next stage, the choice is yours. You are never alone here. You are always in the hands of the Guides; you would probably fancy them angels.

There is a heaven but that is for those who have completed the journey. And that takes many, many different kinds of deaths. Being dead is a wonderfully freeing experience, if you take it with the proper attitude. But if you expect anything other than a continuing of your personal journey back into assimilation with the Godhead, then you are in for a deep and sad disappointment.

Even in death, you must do the work yourself. You cannot be granted enlightenment. You must accept the burdens that go along with opening your spirit to the Light in order to reap the benefits of the Light. To put this in Christian terms, there can no be no Resurrection without Crucifixion and Death. It is impossible any other way. Can you understand any of this?" the young man said to the older one.

" I am not really sure!" the older priest said.

"No matter" McGurk said, "Like all of us, you will relearn in your own time for your own sake." Jamie McGurk looked kindly at his friend, Monsignor Glenn. Finally he said, "Now, onto the problem at hand!"

"So, it's leaving the priesthood that this visit to Ireland is all about, is it?" the McGurk said to Glenn.

"Yes," and then he added "and just what does Jamie McGurk, the young seminarian, feel about my predicament?" The young McGurk thought for a moment and then spoke.

"Bill, priesthood or no priesthood, you are a Christian and you have a Christian duty to live the Christ reality as best you can and in a manner that totally befits your soul, your piece of the Godhead. Whether or not you stay a priest is nowhere near as important as how you choose to see the Christ within you and how you decide to live that Christ toward others. We both know that a Christian may be the only Christ that anyone ever sees. So the real question here is this: in what fashion do you wish to live the reality of Christ while remaining true to who you are and extending that truth toward the rest of humanity? Once you answer that question, whether or not you stay a priest will come to your mind naturally." The two men looked at each other, shook hands and departed. Bill Glenn woke up immediately and left his bed and prayed on his knees. He had received his answer.

Glenn spent two more weeks in Ireland. He wandered slowly throughout the island and then returned home to Philadelphia. He asked to see the Cardinal Archbishop and was granted fifteen minutes. He had been replaced and was currently on hold for assignment.

Monsignor Glenn and the Cardinal met and Glenn asked to be reassigned to Bishop McDevitt High School as its chaplain. He would stay a priest and continue to live at the rectory at Queen of Peace in Ardsley. The Cardinal Archbishop agreed. The men were polite but distant and businesslike with each other. The archbishop did not look at Glenn as he left the suite. Glenn gathered his things, emptied his office. Father O'Bardon who had just returned from a short vacation himself, drove him back to Ardsley. Monsignor

Glenn told the pastor at Queen of Peace Parish, Father Traczska, that he was going to stay at the rectory and told him of his new assignment. The pastor said nothing, smiled and shook Glenn's hand and welcomed the news. He would still have an extra priest at the parish. That was always good news.

LIAM AND MARTHA BACK IN PHILADELPHIA

Their very short private time in Chicago came to an end all too soon. Liam flew home within a few hours of last making love to Martha. Martha followed back to Philadelphia within a week. They dared not call each other on the phone. There were too many ears to hear and eyes to see the emotions coming from them when they were together; they were smart enough to see that and recognize the danger. So they stayed physically far apart, communicated by email and deleted all emails as soon as they were read. They had to be careful now, major decisions had to be made.

By this time it was midsummer and Liam was working hard on the final document that he was to present to the Cardinal Archbishop concerning competing versions of the Jesus Story and the actions that could be taken to keep the Church's version paramount in the minds of people. He was working directly for the Cardinal now, the priest that had replaced Monsignor Glenn was not given responsibility for Liam and his projects. The Cardinal seemed to appreciate Liam's work and he was usually left alone to finish his project without any interruption from above. Liam grew accustomed to this newfound workplace atmosphere since

Bill Glenn was something of a micromanager. Work was more comfortable for Liam than it had been for years.

Liam knew that if he wrote what he was thinking it would be rejected by the Cardinal out of hand, it would never get to Rome. He also knew that if he towed the line and simply wrote the normal traditional Catholic pabulum for general consumption that the Cardinal would be happy and the document would have no impact whatsoever. His challenge now was to find an acceptable Catholic way to tell the Holy Father and the Curia that the old Jesus Story was dead. People were too bright now. They would not accept as history first century propaganda meant as a diatribe from one Jewish sect against another. This was an Age that demanded proof and systematic research into any subject matter. To expect highly educated and informed Catholics to continue to accept a politically motivated broadside written by early Jewish Christians with an axe to grind against the leaders of Second Temple Judaism in a literary style that resembled a fairy tale to the modern mind was ultimately dangerous to the continued existence of the Church as an organization. It was even fatal to the Faith. But how would he meet this challenge?

And then, there was Martha. He and a nun had made love in Chicago and were in love back home in Philadelphia. How could either of them continue to reconcile their sexual lives with each other with their vows of celibacy? How could they continue to live as Religious when they were having sex against the very vows that they had given to God? No easy answer was to be found here either. And there was another problem. Martha was pregnant.

She was caught vomiting in the morning twice by the mother superior of the convent who said nothing. She simply looked at the nun with a very odd and questioning face. Martha had told Liam right away about their predicament. A decision had to be made by both of them very soon, in fact they had to decide what they were going to do. They made arrangements to meet at St. Joseph's University in the Library to talk things over.

Liam arrived at "their spot" in the library early. He was not wearing priest clericals although Martha did wear her nun's habit. They usually sat in the sound room where there were booths and headphones to listen to audio recordings. Generally, no one was usually in the room at dinnertime and that is when they usually would meet. Tonight was not usual. Martha was on time, dressed in her habit and looking white, weak and washed out. Liam grabbed her hand when she entered the room and steadied her. He placed her quickly in one of the chairs in the room.

"Martha!" he said anxiously. "What is wrong?" Martha looked at Liam with fear in her eyes.

"Liam I have been bleeding all day. Something is wrong. I didn't know whether or not I could make it here tonight. I think I am going to lose this baby!" With that, her eyes traveled up into her head and she slumped in the chair. She started to hemorrhage and her legs were dripping blood. Liam screamed for help.

Two students helped get her to the floor and a third ran to the phone to get help. Within minutes Martha was in the ambulance and on her way to Hahnemann Hospital a long drive even in an ambulance. Liam rode with her to the hospital where she was immediately taken to the emergency room and Liam, waited. He headed for the hospital chapel, sat down and he prayed.

Martha's gynecologist was called to the hospital and soon arrived. Doctor Esther Tishman M.D. was an older Jewish woman and had actually taken her medical degree in Philadelphia and had practiced there for over forty years.

She realized what was happening immediately and once Martha was stabilized she was taken into a semi-private suite. Martha was given a transfusion of blood and slowly regained consciousness. When she awoke, Dr. Tishman was at her side. It was 2:00 AM.

"How are you feeling Martha?"

"Doctor Tishman! What happened?" Martha asked weakly.

"Martha, you are weak and will be going back to sleep soon. You had a miscarriage. You have lost a lot of blood but with rest, and you should be fine. The doctor looked down at the younger woman lying in the hospital bed and smiled warmly. "Get some sleep, Sister, we will talk tomorrow."

Martha then said, "Will you find Father O'Bardon and tell him I am all right? He is probably in the hospital chapel." Doctor Tishman agreed.

She found Liam. He was almost asleep on his knees.

"Father O'Bardon?" she asked.

"Yes?"

"I am Sister Martha's doctor, Doctor Tishman." They both sat down in the pew and faced each other as they sat next to each other. "Martha had a miscarriage. She should be fine."

The doctor looked at the young priest for about twenty seconds and then asked him, "Father, would you like to see her now?"

"Yes," said Liam.

"It has been a very difficult day for all of us I'm afraid. May I tell you about my day for just a minute before we go up to see Martha?" Lian nodded his consent."

The doctor looked at Liam. "Early this morning my 43 year old daughter calls me in a panic to say that her 17 year old son is running away from home to enter an ashram, study Eastern philosophy and sit in the Lotus position all day! She and her husband spent $50,000 dollars on his Bar Mitzvah four years ago. He has attended private Quaker schools his entire life. The plan was that he would go the Penn, then law school at an Ivy League college and then practice law with his Uncle Morty. I don't think saffron robes, a shaved head and chanting are going to be in line with that plan." She shook her head in wonderment.

"By lunchtime my ex-husband had convinced my oldest son Saul, he's 40, that he may not be his real father and in fact I was having an affair with the owner of the local Jewish Delicatessen all throughout our marriage. My idiot of an ex told my son that his real father is the Kosher butcher and that I was sleeping with this guy all along. I wasn't, but looking back on it, I should have been! My son calls me in a fury wanting to know if his father is the butcher. I tell him no, his father is not the butcher, his father is the idiot that he spent the day with. "

"I get home from work, and sit down for an early dinner and I get a call on my cell phone that Sister Martha, one of my patients, has been admitted to Hahnneman Hospital. I find out that she has miscarried. A red banner day!" Liam just looked at her. He was as exhausted as she was.

"Liam, are you the child's father?" the doctor asked. The priest said simply, "yes" and waited for her response.

"Look, I am aware of the difficulty you both are facing now. Sister Martha's medical record is her own business, but I happen to know Mother Edwina will very quickly figure this out, no matter that she cannot legally be told anything that Martha does not want divulged. Is this going to cause problems for you?"

Liam looked at her and said, "I don't care, as long as Martha is going to be okay. We can work this out."

The doctor squeezed his hand and got up to leave. "Thank you doctor" Liam said quietly, "thank you for understanding." The doctor left the chapel. Liam took the elevator to Martha's room, and sat in the chair in her room next to her bed. She was out of danger now. He squeezed her hand gently, and fell asleep. He slept until morning. The nurses on the floor let him sleep.

When Martha woke up the next morning Liam was still asleep. She loved him so much that trouble didn't matter. They were in trouble with their church, their families and at least theoretically, they were in trouble with their God. But that could all be worked out if they remained loving and open to the Will of God, Martha thought to herself. She fell back asleep. Liam did not stir.

By 10 a.m. Mother Edwina was in the room accompanied the senior nun in the convent. She woke Liam and asked him and the other nun, a Sister Elizabeth, to leave the room so she could be alone with Sister Martha. He quietly complied. He said nothing to either of them. They did not look at him.

Mother Superior sat down in the chair that Liam had warmed and waited. Martha woke, looked over, expecting to see Liam, but saw Mother Superior instead.

"How are you feeling, Martha?" Mother Superior asked her.

"I have pain. I am weak and tired, but other than that, I am fine. Thank you for coming Mother." Martha said.

"Of course I came. You are my responsibility!" Mother said.

"I asked the nurses at the station what happened. Is there anything you want to tell me?"

"Well", Martha said bravely, "I had a miscarriage. I cannot really add anything to that!"

Mother Superior simply looked at Martha. Finally she said, "Have you decided what you want to do at this point? I take it that you will not want to stay at the convent. Should I query Rome about you? I take it that you will want to be released from your vows. Do you wish to leave the convent? I can say that you are on convalescent leave at another location. No one needs to know anything else."

Sister Martha's answer was immediate. "No Mother, with your permission I would like to return to the convent as soon as I am released from the hospital. Would that be possible?"

Mother Superior was kind but firm. "No Martha. Given the circumstances, that would not be possible. I could possibly arrange for you to travel to our Motherhouse in central Pennsylvania and you could stay there until your situation becomes clearer in your mind. Would you be willing to do that? If so, you must do penance Sister Martha for what you have done. But I can arrange for this to be done privately and without too much melodrama. Are you willing to go?"

Sister Martha thought hard and finally spoke. " I don't feel that I need to do penance for anything. I don't regret what I did. I know that this does not fit into what we have been taught is right and wrong. But I cannot feel sorry for the life I carried within me, no matter how wrong it must seem to you."

Sister Martha continued, " I will simply go home to Chicago. You can tell the other sisters whatever you want. I will sign whatever paperwork you need me to sign in order to be released from my vows. But I cannot say that I am ashamed for loving someone else. I just cannot do that, no matter how the circumstances must look to you right now."

Mother Superior physically flinched. She did not expect this from Sister Martha. Finally she said, "All right Sister. The Order will pay for the hospital stay and to send you home to your mother in Chicago. Then we wash our hands of you. Do you understand?'

Sister Martha said bravely, "Yes I do Mother. I am sorry for the trouble that I have caused you. But I am not sorry that I am in love. I hope someday that you will understand that." Mother Superior left the room and talked quietly to the head nurse. She kept Sister Elizabeth at a distance so as not to overhear. They both left the ward floor and Liam reentered the room.

"Well, what now?" he asked Martha.

"Well, I am apparently out of the Religious Life as of right now. When I am released from here, they will petition Rome to have me released from my vows. What are we going to do Liam?"

Liam looked at Martha lovingly. "I do not know sweetheart, but whatever we do, we do it together."

"Well I am glad that you said that. Why don't you let me fly to Chicago, break the news to my family and you continue here as an active priest until we can figure out what to do? Are you open to that?" Sister Martha asked her man.

"Whatever you want, Martha. We will do whatever you want to do."

LIVING AT SAINT CHARLES BORROMEO

The retired Cardinal Archbishop of Philadelphia, Marco Bertelli, was bone tired from a life of faithful service to his church and now in retirement. His professional life had crashed to the ground when he was summarily chastised and revealed as ambiguous about protecting children by the District Attorney's Office. The local media and legal adversaries portrayed him as an associate to crime in the worst way. He hid the church's complicity in child rape from the eyes of the law to save face for his church and save money for the Insurance Companies insuring his priests for misconduct. He was the consummate company man, and he paid a high personal price for that distinction. He was ever so slowly beginning to realize this.

To this very moment, he saw his role in the sex abuse scandal as one of protector of the church, prefect for its resources, pastor for its power and servant of its needs on the material and spiritual levels. He sincerely could not see why he was being vilified by the local media in public and in private by some churchmen for his role in the scandal. He wanted then what he always wanted for his church, that she should be delivered unscathed from attacks that he considered to be anti-Catholic and filled with hatred and envy.

In short, Marco Bertelli was out of touch with reality on this issue and full of rationales for his role in what was increasingly being seen by observers as the worst church scandal since the papal excesses of the Middle Ages. The international clutch of 3,500 diocesan bishops worldwide knew that serial child rape was happening all over their dioceses, their provinces, their nations. And they did very little to stop it. That was undeniable. The Catholic in the pew would not forget this for generations. The shepherds had turned the flock over to the wolves on a routine and systematic basis. Exactly why they did it, and continued to do it, was a much more difficult thing for anyone to grasp, even those who studied the situation closely.

Bertelli lived on the grounds at the seminary in Overbrook, just off City Line Avenue and a couple of miles down the street from the official residence of the present Cardinal Archbishop. He had wanted to build a home on the grounds for his retirement, but the political backwash from the sex abuse scandal made that impossible. If he had built an expensive residence on the seminary grounds, he would not only be seen as arrogant and princely in the face of the scandal, he would be seen as unrepentant. So, he chose instead to spend his retirement in the faculty wing of the seminary. It was easier than trying to explain to Catholics why he was using their money for his comfort after he and his predecessors had been so cavalier about the safety of their children in the hands of predator priests, nuns and lay brothers. He had already betrayed them in the matter of their children, he did not need to rub salt in their wounds with seeming extravagance.

He was in his eighties now and feeling used up and spent. He certainly never expected that his retirement would be spent in this type of barren environment. He had few friends, almost no family left and very few visitors. He would often explain that he was spending time in prayer and penance, but in fact, he was just alone and growing lonelier by the day. No one seemed interested in his fate. Out of power, and no longer one who could deliver many favors, he was seen as ineffectual and expendable by the clergy that surrounded him. He was sad. For all intents and purposes, he was a man adrift. Rome was polite and officially open to any request he might have, but "old friends" did not call and it was growing harder for his views to be heard at the top. He was out of power and out of influence, and that much was obvious to even the casual observer. He had served the Catholic Church in America and in the Vatican his entire life as best he could. He had been a loyal soldier and one who could always be counted upon to deliver for the Holy Father. He always got the job done. He was a true son of the church. The problem was that he never truly understood what the word 'church' ultimately means.

Bertelli always took the word 'church' to mean the curia, the magesterium, the Credo, the organization, the trappings of power and position that seemed to signify 'church' to him. He could never completely comprehend that the word 'church' simply meant the indwelling of the Holy Spirit within the People of God. That concept eluded him even now. He was fiercely loyal to an organization. But the ethos of 'church' escaped him completely. His church had no people in it. It was more of an idea than a reality. There was no flesh and blood wrapped around his view of 'church'. That made it all the easier to betray the people and their children; they were only part of the church in an almost accidental way in his view. Bertelli's church was majestic, ancient, beautiful, powerful, filled with history and tradition, a place of privilege for clergy and Religious, and it was completely bereft of soul. It was an empty place. No humans lived there. It was a beautiful idea that could never see the light of day on the human plane. It was an idea whose time had come...and gone. It was a theological construct right out of the Middle Ages. No one lived in Bertelli's Church, it was all theology and no humanity.

The Second Vatican Council of the 1960s convened under Angelo Roncalli had tried desperately to put an end to the extreme ritualistic piety codified in Vatican I about a century earlier. Ultimately, it had failed. In fact, an argument could be made that it was the catalyst for an even more extreme and reactionary Catholicism eventually taking hold that was militant in its mindset and medieval in its worldview. The documents of that council spoke of the priesthood of all believers and the People of God containing the Holy Spirit. Relative to structural change within the church after the council, those concepts were ignored. Roncalli tried. Roncalli failed. Bishops like Bertelli made sure of that.

Bertelli would spend his days walking through the seminary grounds, saying the rosary, reading his breviary, taking calls from various priests throughout the archdiocese and occasionally from overseas. But mostly, he was a gray, lonely old man though he never let his psyche view his life in that way. He had been in power too many years to dwell very long on things he could not change. He had learned that lesson well. It is an essential element of wielding power. Do what can be done. What cannot be done must be forgotten and discarded. Idealism and power cannot occupy the same space.

As he continued to age, he spent more and more time thinking about his eternal reward. He could not help but think it would come soon, even though his doctors constantly told him that he would live many years longer. His health was not bad, his heart was not weak, his mind had not cracked. He had many years to live yet. This prospect did not always thrill him. In fact, after the drubbing he took by the Philadelphia Grand Jury Report on Sexual Abuse in the Church, he looked forward to his own demise. But life was not going to be that easy for Bertelli. It was going to drain out of him slowly, very slowly. Much to his chagrin, he knew he had many years yet to live.

Every now and then another bishop would call or visit on his way through Philadelphia. He would stay at the seminary for a day or two and they would talk about days gone by and never once mention the sex abuse scandal that cast the entire American hierarchy in a sad and ugly light. The bishops went to great lengths to avoid talk of the scandal in any conversation with each other. It was as if the entire thing as so traumatic for all of them in its continuing unfolding that the only respite they had was when they were in each other's company. At least then they could be sure that the subject would lie dormant. It can be imagined that lepers rarely talk about their disease. The same was true here. Bishops were the social lepers of the Catholic Church. They knew it and acted accordingly when they were in each other's company. Being a bishop in the Catholic Church was fast becoming like being a member of the Brotherhood of Damned.

194

When they were young priests, becoming a bishop was the epitome of holiness and clerical astuteness. Now they were old men and bishops themselves. Now they knew better. They were made bishops because they were company men, in the worse sense of that phrase. Only the most honest of them would admit that to himself, and there were very few of that type of men among them.

It was a Saturday night in the late summer and the retired Cardinal Archbishop of Philadelphia turned in early after a day visiting parish priests whom he considered friends. Earlier in the day he had stopped in at St. Michael's Parish in South Philadelphia, the initial Irish American parish for the archdiocese. The church had been reconstructed in its original glory and it looked beautiful. He was very impressed with the job that had been done. As he lay down to sleep that evening, it was the altar at St. Michael's parish that he was thinking about as he drifted to sleep. He began to dream shortly after falling to sleep.

"Your Eminence!" a voice said to Cardinal Bertelli from behind. He turned and looked. There in front of him was a priest of about 40 years of age and from the sound of his brogue, an Irishman.

"Father, I don't believe I know you. And I thought that I knew all of my priests!" the Cardinal intoned to the younger man.

"Well Eminence, strictly speaking, I am not one of your priests. You see we both serve the Catholic people of Philadelphia, but at very different times!" It was then that the Cardinal looked closely at the priest and saw that he was wearing a cassock that went out of fashion many years earlier.

"What year is this Father?" the Cardinal asked. "Why, it is 1881 Eminence. Would his Eminence like to take a seat?" and with that the younger priest waved his hand toward the closest pew.

"I think I will at that!" Cardinal Bertelli said. Both men sat down and Bertelli spoke first.

"Father, am I dreaming?" the Cardinal asked genuinely.

"Well, Eminence, let me answer your question this way. We are all dreaming! It is just that right now, you are dreaming in the traditional understanding of that term." Bertelli chuckled. He liked this priest. There was something refreshingly genuine about him that was undeniably pleasant.

"So, Father, what can I do for you?" Bertelli asked. The Irishman laughed heartily. The people praying in the pews shot him a glance and a few actually shushed him to be quiet.

"Sorry!" the priest turned and said in a loud stage whisper to the parishioners, "It won't happen again!" he said.

"He always says that!" and older gentlemen who was praying said in a brogue with great irritation, uttering a stage whisper himself.

"Eminence, the more pertinent question is this: what can *I* do for *you*? You have come here for a reason. You have come here to seek out a priest. Now you've found one. So the question becomes this: what is it that *I* can provide to *you*?" With that the Irishman looked at the Cardinal with kindness and waited for his answer.

The Cardinal Archbishop was embarrassed. He stammered at first and then regained his composure.

"Well, yes, actually, you are right Father. I *have* come to seek *you* out, haven't I? And the truth of the matter is, I have not the slightest insight as to exactly why! I must have come here for a reason. Now why did I seek you out? By the way Father, your name is....?" Bertelli's voice trailed off waiting for the priest to reply.

"My name is James McGurk and I am the curate here at Saint Michael's Parish. And you are ...?" this time McGurk's voice trailed off waiting for the Cardinal to answer.

"Oh yes, of course, you would not know. I am Marco Cardinal Bertelli, Cardinal Archbishop Emeritus of Philadelphia. I am lately retired and frankly, I spend my days wondering what to do with myself!" Both men laughed.

McGurk got shushed again from the Irish parishioners in their pews. "Sorry!" he said again in a stage whisper to no one in particular.

"Perhaps you should just begin by telling me about your life, about your circumstances, your Eminence. Perhaps you should just start talking and the two of us will decide at that point what it is you are hear to tell me. Can you do that, now?" the Irishman asked.

"I think I can, Father; I think I will." And so the Cardinal simply started to talk.

He told the priest about his younger days as a seminarian in New York and then his early days as a priest, his studies and his high profile assignments. He talked about how his family supported his priesthood in every way, how proud they were of him and how proud they were of themselves for giving the church such a successful priest. As he climbed the ladder up the hierarchy, his family grew less and less interested in what he was doing. It seemed that working class Catholics have little time for bishops, no matter how faithful they are to church matters. Bishops are above the people and everyone knows that. It could make for a very lonely existence. It did for Bertelli. It does for everyone who attains the rank of bishop.

Bertelli talked on and on and McGurk listed intently. Finally Bertelli said, "So, Father, do you have any idea why I am here yet?"

McGurk said, "Of course, Eminence, you are here to come face to face with yourself, with your past. All that I am doing is giving you a priest toward which you can direct your thoughts. The truth is , I am just a clerical set of ears to hear your story. The miracle is not in the listening of a life's story, it is in the telling." Bertelli stopped and thought hard about what he had just heard.

"So, you are saying that by just telling my story I am healing myself?"

McGurk answered, "Yes. You are healing, you are getting to know yourself now at the end of your life like you never knew yourself before because you have the time now to reflect on what you have done with your life. You have the time you never had before you left your work at the Chancery. Use your time wisely, Eminence. At some point, time will run out. Reconcile yourself to your past before that happens, before time runs out on you. It matters not one whit what others think of Marco Bertelli. The only thing that matters to the Eternal is this: what does Marco Bertelli think of Marco Bertelli? Once you have come to peace with yourself, with your past, with all of your courage and drive and all of your cowardice and weaknesses you will arrive at full humanity. And in that humanity you will find divinity. "McGurk stopped talking and simply smiled at the Cardinal. The Cardinal sat silently and slowly left the church. The dream faded.

Marco Bertelli woke with a start. It was the middle of the night. He looked at his clock. It read 3:33 AM. He was being cradled in the arms of his God. He dropped to his knees next to his bed. He prayed. He wept.

The following month, a very strange series of events shook Monsignor Glenn and the Cardinal Archbishop Emeritus of Philadelphia, Marco Bertelli, to the very core of their beings.

Bishops and high-ranking priests from all over the country had been calling the Seminary Rector's secretary, Mrs. Navotney, all week. She had been fielding calls from at least three different chanceries asking for directions from the airport to the seminary grounds and all of them wanted to know the exact location of the seminary chapel relative to anyplace else on the seminary grounds. They all asked how to enter the archives from the chapel. The conversations were strange to say the least.

Cardinal Archbishop Bertelli was aware of this only because he would walk down to the Rector's Office every afternoon to pick up his mail and on two occasions, Mrs. Navotney asked him about his brother bishops coming to visit him. He was not sure what she was talking about but did not think to ask her about it any further, since chanceries called all the time asking for various bits of information about all sorts of seminary related subjects. Still, he did find it odd that so many bishops were interested in the physical makeup of the seminary grounds in Philadelphia all at the same time. He just put the whole thing down as serendipity and forgot about it.

Monsignor Glenn had taken a Sunday afternoon and driven out to his alma mater, Saint Charles Borromeo Seminary, to visit his old boss and mentor, Cardinal Bertelli. Bertelli had not had a visitor in a couple of months and was glad to see Glenn. The two men had always liked each other and worked well together, although they had their rough spots. Bertelli was not exactly the easiest man in the world to work closely with...God knows Glenn knew that! But they let any rough spots between them stay in the past and Glenn and the retired archbishop spent a few hours walking around the seminary grounds and talking about old times, vacation plans and other superficial things that made the day light and memorable.

Along about dusk, when light was fading from the sky and Glenn and the cardinal archbishop were on the extreme end of seminary property heading back toward the faculty wing in the college division where the cardinal had a suite of rooms, they beheld an odd sight. Several black limousines pulled into the seminary grounds and headed directly toward Saint Martin's Chapel. The drivers parked the cars and waited inside the vehicles with the windows up. The windows were dark and it was impossible to see inside the cars but it was clear from the purple fringe on the cassocks that the three occupants of the three different limousines were wearing, that at least three different bishops had just entered seminary grounds. Monsignor Glenn and Cardinal Bertelli fully expected that the cardinal would be visited by any visiting bishops. Protocol demanded that such a visit take place, so the two men hurried back to his suite in the faculty wing of the seminary to receive his guests. Within twenty minutes they were in his apartments and the cardinal archbishop waited patiently for over an hour to receive the bishops. No one came to his room. So, the cardinal archbishop emeritus sent Monsignor Glenn to find the men and invite them to his suites. He was more than just a little upset at his fellow bishops but he did not let Glenn see his irritation.

Monsignor Glenn walked down the long front corridor of the college building, normally referred to as the Lower Side and immediately saw that all was not right. Something was odd, very odd. Outside of the sacristy of Saint Martin's Chapel and near the front door of the seminary chapel, just above the steps to the seminary archives in the basement of the chapel, there stood two large men, both wearing black suits, white shirts and black ties like seminarians. But they were uncharacteristically old for students and Glenn could tell from their demeanor that they were not seminarians at all. They acted as if they were bodyguards of some sort. And something else was odd, they were wearing sunglasses inside the chapel. Seminarians would never do that. These men were placed at the door of the sacristy to ensure that no one entered and took the stairs down into the archives. They did not see Glenn and he stayed hidden behind a statue of Michael the Archangel to keep himself out of their field of vision. Something very wrong was going on here.

As that last thought entered Glenn's mind, he heard a strange sort of mumbling, almost like a communal humming coming up from below his feet in the corridor. It was coming from below him in the Archives. The familiar cadence of communal responses could be faintly heard. Monsignor Glenn was afraid.

Monsignor Glenn removed his shoes so that he could not be heard on the marble flooring as he was retreating back to the Cardinal Archbishop's suite in the faculty wing. He almost ran back to tell the Cardinal what he had observed. When he was finished telling what he saw, the Cardinal Archbishop seemed very shaken. He said nothing for a little while and then he looked at Glenn with a very strange look.

Finally he said, "Monsignor, do you have any idea what is happening? Tell me true." The priest looked at the retired Cardinal Archbishop and said flatly, "I suspect secret rituals are taking place at this moment down in the archives beneath Saint Martin's Chapel."

The Cardinal Archbishop looked surprised, not at what he heard, but at the surety with which Monsignor Glenn presented his judgment on the situation. "I suspect that you are absolutely correct" the Cardinal Archbishop said firmly and without flinching, all the while looking directly into the Monsignor's face.

"What are we to do?" Monsignor Glenn asked the older man. The Cardinal turned away from Glenn for a minute and stared out his window. He finally spoke.

"You do realize that if those activities are in fact taking place in this building that our discovery of them will place our lives in danger, don't you?" the Cardinal asked Monsignor Glenn.

"I do" was all Glenn answered. Monsignor Glenn then added, "So I ask you again, what do we do?'

The Cardinal Archbishop simply said, "I have to make a phone call. Wait here." With that the Cardinal Archbishop walked into another room and dialed. He asked for 'Captain Maslow' and then said, "I will hold." After about a minute Glenn heard the Cardinal Archbishop tell someone on the other line, "Simon, this is Marco. Well, the day has arrived. You know what to do. They are in the archives below the chapel on the seminary grounds. Bring what you need to bring and make it quick. There is very little time to lose." He then hung up the phone, re-entered the room, looked at Monsignor Glenn and simply said, "Follow me. And for the love of God, be quiet! Our lives depend on us keeping our heads. Whatever you see, whatever you hear, keep it completely in your head. You are going to need to remember it and recall it exactly as it happened at a later time."

With that the two men walked out of the Cardinal's suite and headed down the corridor, a quarter of a mile directly into the Chapel Sacristy where they were stopped by the two very large men in black suits. Immediately, the Cardinal Archbishop placed his left hand over his heart and said to the men who were Keepers to the Gate of Hell, "Hail Satan!" Monsignor Glenn did the same. They were allowed into the sacristy, given robes which they immediately donned. Bertelli made sure that neither of their faces could be seen, as he pulled the hoods well over their faces. They then went down below to the Archives. Once there they beheld a scene that was unspeakable.

A small girl of perhaps eight years old was totally nude and laid out on a low altar and was being raped by a man in a hooded garment fringed with odd symbols. She did not move and did not cry out. She was surrounded by fifty people, all hooded with the same dark robes, with symbols embroidered onto the hems and arms. They were all humming or chanting. They were swaying back and forth as they hummed and the man doing the raping was slow, methodical and entering the little girl in time with the swaying of the group. The entire thing seemed to be tightly orchestrated, choreographed and it seemed to follow a strict sense of order. Bertelli and Glenn stayed behind the last row of the crowd but could behold the full horror of the scene.

There were swords, daggers, pikes and all sorts of sharp instruments in the hands of many and at one point, off to the left of the altar on which the little girl lay, there seemed to be some sex act going on between a man and two women. The room was dark, lit only by candles, and there seemed to be chants and responses assigned to the sex acts taking place. The whole thing seemed more like a play or following a script than to be spontaneous debauchery. It was bizarre to say the least and Bertelli and Glenn fought to keep themselves calm. Like everyone else in the room, their faces were hidden by the hoods.

Within minutes the group was breaking down into subgroups and all of the subgroups seemed to have pre-assigned duties that they all seemed capable of doing without speaking. It became obvious to Monsignor Glenn and the cardinal archbishop that they would be discovered as frauds in a moment or two since they did not understand the ritual's expectations. So they quickly hid behind two old Confessional screens that were placed back near the wall away from the ritual. They hid and held their breath. If they were discovered they would almost certainly be killed.

The ritual seemed to go on and on. Members of the group seemed to be swaying more slowly, and the rape of the little girl ended. She was shivering and seemed almost as if she did not know what was happening to her. She was placed in a red robe and handed off to some sort of priestess beside the altar who took her to the back of the room and began to swab out her vagina with some sort of liquid that smelled strongly of vinegar. Apparently, this was some sort of ritualistic attempt to either stop a pregnancy in an older girl or to teach the younger girl what to do later on when she became of childbearing age. In either case, it deeply disturbed Glenn and Bertelli. This was dehumanizing to watch. It was all so mundane, so organized, so completely orchestrated with the sense that this had all happened before and would all happen again. True evil is not horrific in a melodramatic sense, it is organized, mundane and absolutely scripted to the point of imitating normality. Bertelli and Glenn could see that now.

Without warning there was shouting and a large commotion above them. There was only one way out of the archives and the entire coven stood frozen in place and watching the stairwell. A platoon of policemen appeared. There were State Policemen,

Philadelphia policemen, local policemen from the Montgomery County borough and federal agents. The Satanists were placed under arrest one by one and their hands put in plastic handcuff ties. As the police arrested each person, they pulled the hood down off their faces. Monsignor Glenn and Cardinal Bertelli came out from behind the confessional screens. Bertelli yelled "Simon, over here!" and a tall Jewish man walked over to them and was preparing to arrest Glenn when the Cardinal Archbishop Emeritus of Philadelphia said to his friend, "No, he is with me. Monsignor Glenn, this is Captain Simon Maslow of the Pennsylvania State Police." The two men shook hands as the various Satanists were led out of the archives and out of the chapel building onto the grounds outside the chapel.

The commotion among the seminarians was immediate and considerable. They all stood on the grounds outside the chapel watching as the lowered hoods revealed three Catholic bishops, ten Catholic monsignors and several prominent members of the Catholic Church in the Philadelphia area. The three bishops had all attended the same seminary as young men and all at roughly the same time. One priest who was arrested, a Pennsylvanian named Father Robert Benestane, was a personal friend of John Cardinal Kraske and had in fact been the very priest to lay the linen cloth over his face at the funeral Mass before he personally closed the Cardinal's casket so many years before. He was known to be a shaker and a mover and was a large fundraiser in Catholic circles in Pennsylvania. His very presence in this Satanist Circle implicated John Cardinal Kraske in Satanist suspicions from many years before. Evil is very powerful, but it is not eternal. Truth is. All who cared to look could now see that.

Monsignor Glenn and Cardinal Bertelli stood in awe, their satanic robes removed, as a squadron of police vans and cars left the grounds of the seminary. They were all under the influence of drugs and most were charged with possession, trespassing on seminary grounds. All of them had their pictures taken in their Satanist robes and the ritual rapist was arrested for child rape. He was a priest from Ohio and a seminary professor in the Midwest. Glenn and Bertelli agreed immediately to be witnesses. Captain Maslow thanked both of them for their courage. Finally, a Satanist ring had been found and exposed. And Monsignor Glenn had met his assignment parameter after all. The fact that he had finished the job after the job had been taken away from him meant little to him. He had found the proof. He had served his Lord. He had redeemed himself. Cardinal Renatto could go to hell for all he cared!

As for the eight-year-old girl, it was found that oddly enough, she was a little Lutheran girl from Central Pennsylvania, a full sixty-five miles away from the seminary. She had been brought to Philadelphia by the priest Benestane for these rituals. He had specifically groomed her since she was a much younger child to be his Satanic Wife in these rituals. In fact, he had 'married' her the year before in a ceremony that claimed her for his and only his sexual use. Taken away from her parents who were later found to be Satanists themselves, she had to face a childhood and young adulthood filled with extreme psychological pain. She was the most innocent of all, the bravest of all, the most damaged of all. She was the one instrument of God in this entire sordid affair that was truly crucified and broken. She was too young and too damaged psychologically to be able to be a credible witness to the evil that befell her, but her courage haunted Glenn and Bertelli for the rest of their lives. She retreated into her own psyche, was diagnosed as a multiple personality and did the best she could to live her life. She would eventually become a nurse and marry a fireman and have a beautiful daughter. In her later life, she would lead a crusade against Satanist activities that would gain her worldwide fame. This is how God operates. He is never easy to figure out, but ultimately, He is always just.

As for the final outcome of the day's events, the arrests were all over the Philadelphia and Pennsylvania newspapers for months. The current bishop of Philadelphia, Cardinal Archbishop Julian Renatto, remained strangely silent and had no comment. He was immediately summoned to Rome and had to explain the situation personally to the Holy Father. But even with that, Monsignor Glenn was surprised at his silence. Cardinal Archbishop Bertelli was not. More would be revealed in years to come. Monsignor Glenn realized now more than ever that everything and everyone is not what it seems. Still, he had acted as a priest and shown courage in the face of pure evil. Monsignor Glenn was thankful that he was chosen to serve his Lord in this manner. And for that matter, so was the retired archbishop of Philadelphia, Marco Bertelli. The two men grew closer after that and Monsignor Glenn offered to write the Archbishop's memoirs. The Cardinal Archbishop Emeritus accepted. A real friendship had been born out of their refusal to allow evil. They had both learned how to be good priests that afternoon. They were both grateful for the chance to participate in this act of priestly redemption.

Martha Konscikowski flew home to Chicago, no longer an active Religious. Her mother and her sister were waiting for her at the airport. They kissed her and hugged her as she got off the plane and drove directly to her mother's apartment. Their talk was superficial and did not touch on the weighty matter at hand. Her family knew that she had been hospitalized but they were vague on the exact details. Martha had decided not to lie to them. If they asked, she would tell them.

Once home Martha saw that her mother had made up the extra bedroom in her apartment for Martha to live in. Martha smiled and kissed her mother. She said to her mother and sister, "Let's sit down and talk." The two women looked at each other, then sat down silently. They waited for Martha to speak.

"I am going to tell you exactly what happened. I was pregnant with the baby of the man I love and I miscarried in my third month. Mother Edwina asked me whether I wanted to be transferred immediately to our Motherhouse in order to accept Penance for my behavior or whether I wanted to leave the convent. I chose to leave. I am home now but I expect to travel back to Philadelphia very soon to make accommodations so that I can be near the man I love. Do either of you have any questions for me?" She looked at the two women, the only family she had. They were in shock. They did not know what to say. The three of them sat there in silence for about a minute.

Finally, Mrs. Konscikowski said to her daughter in a thick Polish accent "Martha, you are home now. It has been a trial for you. Whatever you have done, you are my daughter. I want here with me now. Can you at least stay for a little while and let me have that pleasure?" Martha nodded yes. The three of them cried and held each other for a long time.

LIAM'S REPORT TO THE CARDINAL ARCHBISHOP ON THE JESUS STORY

I t was now October, nearing November 2007. Liam was writing his report on the Church's options for telling the Jesus Story. Jesus was no different to the modern mind than Julius Caesar or Hippocrates or Pliny. It was pretty much as simple as that. Jesus would be treated by modern scholars in the same manner as any other personality from antiquity. Any expectation that things were going to change was naïve. That was the major point that Liam wanted to drive home to the Curia with his report.

Martha and Liam were secretly planning a life together. Eventually, that would mean that Liam must leave the priesthood. But before he would do this drastic move that would upset his life, his family and his belief system he wanted to deliver his report the Cardinal Archbishop. He considered it his final gift to his Church. He worked on the report constantly, sometimes for ten hours a day. Gathering the facts and quoting the authors was the easy part and now that was finished. It was the Executive Summary that would be difficult for in that section, in those few cover pages of the report, Liam would bare his soul to his Church. Finally the executive summary was ready to be written. Liam proceeded with great diligence and care. He poured his soul into it. In four days he was satisfied that he had done what he could do. His report reads as follows:

Executive Summary

During the year that this report was written, dozens of biblical exegetes were interviewed and many submitted written explanations and rationales for their work. They are attached to this report. In short, it is perhaps easiest to state immediately that the Church's philosophical right to be the primary source for all facts and nuances of the story of Jesus of Nazareth have been successfully challenged by academia, and by extension, by the media and anyone with an interest in relating the story in the world at large. The basic tenets of free expression in Western democracies and the norms of modern scholarship have changed the intellectual landscape forever in this regard. The Church must learn to survive with competing versions of the Jesus Story ever present in the mind of the people. That is the hard and cold reality of the state of affairs regarding Historical Jesus Research throughout the world.

It is equally true that as the world's population gains in its intellectual capacity through formal education and that informal education provided by the media, any hope that the common believer will adhere to an ancient cosmology as described in the New Testament must be abandoned. The New Testament writers wrote in a genre that virtually all serious biblical exegetes now see as more of a political broadside than history. In short, the Gospels and Acts of the Apostles are not history and almost certainly were not meant to be seen as such. The New Testament was a genre of literature that was extant in the ancient world to a greater or lesser degree in all mystery religions and cults of that time. They were written long after Jesus allegedly resurrected from the dead and they were written in a manner that seems to indicate to modern scholars that grievances were being settled by various sects of Jews in those writings. In short, a minority party of Jerusalem Jews (i.e. the Christians) seemed to be using the New Testament writings to, at one and the same time, indict the majority party (mainstream

Second Temple Jews) for their unbelief in Jesus as messiah as well as spell out their core beliefs in that messiah.

The Gospels speak of things that are far outside the human norm. Jesus is transfigured in light in the presence of ancient prophets, he heals people with his touch and is noted as healing the blind and lame, he raises a dead girl to life, he arises from the dead, he ascends into heaven. If this is history, the modern mind cannot accept it. If this is metaphor, it must be explained as metaphor. The Church must take an honest intellectual stand on the issue.

The only people who seem to consider the New Testament as history are extreme fundamentalists who deny evolution, believe sincerely that eschatology is now coming into its final stages in our lifetime and that final judgment is imminent. If this view is correct, then it is outside the norms of human experience and also stands completely and irrevocably outside of modern standard biblical scholarship. There is scholarship and there is Faith. If we are going to attempt to meld them both, then we must be absolutely true to both traditions. We cannot deny one, even in a small matter, in order to prop up the other.

Perhaps there can be a fusion of Faith and Science in the Cosmic Christ or the Christ Consciousness concept that has been written extensively by Teilhard de Chardin or Matthew Fox. Both men are now seen as pariahs to the Curia and seem to stand outside of traditional Catholic theology. I hasten to add that Francis of Assisi, our most revered saint to the masses, wrote a poem to Brother Sun, Sister Moon. Has he been rejected out of hand by the People of God for his pantheistic tendencies? Of course not! He is loved by all. Why is Chardin rejected for his attempt to reconcile Christ with evolution? Why is Fox rejected for his extreme pantheistic tendencies related to Christ Consciousness? Is it because these men are wrong? Or is it because we are afraid that their vision will lead us in directions we do not wish to go? In either case, we had better decide soon. The time for intellectual feet dragging has ended. The journey toward a new mode of Christianity has long since begun. The Catholic Church has refused to join in the journey so far, and by doing so, it is in extreme danger of becoming completely irrelevant in any serious discussions concerning the future of Christianity.

The people have already decided. The Faith in the West is largely dead and we are looking to Asia, Africa and the poorer regions of Latin America for our survival. But these areas of the planet will also have universal education soon. We cannot hope to save our version of the Jesus Story on the gamble that uneducated masses will simply accept what we tell them. That world will soon be gone. A new world of intellectual honesty and sincere grappling for metaphysical and historical truth is now upon us. Do we have the courage to respond to that truth as it presents itself? Or will we continue to use our old paradigms to bring Christ into a world which no longer recognizes such ancient cosmology as valid or useful?

The choice is ours. We are out of time. Modern and educated minds reject our version of the Jesus Story out of hand as folklore or worse, deliberate manipulation of the facts in order to gain power over the unsuspecting and desperate. The decision to proceed toward a more realistic and ultimately, a more fulfilling Jesus Story, is upon us. May God help us in our decision to proceed. Amen.

Father Liam O'Bardon

Philadelphia, Pennsylvania

November 15, 2007

The report was written and turned into the Cardinal Archbishop. The Archbishop read the report, all two hundred pages of notes, research abstracts and footnotes. He then threw it in the trash. He said nothing to O'Bardon but the office secretary saved his report from the shredder and returned it to him. O'Bardon merely laughed. Honesty does not always pay, especially in religious matters. He had done what he was asked to do and it was rejected out of hand. The Cardinal would not even look at O'Bardon and did not speak to him. He would not even answer when O'Bardon said 'good morning, Eminence'. O'Bardon was glad. It would make his decision to leave the priesthood that much easier. Liam had decided to leave immediately.

He had written a letter of resignation and mailed it to the Chancery, care of the Cardinal Archbishop. It would be received in two or three days. The Archdiocese would then take steps to laicize him. Liam did not care anymore.

Liam drove to Queen of Peace parish and gave Jamie McGurk's journals to Monsignor Bill Glenn with a handwritten note to read them and then pass them on to the Archbishop. Glenn answered the door when O'Bardon got to the rectory and invited him in.

Liam just handed him the journals and said, "I am leaving the priesthood Bill. These are for you. They were found inside the altar when they demolished Saint Kevin's parish last year. Make sure you read them before you give them to the Cardinal. I think there are things in here that you are going to want to know." He then turned and walked back to his car. That was more or less the end of his priestly duties. Liam felt relieved that it was finally over.

MARTHA RETURNS TO PHILADELPHIA

Martha flew into Philadelphia the evening that the report was finished and turned into the archbishop. She and Liam had planned a weekend together in Margate, New Jersey, a small summer resort on the Jersey shore. The O'Bardon family had owned a summer home there for generations and it was a place that he and Martha could be alone for a while and think and talk and plan. Martha flew into the Philadelphia International Airport, and Liam was there to meet her. He was not dressed in clerical clothes but they were careful about showing affection where they might be seen. Liam took her hand gently and said nothing. Martha returned his look.

They walked silently to Liam's car and drove to New Jersey and the shore with very little talk between them. They had missed each other in Martha's absence. Martha held Liam's hand as he drove. The drive took about two hours, and they spent most of it listening to each other breathe. They loved each other. They knew that most of all.

"I have decided to leave the priesthood, Martha. I did what I could do for my church and I can do no more. It is time to leave and start a life for myself. Would you like to be part of my life, and let me part of yours?" he stopped talking and looked at his woman.

"Yes" is all Martha said. It is all she wanted to say. It was all she needed to say.

They arrived in Margate, spent two days making love and eating in local restaurants and walking on the beach. Since it was autumn they were almost alone. Beach resorts are like that in the off-season. Liam had made arrangements to teach basic writing and study skills in a state run vocational school for troubled boys near Philadelphia. Martha found a job as a teacher's aide in a school system in Bucks County, just north of Philadelphia.

The following week they found a two-bedroom apartment in Doylestown and settled in for a life together. They married in the local Episcopal Church just before Christmas. They liked the minister. She had a good head on her shoulders. The following summer Martha became pregnant again and the pregnancy proceeded to term. The baby was a girl. They named her Faith. She was baptized in the Episcopal Church. It just made things easier that way.

Life has a way of coming full circle. What starts out as one thing usually reveals itself as something quite different, quite unexpected when it is examined closely. The lives of Martha and Liam were intertwined with their religious vocations in a way that would have made The McGurk happy. They loved each other above all others and saw each other as a gift from God. They lived the Christ reality in their marriage as best they could, from hour to hour, from day to day. They loved each other for what they are, not for what each would have the other be. They were content to live their life together quietly, lovingly and without looking back.

Jamie and Bibiana approved. Life was being lived the way it was supposed to be lived—with love.

About the Author

Born in Philadelphia in October of 1952 into a Catholic family that had Irish and Italian cultural roots, Tom Barnes was educated in the Roman Catholic school system of the Archdiocese of Philadelphia. He entered high school seminary in his senior year of high school at age sixteen and stayed in seminary until his twentieth year. At that point in his life, he immediately enlisted in the Marine Corps Reserve while finishing college at the Mount in Emmitsburg, Maryland and in 1975 he found himself to be an unemployed college graduate.

He enlisted in the U.S. Coast Guard in April, 1975 intending only to stay for one enlistment and eventually decided to make a career in that Service, retiring as a CWO3 (Personnel Administration) in the Fall of 1999. Tom taught business courses at Woodbridge High School in Virginia for three semesters after he retired from the Coast Guard, and then worked in the Office of Human Resources at the Smithsonian Institution in Washington D.C. as an employee trainer for almost five years following his short teaching career. He is divorced, has two adult daughters and two grandchildren. Tom is a totally disabled veteran and a retired federal worker.

Tom holds two bachelor's degrees (liberal arts and general business) and three master's degrees (secondary education, human resources management and human performance systems). He practices Zen Buddhist meditative techniques, lives a quiet life and is actively involved in progressive politics in Northern Virginia.

Made in the USA
Charleston, SC
02 July 2014